I0599548

1

©2025 Bethany Francis

Cover design by Sofia Sanz
Edited by Victoria Straw

ISBN: 9798998740503
First Edition: May 2025

For more information, visit: @hellboundbook or www.befrancisbooks.com

*To all the women who fight demons that they
don't talk about.*

HELL-BOUND

By
B.E. Francis

Book 1
Pacts of the Infernal

PROLOGUE

The god's elegant boots clicked against the marble.

The other male tried his best to prevent shivers from running down his spine as he watched the deity approach. It had been several millennia, and this creature, this despicable evil thing, could still cause his fear to emerge.

"You did not tell me you would arrive," he said, standing.

The god picked an imaginary piece of dust off of his immaculate robe. "I can come here whenever I want. I *own* you."

The male did not tremble. He was done trembling. He went to that dark place in his mind—that glorious numbness that kept him safe.

"I come to make sure you understand." The god's presence engulfed the room in power despite being shorter and smaller than his companion. "You haven't been doing your job. You are dangerously close to violating your contract."

The taller male held a stony face.

"I have not violated anything. The contract does not stipulate how much work I have to do at a time—"

The god shot towards him, grabbing his face in a violent grasp.

"You will do what I fucking *tell* you to do. Contract or no contract. *Your* soul might be safe, but all these little creatures you care about, all these little minions you have, will suffer a level of pain that only a god can give. And what will you do then? What will feed your power when all others have left you alone and abandoned? You are *nothing*. The fact that you live is by my glorious mercy."

He spat these words, eyes flaring with rage, clenching tighter until the black ichor, in place of blood, flowed from where claws pierced skin.

Bleeding, the injured male felt the warmth rushing down his face, reminding him that he was, cruelly, still alive.

He kept his eyes locked on his aggressor. He would not back down—he would murder this being. He would get the power he needed and maim him. Torture and cut, until he begged for forgiveness, which the male would never grant. He would lock him away for hundreds of years, returning only when he craved seeing the misery and desperation shine through the monsters' eyes—unless he gouged them out first. For the people the god had killed, for those that this evil beast had sucked the souls from, he would cut—small cuts for every. Single. One. The male would say their names in his ear until this unholy god could hear nothing else. He would make him repeat the millions of names, and when one was inevitably forgotten, he would lash him with a whip of just as many tails. The male imagined the sound of those barbs raking on his aggressor's skin.

He would have his revenge. He would be sated. Just not today.

The god finally released his face, pushing him away for good measure.

The blood was running freely now, making small patting sounds as it dripped onto the hard floor.

The male did not move to wipe it away.

The god sighed and picked up a small relic from the victim's desk.

The other hissed his disapproval, unable to hold back his outrage.

"Oh, don't be *childish,*" the god said, placing the trinket in the pocket of his robes. "It's only a bauble."

The male's eyes glared at the thief. Pure venom.

"I don't know why you resist," the god said, tapping his pocket contentedly. "You have nothing to save. Not yourself—not those people you pretend to care about. All you want is power. To be worshiped. That's what we all want, after all."

The blood began to soak the injured male's hair, which had fallen down over his forehead. He clenched his fist as his jaw worked soundlessly.

"You cannot be saved," the god continued, "you cannot be redeemed. Maybe you could have." He exhaled a sigh. "But you're too far gone now. You can't change. You've known nothing else for so long." He laughed darkly. "I could destroy your contract now, and you will still cower at my feet, begging me to let you have power again. Pathetic."

The unholy deity turned his back on the male and walked leisurely to the door.

"Do your job before I destroy everything you have created here. Don't think I don't know what you're up to. I am everywhere."

He looked back only once more.

"Get that, would you?" he said, indicating towards the door.

The male growled despite himself, flicking his hand for the door to open before the ruler of The Hells strolled out.

CHAPTER 1

Renata sat on the docks, gazing at her arm. An ugly scar, about five inches long, marred the skin there. It was discolored, a pink harshness against her pale skin, but to her, it was beautiful. The scar meant that she had lived a life. That she'd had experiences that had changed her—not that she could remember any of them.

During her six weeks on the merchant ship, she'd spent hours imagining how she'd gotten the scar. Had she fallen as a child? Did she get accosted by two ruffians in a back alley? Perhaps she had dropped a knife while making dinner for her lover, Nephele, a person she had also forgotten.

The nightmare began several months ago in the small town of Vergessen.

She had awoken to a stranger lying half-naked in the bed beside her.

Renata recalled her horror and screams for help as the male Elf, who she now knew as Nephele, tried to explain that he was her partner, that they lived together, and that they were in love.

True, he wasn't entirely unfamiliar—with his long dark hair, blue eyes, and pointed ears—yet she could not place them. The space where those memories should have been was blank. He was like a character she might have seen in a play.

It didn't take long to figure out that something was terribly wrong. Renata had forgotten her life. But not quite everything. She could still remember faces and names, yet there was no meaning behind them—no memory attached. She could still remember how to do daily rituals. Her fingers immediately knew the proper rhythms when she pulled at the strands of her hair to plait it—she didn't need to think about tying her boots. It just happened as if her habits had been burned into her body rather than her mind.

She recognized her mother, Clara, by sight but not by recollection—no memories to prompt any emotional connection—nothing to tie her to this wizened Elven female with a kind face. While it felt right to call her Mother, there was nothing else. The same was true for her father, Atlas. Yet Renata was undeniably theirs—with her mother's silver hair and her father's dark Human eyes.

She visited her parents one last time before she left Vergessen. She sat at the small kitchen table, dissociating as she watched the steam rise from her tea cup. Her mother was crying, and her father, much like her, refused to say much.

"You still can't remember...anything?" her mom said again.

Renata finally looked up, forcing herself to meet the lovely female's eyes.

"I...no. I mean—not really. I know who you are. I remember people, I somehow recognize them—but none of our...interactions. If that makes sense?"

"No, Renata...it...it doesn't!" Clara stammered, anguish in her wet eyes.

Atlas just shook his head wordlessly. His eyes were creased on both sides, looking much older than his wife's.

The older woman reached across the table to hold Renata's hands. As skin touched skin, Renata's first instinct was to pull her hand back, not yet used to physical contact. But they felt warm, comforting even.

She held her mother's gaze.

"You can fix it. Say you can fix it."

Renata's jaw worked. "Mother. I don't know what this is. I...don't know what happened."

She felt, in that moment, that she should be sadder. That she should be heartbroken, like these two. That she should feel something for them besides pity. A flicker of affectionate feeling. But she was blank. She knew they had been close, or that's what they'd told her. Stories of her chasing bees 30-something years ago and playing a small piccolo in the garden to the plants so they would grow faster.

Clara continued to desperately share these moments to trigger some sort of recognition rather than the ever-present frustration.

"And Nephele? Have you seen Nephele?" she asked, sniffling.

"Not yet."

The weeks that followed were a cacophony of tortuous interactions. Everyone was so upset that she couldn't remember.

"But surely, *me?* We see each other every fortnight!"

"Don't you remember? I've known you since we were youngsters."

"Be serious, Renata. You order the same thing every week!"

And Nephele, most of all.

The last time she had seen him was at a quiet tavern near dusk. She had avoided the encounter, but as she was leaving in the morning, she couldn't put it off any longer.

Nephele's eyes were bloodshot shadowed with tiny purple curves underneath.

Renata sat silently, as she'd learned to do in many circumstances lately.

"Renata..." he started, breathing out a shaky breath. "I heard you're taking the ship out tomorrow. To...Ataria?"

She nodded slowly. "Yeah...I got a letter," she said, scratching her arm nervously. "The sender said that I would find answers there. So you don't have to worry," she said, plastering a smile on her face. "I'm sure I'll be back to normal in no time..."

Her words trailed off, hanging in the air awkwardly.

Nephele's eyes began to glisten, but before tears could fall, he wiped them away on his sleeve.

Renata's heart clenched.

She wished she could give this male what he wanted. From what Clara and Atlas had said, he was genuine and kind.

Nephele cleared his throat, trying to steel himself.

"I don't think leaving is the answer—"

"But I don't even—"

"Please, Renata, let me finish," he said solemnly, lips trembling. "I think leaving is a mistake. What if you forget how to get home?" He looked at the table hopelessly. "But...I love you, so I...respect your right to choose this path yourself."

Renata clenched her fists, frustrated. How was she even supposed to respond to that—to defend her decision? Did he not understand that she was scared, too? That the only thing that felt more terrifying than leaving was staying here? But she pushed down her aggravation—he was hurting, and if nothing else, she could understand that.

"You will always be the woman I love," he continued sadly. "The woman that showed me what it meant to be alive. The woman who challenged me to be a better man and inspired me to help others, no matter the cost."

Renata blushed, feeling undeserving of such an endorsement.

"It is because of how true I know our love is—was— that I know I have to let you go. If this is what you chose, perhaps you should live that life." He let out a small sob. "But, selfishly, I can't give up—don't think I can move on knowing that you might return to me one day..."

Renata finally found her voice.

"Did I not...mention anything before? Did I not explain?" she asked desperately, knowing the answer before it came.

He shook his head mournfully. "I wish you would have. Perhaps then we both wouldn't feel so lost."

Renata came back to herself as a small wave splashed upon the docks. It was some kind of cruelty that the only memories she had now were of confusion and hurt faces. Of conversations that led to tears—tears she couldn't understand. So when Leonardo's letter summoned her to Ataria, she leaped at the chance to change her fate.

The letter explained that news of her mysterious affliction had reached the shores of Ataria and that, if she was interested, he could book her on a merchant vessel to arrive in six weeks to discuss her affliction.

Renata had no desire to question the letter's authenticity. If it was something false, it was still better than staying in that depressing little town with the pitying faces bearing down on her.

The journey itself was relatively uneventful. She found that she wasn't prone to sea-related illnesses and enjoyed the water spray and how her skin stung mildly from the salt that constantly coated it.

But the best part was the freedom—freedom from the expectations and the sadness. No one on the vessel knew her. She could be anyone and didn't have to answer impossible questions or be affronted with tales of the past that made very little sense to her.

She wasn't angry at the people in Vergessen. Most were trying to be helpful. But it was incredibly irritating to be *told* who you were.

"But you *used* to love oysters! How could you not like them now? No, no...you're mistaken. Renata loves oysters!"

On the sea, she could breathe. She could rock gently side to side with the waves and listen to them crash against the vessel's side. If she ever found herself melancholic, she would retrieve a small piccolo from a satchel, the only real item of note she had brought, and play a gentle tune.

She had shocked herself back in Vergessen when she lifted the piccolo to her lips and immediately began playing. She almost cried with relief and joy as the notes twisted through the air. It felt almost miraculous that her ear recognized different notes. Memories of people were lost to the mysteries of her mind, but when it came to music, to the melodious sounds that made her blood quicken and her heart beat a little faster, she would never forget. Perhaps it was too much a part of her—something that made up so much of not only who but *what* she was—that it couldn't be torn from her mind.

She also made a friend on the ocean journey, a young urchin named Benji.

He wasn't on his way to Ataria. Instead, he explained, "I've been workin' on this ship for years! Best home a man could ask for!"

Benji wasn't, in fact, a man. He was Human, but he barely reached Renata's shoulders and still had the round cheeks of a lad. They formed a fast friendship as Benji loved to tell stories of his adventures on the *Sea Walker*, their vessel. Renata was always fascinated by his tales.

He would regale her with stories of different ports, foods from all over the world, and times when they'd almost wrecked and *surely* would have died if not for his heroics.

In only his few years, Benji had lived such a spectacular life that she couldn't help but feel jealous of all the adventures he could share. Renata was woefully unable to reciprocate.

But the friendship wasn't one-sided. If there was anything Benji liked more than spinning tales, it was money.

One night, he snuck into the guest quarters and pushed Renata's hammock, jolting her awake.

"Heya, Ren! Follow me! I have an idea."

Renata, bleary-eyed, slunk out of her hammock and followed him up on deck. It was pitch black, save for the glow of three lanterns. The night sky was absolutely breathtaking—glittering like millions of gems and somehow wholly different from those in Vergessen, which looked dull in comparison.

"Hey! Ren! Did you hear what I said?"

"Ah. Sorry, Benji. No."

Benji gave an irritated sigh.

"I said I found a way to get some money. See, I've been watching you. You're like a dang cat when you move—you barely make noise! Probably because you're so small," he said thoughtfully.

Renata knew better than to mention their height disparity.

"So, the way I see it, we can both get good if you just sneak into a couple of chambers and snatch some coins. Maybe from old Simon?"

Renata couldn't really remember much about the cultural connotations of money. But she did know that stealing was frowned upon.

"Benji, I don't think we should be taking money. What if they kick us off the ship?" she whispered.

Benji waved her off. "No *way*. Besides, Simon takes money, too! Remember when he was playing cards with Sean? Sean called him a *lying thief!*"

She supposed that was true. That *did* happen.

"It's all about strategy. Whoever has the best *skill,* like in cards, gets the most money!"

Renata had no argument for this.

In the end, they both made off with a stash of gold pieces each, stolen from pockets, socks, and deserted cabins.

Benji was right, though. No one even noticed Renata as she slipped her hand silently into their trousers. Her favorite find was a small mirror that Jon Jon had left in his hat.

Renata had no particular plans for her spoils, but Benji told her that she would find something in no time and that *he* was going to buy the best cakes in Ataria.

One night, as they lay together on the deck, Benji became wistful. "Say, Ren, what'd you buy if you had all the money on The Mortal Plane?"

She immediately knew what she should say. *My memories!*

But she hesitated. Renata felt she had to at least find out the *reason* for her affliction. Perhaps it was just some illness that she had unwittingly contracted one day. The medical magicians in a city as big as Ataria would surely have the cure.

Remembering her time with Benji on *Sea Walker* gave her courage. It meant that no matter the answer to her affliction, she was at least still capable of making memories. Perhaps one day she would share the stories of Benji with another—keep them alive for him so they would never be forgotten.

Then, in her small moment contemplating her own menial memories, she stood purposefully, dusted off her pants, and made her way to The White Whisper.

CHAPTER 2

The entrance to The White Whisper had no door. Renata could hear the laughter and music wafting into the streets.

The violin music was jovial and sweet. The perfect music for a bar with a broken door.

Walking into the tavern, it was obvious that this was one of the rougher places in town, and yet the ball in her chest immediately began to loosen, and her fingers, previously clutching her bag, began to relax.

Most of the tables were occupied with a variety of different races and creatures. She saw other Half-Elves, Orcs, Gnomes, and one man she swore was just a noodle with eyes.

But no Fae.

She sighed, realizing she always got nervous around the Fae despite their shared features. For her, it wasn't hard to tell them apart. Fae typically had longer, more pointed ears and pointed teeth. They also varied in some special features. Some had wings, others tails, some horns, but they always smiled.

A trickster, wicked smile—an intrusive thought.

This line of thinking confused Renata. She couldn't place why she had this—they were just there. She wondered if she should abandon these beliefs until it proved otherwise necessary to have them. It seemed somehow unfair of her to react so harshly to people she hadn't had a chance to talk to.

The only table with a lone inhabitant had been pushed into the corner of the tavern. It was occupied by a middle-aged Human scanning the common room. He was handsome, with long white hair that he'd secured in a low tail. When his eyes landed on Renata's, he smiled and waved her over.

As Renata hesitantly moved towards him, she smelled the musty scent of spilled drinks mixed with the delicious aroma of boiled potatoes.

Her favorite?

She even enjoyed the sticky feeling under her boots.

"Good afternoon. Renata?" he said, tilting his head toward her and gesturing to the available chair across from him.

"Leonardo?"

He smiled slightly.

"Yes, I've been looking forward to our meeting."

He sat stock-straight in his chair, looking her up and down as if searching for something.

"You've made a long journey. Please, let me buy you a drink. I've heard you're quite fond of ale."

Renata furrowed her brow and sat.

"I'm starting to get nervous that everything keeps saying that about me."

Another smile.

"Oh, don't worry. All of us have our vices, and from what I hear, it only makes the stories about you all the more celebrated. You're something of a folk hero outside of that small town of yours. The Defender of The Planes, they call you," he said, leaning back thoughtfully.

"Uh, yeah. I am sure it does," she said, punctuating the statement with an awkward smile.

The man cleared his throat as if equally embarrassed, perhaps thinking Renata would've been flattered.

"That ale, then."

As a round-faced waitress set two frothy ales in front of them and Renata found herself wishing she were there for pleasure. The violin was calling to her, and the tankard was alluring, dripping with sweat. She craved losing herself to the atmosphere.

"I guess you're wondering how I know about your predicament?"

Leonardo's voice snapped her out of her reverie.

"Well, let me get right to it—I am a member of an organization called The Gilded Triangle. We are worshipers of Nainaur. More importantly, we work *against* infernal beings that occupy the deepest layers of the planes of hell."

Bells went off inside Renata's head.

Yes, this was information she had heard of, the simplest version. Nainaur good. Hells bad. She knew that there were a lot of people in her village who worshiped Nainaur. There were several temples to him. Her parents even had a small mantle with incense to ward off spirits from The Hells.

"I'm sorry, but I'm not religious. I don't think praying would—"

"I apologize for the misunderstanding," he said, holding up a hand. "I'm not here to convert you—not yet, anyway," he murmured. "The Gilded Triangle believes you've had some involvement in The Hells."

Renata wet her lips. "You'll have to explain. How do you know this?"

Leonardo blinked patiently at her.

"Oh yes, the memories." He cleared his throat. "Where to start? Mortals—those from our plane—often fall into temptation and sign contracts with infernal beings, mostly Devils, in exchange for their souls. We, The Gilded Triangle, try to help these people by finding areas of ambiguity in their contracts, taking advantage of these, and setting their souls free. Souls that Nainaur can then redeem."

He lifted his chin proudly.

"Why would you think that this happened to me? No one in Vergessen mentioned anything like this."

He nodded sympathetically.

"The Gilded Triangle has access to many resources. We recently had an operative enter The Hells, and he overheard that a Devil had signed a new contract—an important one. With you."

Renata's eyes widened.

"No, sorry. You must be mistaken. Even *I* know that it would be foolish to sign away my soul to the service of a Devil." She scoffed. "There must be some other explanation. Devils are known to be dishonest, right?"

He took a moment and looked at her, probing for something in her expression.

"Renata, please do not disrespect my time by lying. The Gilded Triangle is not in the business of working with the soulless, but I am afraid we have no other choice. Even now, I can smell the infernal scent on your skin."

He wrinkled his nose.

Renata felt momentarily taken aback by his harsh words while simultaneously resisting the urge to smell her pits.

"Excuse me!" she sputtered, feeling her face redden. "If I have a *scent,* it would be the six weeks of travel on that ship I took to get here to listen to your insults and ridiculous theories! What a waste of time."

She moved to stand.

"I'm sorry, please," he said, raising his hands apologetically, face suddenly worried. "I didn't mean to offend." He paused. "I realize I can sometimes be severe—but I want to help you—and I hadn't realized that your memories were part of the contract. In truth, my colleagues and I assumed you were feigning forgetfulness to hide your involvement with the Devils. But this certainly complicates matters." He scratched his chin pensively. "Renata, I need you to be as truthful as you can. Is there anything you remember from your time in The Hells? I won't judge you. I am here to help, as my lord commanded."

Renata, face still warm, clenched her jaw, trying to keep the anxiety from rising. Had she really been so stupid? That other woman, the real Renata, was a stranger to her.

She felt like an entirely separate person. What if she *was* that stupid? What an embarrassing thought.

"Are you saying that I did this to myself?"

Her breath faltered, panic tightening in her chest.

"Why would I *want* to forget?" she asked, confused. "I don't remember The Hells or...a contract, and I'm...absolutely miserable—are you sure one of the Devils didn't just curse me or...something?"

"No, no, Renata," he said, shaking his head for emphasis. "We are absolutely certain that you have a contract. I must insist that your soul is lost, and this is most likely the reason for your current...state.

"But either way, there is an easy way to prove this. You should have your contract." He glanced at her satchel, still clutched in her hands. "I'm sure it's there."

Her eyes shot to her bag.

"No, I'm sorry, but you're wrong. There isn't anything in there besides some letters and other...personal effects."

Again, she tightened her grip on her bag.

"Renata, these contracts are magical. You cannot escape them. It may be hiding in your pocket or bag, and you haven't even noticed. They aren't always obvious. They sort of...follow you. You might try to tear them, throw them away, burn them, but they always come back, eventually."

"I'm telling you." She spoke through gritted teeth, getting impatient. "There is nothing in my bag."

The man breathed out steadily, also seeming to lose a bit of his decorum.

"I'm positive we can find it."

He tried to give a small, encouraging smile, but it looked strained.

Renata wracked her brain. She had been through her bag hundreds of times—reading letters from her family and Nephele—playing her piccolo.

"Maybe look again?" he asked cautiously. "Now that it knows your intention to read it."

His forehead furrowed determinedly.

Renata huffed.

"Sure."

She flipped open the flap of her satchel and pushed aside her piccolo only to see the scattered papers, all the letters from home, some coins, and an apple.

"See?" she said, spilling the contents on the table and crossing her arms. "Nothing."

Leonardo looked disappointed and poked gingerly at the apple as if it would transform into an infernal contract.

"Well, we can't figure out how to break your contract if we can't locate it."

Renata stared at the sad belongings covering the table. This was all she had to show for herself now. She had a house back in Vergessen, but she couldn't remember buying it or even why *that* house. She actually felt it was pretty cramped.

But these items—had all been selected by *her*—the Renata she was now. The letters to remind her that she used to be someone, the piccolo because she found that she loved to play, and the apple because, well, she got hungry sometimes. This observation made her deeply sad. She felt pathetic. As insignificant as the crumpled papers she hastily dumped on the table.

She steadied herself.

"Let's say I believe you. Why did I do it? And...what do I do now?"

Leonardo looked up at the ceiling thoughtfully.

"I cannot know the reason you did this any more than you can, I'm afraid. But I do think we can help each other."

"You mean, a deal to break a deal?"

An amused smile crossed the man's face.

"I suppose you could think of it like that. We, me and the members of my temple, can help you find your soul. But we also need you to help us retrieve an artifact stolen from our church."

"But why don't you just go yourself to get it?" she replied skeptically.

Leonardo waved a hand dismissively.

"Entering The Hells is difficult on the best of days, and as for the followers of The Almighty, it is tantamount to suicide. Just as I can sense your involvement with a Devil, they can sense our holy dedication and piety and will stop at nothing to purge it from their plane, whether through acts of violence or temptation. It is for these reasons that we need *your* help. As a soulless, you will not be an immediate target of their machinations, and your history defending the planes makes you the perfect candidate."

Renata's throat bobbed.

"Leonardo—"

"Leo for now," he said, smiling again.

"Leo. I don't know if I'm equipped to do this. I don't know anything about The Hells. Even if I did, I have very few memories now. Whoever I was, whatever people remember me to be, I am not that anymore."

He paused for a moment.

"Renata, there is nothing I trust more than the words of my god. He trusts you—he believes you are still our best chance at retrieving our relic. Even if you can't, you deserve a chance to save yourself, right?" He began to nod encouragingly. "I think that you will figure out how to handle this task. Maybe you can break the contract first, recover yourself, and then find the relic? Either way, you're still *her* somewhere inside."

Renata wasn't so sure. The wall blocking the memories of who she was, seemed to get stronger each time she approached it, yet the offer was tempting. It *was* what she wanted. Their goals *were* aligned, and she didn't feel there was any other way to figure herself out. And if she didn't accept, she would have to admit that this journey had been a colossal waste of time.

"Okay. I'll do it," she said, sounding more determined than she felt.

"Excellent. Most excellent," he said, sighing with relief. "I can help you cross the planes, but only when entering. Once you get there, it is up to you to find a way back."

"Ah. Okay. And how would I do that?"

"Oh, I'm sure you'll find a way. They always do." He shrugged. "Just don't make a deal with a Devil," he said, raising an eyebrow.

Renata grimaced, an annoyed feeling rising again.

"Yeah, of course. Any other useful tips?"

"You must blend in. On the surface, you should be safe—you are already bound to The Hells, but any conspicuousness could mean that The Gilded Triangle's mission is compromised. You *must* take care.

"The Hells are not like The Mortal Plane or The Fae Plane, of which you are—were—familiar. They are ruled by one king, a creature that lords over his subjects like a tyrant, enslaving both Devils and Mortals for his evil designs.

"The king, who is also their god, has many lords and ladies that rule the different city-states of The Hells. Each lord is capable of stealing souls. The High Devils comprise the upper class, while the Lesser Devils are the workers and lower-class citizens.

"Avoid the High Devils. We still do not fully understand the extent of their powers, but we know that they can sense Mortals and even control them.

"The most important things you must remember to survive are," He began to count on his fingers. "One. Devils will rarely directly lie, but their words are honeyed with trickery. Nothing gives a Devil more pleasure than trapping a Mortal into a deal. *Never* trust them. If you are forced to engage, use flattery as worship. Adoration is what they crave most.

"Two. Do not give in to temptation! They are the epitome of gluttony and vice, always surrendering to their most carnal desires. There is no line they will not cross when it comes to seeking their pleasures.

"Three. There are no good Devils—they cannot be saved or redeemed, no matter how innocent or nice they may appear on the surface. They are evil by essence and will try to corrupt you.

"Four. Never tell them who you are. You are too powerful—too important to remain trapped within their schemes."

The familiar feeling of awkwardness filled Renata. Should she be taking notes? This suddenly had become very overwhelming.

"I see. Avoid Devils at all costs. Stay away from temptation." She hesitated. "And what happens if I *do* give in to it?".

Leo's nostrils flared.

"Then let's hope you have a very strong constitution for...undesirable experiences. We cannot guarantee your safety, Renata."

She swallowed but nodded. Her decision had already been made, and she wouldn't turn back.

"But I believe," he said hurriedly. "With your history, you are the right choice."

Despite his words, for a brief moment, Leo seemed worried, then recovered himself.

"We need to act with the utmost haste. If you are willing, I can transport you there first thing tomorrow morning." He reached into his bag and pulled out three gold coins. "This should be more than enough to pay for your room and board here tonight."

She looked down at the gold coins and immediately thought of how Benji's eyes would sparkle at such a fortune.

"So that's it?" she asked, sliding the gold towards her, "We just met, and I'm going to wander The Hells until I find this thing you want?"

Leo waved his hands again, unconcerned. "Tomorrow we will go over the finer details. But you won't be completely alone. We will be able to communicate once you arrive. While The Gilded Triangle can't enter, our lord still has ways to use his powers within."

He stood and cleared his throat.

"I think that just about does it."

Renata also stood up, uncertain as to the correct social decorum.

She discovered early on that social situations were mostly agreeing with people and mimicking their movements.

Leo offered his hand for a shake, and Renata copied the gesture.

"May The Almighty protect and guide you. Remember, he is always there with his loving embrace to protect you."

He paused for a moment, meeting her eyes expectantly, but Renata wasn't sure how to mimic this behavior, so she just stood there.

Leo, seemingly realizing the moment had passed, gave a slight bow, rounded the table, and left without another word through the doorless opening in the wall.

Relieved, she plopped down and grabbed her tankard, realizing too late that it was empty. She must have drunk the whole thing during their conversation. Leaning over the table, she saw that Leo's was still full and unabashedly slid it towards herself.

"I need this," she said, taking a long pull and settling in.

With nowhere else to go, Renata decided to take part in what had become one of her favorite pastimes, drinking a mildly warmed ale that she didn't have to pay for. She closed her eyes to listen to the jolly tune of the violin. It didn't exactly fit her mood, but it was pleasant nonetheless.

Suddenly, she felt a warmth in her lap. Her head whipped down, startled. Her bag had suddenly become very toasty.

"What the—"

She reached in and searched inside.

It wasn't hard to locate what was happening. Her piccolo was gently vibrating and quietly whistling a tune.

Renata looked around the tavern. There were several tables very close to her, but no one else seemed to hear the noise. Reaching in, she delicately touched the small instrument. It immediately stopped vibrating as if relieved at her touch. Abruptly, the overwhelming feeling of musical desire flooded her mind, and she itched to stand on the stage and play.

She looked towards the player currently occupying the space. He was easily identifiable as a Gnome with his short stature and nubbed ears. It was hard to tell his age, as Gnomes, like Elves and Fae, aged very slowly. He looked youthful and didn't have the marks of someone who had been through many trials in his life.

Renata, despite being young for someone with Elven heritage, had faint lines on her face like small grooves carved into her skin—another outward reflection of her past. She still looked youthful, but she knew that these marks were indeed evidence of a life lived, one that, despite what people had told her, might have had hardships. Others her age in Vergessen didn't seem to carry so many worries drawn upon their skin.

Renata stood and let her body walk her to the stage. The Gnome glanced down, indicating that he had seen her as he finished the last few notes.

He bent down from the small stage, which was high enough to where, even with his short height, made him taller than her.

"Hi, Miss, what can I do for you?" he asked politely, his foot edging a small, ragged felt hat in her direction.

The hat had several copper pieces and some silver inside. Taking the hint, Renata dug around through her bag and placed one of her gold pieces inside the hat.

His eyes widened, and his mouth gaped.

"Oh wow. Uh...can...I play something for you? Any special requests?"

"Um... sort of. I don't want to intrude—I'd like to play a song on my piccolo if you wouldn't mind?"

The male smiled, grinning from ear to ear.

"Honestly, Miss, it'd be a great relief to be able to take a break."

He hopped down and motioned for her to take the stage.

Renata smiled in thanks before deftly pulling herself onto the stage and looking around the room. No one seemed to notice the pause in the musical interlude or that there had been a change at all. People were busy cajoling, talking, playing games, and having conversations with their heads leaned close together.

Renata dropped her bag on the stage and kicked it behind her. She looked down at her piccolo—anticipation and excitement rising. She hadn't played her piccolo for a large audience before or in recent memory. But she was surprised that she wasn't nervous. In fact, she felt glee at the prospect. But what to play?

When she played to herself on the ship, she had felt her melancholy through the notes.

That wouldn't do.

Happiness.

That's what was appropriate here.

But a happy memory? That wasn't yet something she could grab onto. But she did have something. She raised the piccolo to her mouth, closed her eyes, and began to play.

A song languidly came forth from the small holes, a delicate song, not jovial like the others being played before but happy, nonetheless.

It was reminiscent of the wind and the salty air in the ship as it rode the waves. Playing felt familiar—as so few things did—and she relished the sensations across her lips. She didn't know where she had learned the song or if she had *learned* it at all, but it felt right. She couldn't remember happiness, but she could remember being contented and hopeful as she headed towards this city. Taking the ship—coming to meet Leo—was the first true decision of her life, of the life she had now. The first decision she remembered. That was, in its own way, important and something to be celebrated.

She slowed her breathing to a subtle and quiet sound. She always loved this part, the change to a song, unexpected and surprising. It sounded so somber—a short reflection of the uncertainty she felt.

As she played the last notes and pulled the piccolo from her mouth, she realized she hadn't heard voices or movements in the room. When she opened her eyes, she blushed furiously and noticed that most of the room was agape. She hadn't really considered the audience and wasn't yet attuned to interpreting people's faces. She couldn't decipher if they were silently appalled or stunned. She decided the best course of action, either way, was to get off the stage as quickly as possible and buy another ale.

As she bent to jump down, her foot glanced off the old hat, which had been pulled to the edge. It was full. Coins of silver and copper to the brim—even a gold or two. She stared at it for a moment before gathering her bag and walking away.

She felt a tug on her tunic.

"Wait, miss!" It was the Gnome, only about waist-high to her now. "You have to take your earnings!"

He shoved the hat towards her enthusiastically.

She looked at the hat.

"But...it's your hat, and you've been playing all night."

He looked a little embarrassed and scratched the back of his neck.

"Yeah. But eh, I just play at a local bar, you know? How much can you expect from a bard who plays at a doorless bar? And besides, those belong to you. It would be ungentlemanly if I took money from such a talented lady."

He looked bashfully down at his feet.

She smiled small at the male.

"Thank you."

"Say, where'd you learn to toot like that?" he asked, seeming genuinely interested.

"I...uh, you know here and there."

He eyed her suspiciously. Something she said hadn't convinced him, and she didn't know how to escape from yet another uncomfortable conversation.

"Well, thank you so much for letting me use the stage," she said, backing away, trying to put a smile on as a mask. "I'll be seeing you."

She headed quickly for the doorway, hearing the jingling of coins in her bag. She immediately thought of Benji and wondered if he had found the best cake in Ataria. If not, she knew exactly what she would do next.

CHAPTER 3

Benji was ecstatic when Renata arrived to give him half her earnings. He refused at first, "Look, Ren, I ain't no charity case. I get my earnin's fair and square!"

"Okay then, how about this? We play cards and you can win it off me. Fair and square?" she offered, trying to hide her smile,

His eyes lit up.

"Yeah. yeah! I could do that."

They settled in, using an abandoned crate as an impromptu table.

It wasn't the fairest game. Benji was obviously cheating, and Renata couldn't remember the rules, but it was a silent agreement to save egos.

She spent the rest of the day with Benji, learning to play and enjoying how the hard cardboard felt against her hands, perhaps an echo of familiarity there. Benji also insisted that she perform a lively sea shanty.

"It goes like this…dun dun dooooh deeldl dee dee…"

"Um. Like this?"

She tried to match his cadence as best she could but, judging by his expression, failed miserably.

He grimaced.

"Yeah, ugh…that's about it."

Unsuccessful in an attempt to also not wound her pride. But she didn't mind.

"Benji?" she asked as she watched him shuffle the cards with skilled hands. "How did you first begin working on ships?"

Renata was surprised that Benji stopped shuffling and puffed out his chest.

"I was blessed by Nainaur, or my mother was!"

"Really?" she asked, surprised. "How was that?"

The small boy flipped an ace through his fingers.

"Well, my paw left me and my mom—but he said he'd come back! But...after a while, my mom..." He stopped, a flash of pain crossing his face before it, just as quickly, disappeared. "She stopped getting out of bed for a while. She kept saying he'd come back—told me that while we waited, that I was the *man* of the house."

He puffed out his chest again proudly.

"She would only leave bed to go to the temple of Nainaur every evening to light a candle for paw. One day, after I came home with some food, I saw her note. It said she'd gone to join my paw and Nainaur in The Heavens, to not look for her because she had become a special angel." He stopped again, this time looking down at his knees. "It was hard at first, knowing she was gone. But...I only had to live alone for a bit before I found the shipping yard." He looked up at Renata. "And I'm special because I have an angel looking down on me! So nothing bad can ever happen to me!"

Benji looked at her expectantly, but Renata didn't know what he wanted from her. Even though he had so many more memories than her, he was still just a child. It was easy to forget that he was so young, his air being so capable and independent. She wondered how long he would believe this story that he told himself. That if he would wake up one day and accept that his mother had left him. Or if he'd hold on to that story for the rest of his life.

I guess sometimes memories are what you decide they are.

"I'm very happy to hear nothing bad will happen to you, Benji," she responded. "I'll need you to escort me back to Vergessen when I return."

As the sun started to set and she began packing her new set of cards and piccolo, she felt a tug on her tunic. Before she could fully turn, Benji had slung two stiff arms around her neck. She was taken aback at first, but that gesture wasn't entirely unwelcome.

The awkwardness came when she realized she didn't know what to do with her arms. She tried to imitate the gesture as best she could and hoped that her movements didn't seem disingenuous. He didn't let go for a few beats, so she supposed she had succeeded.

This feels nice.

It was warm despite the chilling ocean breeze, she acknowledged before he broke the hold.

She gave one more small wave and walked off the docks, tracing her steps back to the tavern, looking forward to the bitter taste of ale. Her booted feet kicked up rocks as she shuffled down the empty street. It wasn't long, however, for her ears to twitch slightly, hearing another set of footprints scraping stone.

Someone is following me.

But her body didn't want to run, and she didn't feel threatened by the footsteps coming closer and closer. A small whisper in the back of her mind told her to just *keep walking.* So she did.

She walked—still looking at her feet but not sure where she was walking *to.* She passed the tavern, and soon, the streets became dark. There was very little light in this part of the city, making her pulse tick up a notch.

She then felt the hair on her arm stand on end right before a hand roughly grabbed her shoulder and spun her around. She abruptly found herself face to face with a hulking Orc, one of the same she had seen at the tavern.

His skin was a sallow shade of green, like mold on bread. His tusks protruded from the bottom of his mouth and were so long that they threatened to poke holes through his top lip. He was completely bald and had a long scar from his scalp to his cheek.

"Hey, flute girl! Wanna share those coins yeh got there?" he grunted, gripping her arm painfully.

Her ears perked again as she heard some rustling in an alley nearby. He wasn't alone.

"Right, s-sure," she said, reaching into her satchel.

With a start, she realized that her hands were searching for something other than coin. She suddenly felt at war with herself—stuck between crashing thoughts—and froze, one hand still in her bag.

The scarred Orc grunted again as two other males approached from the alley.

"You better hurry, little bard," he said, producing a club from behind his back. "We'z don't care how well you play that pipe. We'll beat the coins out of yeh."

The war in her suddenly stopped. She could feel the blood flood to her ears as she whipped around.

What are you doing?

The losing side of her brain shouted as she raised onto her toes to get eye level with the tall figure. Her patience had run out.

"Fucking *try* it, prick," she snarled.

His eyes widened in surprise.

"Oh, ho, ho." He laughed falsely. "You remind me of me old lady—before I tore her ears off. Tell yeh what, apologize and hand over the coin, and I only tear *one* of those pointy things from yer skull."

A few drops of spittle landed on her face as he dug his grimy fingernails into her arm.

"And I'll take that second-rate instrument yeh got. I'm sure I could sell it for at least a few copper."

As he raised his club, Renata's body reacted to the threat. She spun, using momentum and her lithe body to twist around, bending her arm, causing the beast to lose grip.

The Orc stepped back, disoriented.

"Don't just stand there! Fucking kill her!" he shouted, trying to regain his equilibrium.

Renata shuffled back as the other two Human males leaped forward, grabbing for whatever purchase they could. Unlike their boss, they were quicker and less lumbering.

Run you dumbass, her brain screamed at her.

She was outmatched, outnumbered, and unarmed. Anyone with half a mind would run.

Fortunately for Renata, in her state, she didn't exactly have half her mind, only her two internal voices of self-preservation and instinct.

And she found that the action, the threat of danger, excited her. She couldn't stop the gleeful smirk that appeared on her face.

This was like music. Something inside of her remembered—her body remembered. These echoes lived in her limbs, not her mind, and refused to be forgotten.

She sidestepped the first Human and positioned herself to his back. She then leaped off her feet and threw her weight towards him, lacing her arms around his neck. She was small, but she found that she could feel her muscles flex, securing a familiar grip and blocking any air to his lungs. She somehow knew that if she leveraged her knee in the center of his back and leaned her weight into his neck, he would quickly fall unconscious.

In the confusion, the second human—armed with a dagger—hesitated, his face bewildered as he looked dumbly at his flailing comrade.

The Orc growled, obviously less concerned, and lunged at Renata, knocking all three to the ground. She landed painfully on her back, the weight of the Orc crushing her lungs. She gasped with the impact, momentarily losing her hold on his neck. As the Human scrambled away, the Orc grabbed her and lifted her high over his head, slamming her down again to the ground.

Her entire body was rocked with pain, the air leaving her lungs. The Orc reared back to bash his body into hers, but she rolled to the side just in time for him to collide with the rocky cobblestones.

She was still trying to gulp down lung-fulls of air as she scrambled to her feet. The adrenalin was pulsing through her veins now, constricting her pupils and dulling the aches in her body.

The three began to loom closer, brandishing their weapons and chuckling.

"Is that all?" Renata heard herself say. "Tsk tsk, my boys. Are you going to let a little lady take such easy advantage of you?"

As a response, all three lunged at her, but she was ready. She sprang up and grabbed hold of a protruding brick on the wall several feet above her that she had seen while splayed out on the ground, waiting for her eyes to focus. It was only a foot wide, but she was able to easily perch herself there, balancing on her toes and dispersing her weight by leaning her back against the wall, arms out wide. On her pedestal, she was about six feet higher than her attackers.

"What the?" one of the men murmured as she shot upwards.

Renata gave a wicked grin.

"I don't know if you've ever heard of the Defender of The Planes, gentleman. But I suggest you don't test the meaning of that name."

Of course, it was an empty threat. Even Renata's instincts told her she couldn't take the three males without a proper weapon. Still, it filled her with a sense of satisfaction, of pride.

Theeeeeere you are, my darling. It has been too long. Have you missed me?

That. was *not* her voice.

Thrown by the intrusion, she almost lost her precarious balance. She glanced in every direction, but no other attackers were waiting. Even so, the voice was too close. It would already be upon her if it wasn't..in her. Blinking rapidly, she recovered herself.

Time to go—her own voice this time—insistent.

Remembering the men, she looked down.

They were gone.

She stared at the empty space, uncomprehending. She hadn't been *that* scary. And again, she wasn't armed. They knew that.

She leapt up, grabbed the exposed edge of the roof, and pulled herself to sit, dangling her legs. The ocean wind blew aside her silvery hair, and as it did, a black smoke swirled around her. Another unrecognizable sensation tingled her body as she surveyed her hands and arms. The mysterious vapor was so black that it seemed to absorb the little light that flickered from the lanterns.

"What the hells?"

She gasped, holding her hands out in front of her as if they would burn her if she let them touch her body. She had just bested three attackers, and now she was...smoking? Where would she even begin with processing all of this?

As the minutes ticked by, Renata kept her ears fixed, listening for any voices that could indicate the return of her assailants. But after half an hour of silence, she reluctantly decided the coast was clear. By that time, the smoke had dissipated, and the tingling had stopped.

Satisfied she was back to her new normal, she leapt down deftly from the roof and began retracing her steps to the tavern.

Once in her room, Renata sat on the bed with her knees tucked up to her chest, her piccolo set lovingly on the edge of the sheets, and a beer, untouched, waited on her nightstand.

She lowered her head to her knees breathing out a few shaky breaths, surprising herself as she shed a few tears. It hit her all at once.

It was too much—entirely too much. Everything was spinning out of control, and her mind couldn't grasp any surety. She had woken up, lost and floundering, to an unknown life and a burden of expectations before her. Now, half a world away from those expectations, she was thrown in the middle of a conflict involving gods and Devils and couldn't even explain what was happening to her body.

This body, this vessel that housed her, was entirely unfamiliar. The way it moved, the power it emitted, felt like another stranger making demands that she was unable to fulfill.

How sad it was to think about. That, at one time, she'd had everything—a family, a lover, friends, and favorite places, or so they all had told her. Yet now she had to live knowing that none of it was hers anymore.

As the sheets of the small tavern room dampened from her tears, she thought of Benji. He had no family. He was nothing more than a child, taking money from other crew members to survive. She felt selfish—feeling so lonely and sorry for herself. She wasn't actually alone. There were people who loved her. She should be grateful. Still, she couldn't shake the hurt and confusion. Everything was just...out of control. Her life was happening around her, and she was paralyzed to just watch.

With nothing else to do, she sat silently on her lumpy bed, staring at the sheets. Letting the tears fall until, eventually, she let herself drift into an exhausted slumber.

CHAPTER 4

The next morning, Ren awoke to pain aching through her whole body—the consequences of her encounter the night before—purple bruises having appeared as she slept. Muscle memory or not, it had definitely been a while since she had used her body in *that* way.

She dreaded her meeting with Leo—she wasn't in form to do anything, let alone enter the most dangerous plane of existence.

It was still early in the tavern, and she forced her throbbing legs to carry her downstairs, following the smell of sizzling breakfast meats wafting in from the kitchens. Once downstairs, she saw Leo and two other people—an Elven female and a Half-Elf male—sitting together, whispering. Curious since, while there were a few more people eating around the open area, the tavern was mostly abandoned.

Leo met her eyes and waved her over with a grin.

"Ah yes, Renata! I am so glad to see you are an early riser like myself. Please sit—have some breakfast!"

His two colleagues avoided her eyes, staring at their hands, which were laced together in front of them.

All three were wearing white robes with delicate gold stitching on the ends. The front depicted a humanoid figure alight with stars and had flowing robes forming a triangular shape; the same depiction hung on solid gold pendants around their necks.

"I'd be careful with those," Renata said, sitting and tilting her chin towards the pendants. "People in this city might think they're worth something."

She noticed the female narrowed her eyes at her menacingly.

"Are *you* planning to take them from us?" she asked.

"Obviously not!" Renata shot back, surprised at the hostility. "I've just noticed some... activity in this neighborhood. Just trying to watch out for you."

The female did not look convinced.

"This is Claudia and Brennan," Leo said, breaking the tension. "Two of my most trusted friends and fellow devotees to Nainaur, The Almighty. We are all here to help you cross over into the planes of hell and aid you in finding our sacred relic."

Claudia cleared her throat, and the Half-Elf, Brennan, shifted uncomfortably.

"This relic is of incredible importance to The Almighty," Claudia said curtly. "The existence of which is closely guarded. Only the most faithful know of it, and only because it was stolen. This relic *must* be recovered!"

She punctuated each word by tapping her index finger on the table.

Renata just blinked at her.

"I'm sorry, have I done something to you? You see, I can't remember all—"

"You are given a chance at redemption," she cut in, "a chance you do not deserve. You have no soul, you have betrayed your plane and its people, you have violated the very *nature* of things!"

Renata felt blood rush to her ears. She didn't know if she should apologize or punch this female for saying such things.

But it's true, isn't it?

She was this person. Wasted and soulless.

"Peace, Claudia," Leo said, placing a hand over hers. "The Almighty has declared that it must be *Renata* who retrieves the relic. We are not ones to question His will, are we?"

Claudia looked stricken. "Of course...I didn't mean—"

Brennan interjected, speaking for the first time.

"Yes, yes. Your devotion is without question."

He reached into the pocket of his robes and produced a folded piece of parchment. It was quite old, dry, and crisp on the edges, having been folded and unfolded what looked like countless times. He gestured for Renata to take it.

She opened the brittle page delicately, trying to convey a bit of reverence to the three. It wouldn't do for the acolytes of a god to think she was being disrespectful on top of everything else.

There was just one image drawn on it. A large tome.

"It's called Vutar'ka Zhartun," Leo said, pointing to the depiction. "We know you cannot understand the written language of the damned, but the tome should be almost identical to this depiction. It is enchanted and cannot be altered by any Mortal or magical forces.

"It is most likely kept in the Devil's den, the largest of which is in the city of Ogriazeth. We will send you via a portal to the outskirts. From there, you can make your way to the Denizen's Tower, a tavern where we have secured you safe accommodation. The owner of the tower is already expecting you and will give you more instructions once you arrive."

The words hung in the air.

"And, my contract. Will I be able to find it there?"

Renata observed a slight tick in the muscles of Claudia's jaw.

Leo cleared his throat.

"Yes. The Forked Tongue is the den's name. It will have a denizen of Devils inside. There, you can start your search."

Renata pulled her bag closer to her, suddenly feeling vulnerable as the weight of her task settled in.

"Do you have any questions?" asked Leo.

In truth, she had many. But her mind was still sluggish and unable to properly form thoughts.

She shook her head.

With a pleasant nod, Leo slapped his thigh.

"Well then, let's get to it!"

He stood up from his chair, the wood scraping against the stone.

Obediently, the acolytes stood with him, walked slowly towards the back exit—apparently more of a priority than the front to secure with an actual door—and beckoned her to follow.

Outside was a small alley cluttered with piles of trash and a modest wooden outhouse. The stench of days-old garbage and stale alcohol was overwhelming. Renata wrinkled her nose in disgust, but the others appeared totally unaffected by the assault on their senses.

"We will make a portal here. It's private enough. No one should disturb us. I can't keep the magic for long, so you must enter before it dissipates, as we cannot cast the spell again.

"Renata, I need you to understand—the longer you stay in The Hells, the more likely you are to be corrupted and lose even more of yourself than you already have. Do not linger."

Leo shifted his cloak and produced a glittering dagger. The blade was about a foot long, and the hilt was solid gold. He turned the blade delicately in his hands, passing it to her, hilt first.

She weighed the weapon in her hands.

"This won't be useful," she said, surprising herself. "The gold hilt will be too weak for the pressure needed to break through bone."

Leo smiled.

"There she is. The warrior we've been waiting for."

Claudia and Brennan exchanged relieved glances.

"But this isn't a mere Mortal instrument. It is a holy relic. Her name is The Holy Transgression. She will help you."

Now that he had mentioned it, she could definitely feel a warm, magical vibration radiating off the dagger.

With that, he stepped back, clasped the hands of his fellows, and began to chant.

She couldn't understand the words, but she found them nonetheless comforting as she listened to the cadence of their voices, their own type of musical interlude.

In fact, she was surprised that her anxiety hadn't ratcheted up to an intolerable level. This was happening all so fast. It had barely been a day since the ship had docked, and there she was, leaving the only world she had known.

Her thoughts shifted. Was it really such a loss? She had only been herself, her current self, for a few weeks. Learning from scratch was all that she knew. This would be just another challenge she'd have to adapt to. She would have to fumble around to get her bearings either way, whether it was a new city or a new plane of existence. If she had learned anything last night, it would be to trust her instincts, and at this moment, her instincts told her to *go to hell.*

Continuing to chant, Leo's face began to look pained as it creased, and a bead of sweat appeared on his forehead.

There was a flicker—a small spark like someone had lit a match—and a low rumble thundered through the sky before a fiery circle suddenly appeared. Seven feet tall and just as wide.

Feeling the immediate heat, Renata sprang back.

Claudia and Brennan hit their knees dramatically, continuing to mutter while clutching their holy symbols. Behavior that, despite its apparent effectiveness, seemed a bit theatrical for her tastes.

Leo, still standing, looked towards Renata.

"You must go. Make haste. I cannot concentrate on the portal for more than a minute. Good luck, and please, do what you must, whatever you must, to achieve your goals. The Hells are dangerous, but I have faith in my god, and he has wisely chosen you for this task."

Renata swallowed the lump in her throat, nerves finally revealing themselves.

"So I just—"

"Yes, go!" he blurted, and without another second of hesitation, Renata ran towards the portal.

The heat intensified as she threw herself inside.

The odor of the alley vanished and was replaced by the equally overpowering scent of sulfur and soil. Renata expected to feel like she was whirling through some sort of tornado—but instead, she felt frozen in time, seeing only the slight shifts in the red flames. The only other discernible change was the growing noises around her beginning to dissipate and reform before a pop and a yank, halting her abruptly despite the apparent lack of motion. It felt like hitting a wall.

As her vision cleared, new colors began to take shape. Even in her first seconds of clarity, Renata knew there was no doubt that she was in Hell.

She found herself standing in a forest clearing, if this sad foliage could still constitute a forest. The trees had no leaves and were scarred by fires. Nothing was growing. The soil under her feet was ash, and the only color she could see was gray. The sky, too, had only dark gray clouds hovering above her. There was no sun. Instead, the sky was streaked with stagnant lightning, making no sounds but lighting the plane with a purple glow.

Renata clutched the strap of her bag, standing perfectly still, half expecting someone to attack her again. But there was nothing. Oddly nothing. No animals rustling, no rippling brook, not even the shift of her hair in the wind.

All was still.

Vacant.

The only sign of life was about a half mile in the distance, where she spotted a collection of angular-shaped buildings. She crouched low, trying to not make noise as she cautiously approached.

She needn't worry, though. The lack of vegetation made her movements essentially silent.

Drawing nearer, she noticed how the purple glow was refracting off each structure, reminding her of the light of the stars shimmering on the ocean waves.

Sneaking around the back of the buildings, she observed that they were made of a reinforced mountainous rock filled with gemstones that adhered the various parts together. Blues, greens, reds, a rainbow of splendor crisscrossed each facade. It was magnificent. The veins looked simultaneously sinister and expensive. The rough, porous rock gave way to the smooth iridescent crystals. Once close enough to touch, she ran her fingers over the wall. The contrast in texture sent ripples of pleasure through her fingers and up her arms.

Why would anyone value cold coins of the Mortal plane when these glorious jewels existed?

She wanted them.

She imagined people looking on in envy and admiration. She saw herself adorned in exquisite jewelry, surrounded by people from all races and classes, smiling and asking if they, *too,* could touch the glittering treasure.

Darling. Don't tease me, she heard purr in her ears.

That voice again. But this time she truly had *heard* the voice. Like a gentle whisper of someone leaning in to share a secret. The caress of a breath. A male's voice, more identifiable now.

"Hello? Is someone there?"

She waited for a response, eyes darting around wildly, gripping the dagger that was secured to her belt.

No response.

"Show your face," she hissed, trying not to raise her voice above a threatening whisper.

A chuckle.

You can't help yourself. That's fine. You'll get used to that, pet.

The stroke of breath on her ears caused an involuntary shiver.

"Who are you!?" she demanded.

No response.

It's just this place, she thought stubbornly, barrelling forward as if she could out-walk the specter. As she dashed, he noticed the trail of black vapor she left in her wake.

Not good.

She kept herself out of sight, darting from the back of glimmering buildings until she felt alone again. To her dismay, the distraction had forced her several miles into the city, and now had even less of an idea of how to get to the Denizen's Tower.

She poked her head out from behind one of the smaller edifices and spotted the first inhabitants of Ogriazeth.

They were dressed in what could only be described as rags. Renata could not qualify these gray and brown fabrics as something resembling clothing. Her pants and tunic, road-worn and in need of washing, looked positively regal in comparison.

The people walked sluggishly as they made their way through the city, faces dirty with soot and walking with their backs arched as if carrying an invisible load.

To her surprise, not all of them were Devils. There were people from her world—from the Mortal Plane. Humans, Elves, and Fae were all walking and groaning as they meandered to their various destinations.

One woman was tugging at a smaller Gnomish male, trying to keep him on his feet while he staggered wearily. Another tall, Elven male was coughing, spewing black liquid from his throat. The several others she saw weren't faring much better, looking gaunt and pale.

Renata felt nauseous. She had never seen such suffering. She had never experienced, from her recollection, such misery.

Her sadness quickly turned to fear. Was this to be her fate? Was this what was supposed to have happened to her? Was sending her to Hell all an elaborate trick to trap her into this existence?

She felt an overpowering urge to grab each person and throw them into the portal—rescue them from this torment. But her portal was long gone, and she could not call it back.

Renata swiftly reached into her bag and pulled out her piccolo. She wasn't quite sure what she hoped to do, but her internal musician demanded something of her. The piccolo thrummed in her hands encouragingly.

Breathing steadily, she walked into the open street, closed her eyes, and played.

This song was mournful. She wasn't sure if these people would appreciate something dismissively upbeat. Instead, she decided to play from her heart. The side of it that felt lost and scared about the future, but even more scared about the past.

She spared a moment to open her eyes and saw several people begin to gather, their own eyes large. None gave money, and it didn't look like they had anything to give, but it didn't matter.

She continued playing and tried to make meaningful eye contact with several strangers, wanting to show them that she played for *them*. But they all stared back through unseeing eyes, swaying gently from side to side. Her eyes caught on a thin, Fae male. His ears were almost as long as his head, and he wrote a ratty brown hat over one eye.

Momentarily distracted, Renata didn't see the Devil approach. He snatched the piccolo out of her hands.

"Stop that racket!" he barked.

After recovering from the initial shock, Renata felt rage rise inside her. How dare he interrupt her song. Her music! How dare he interfere with such an intimate moment and *touch* something so personal.

"If you damage that piccolo. I will kill you," she heard herself say.

What are you doing? Her inner voice screeched in her head.

The male Devil was about a foot taller than Renata with blue skin, sharp, pointed teeth, and four jagged horns, which rose from his forehead and bent back toward his crown. He flicked a long barbed tail threateningly and clenched his fist tighter around the piccolo. Renata could almost feel the instrument strain against his grip.

"This is your only warning. If you do that again, if you disturb the sleepers, I will report you. Then you'll hope death is the only thing that happens to you."

The people around her had already scrambled away.

"Excuse *me*," she snarled, snatching back her piccolo, "but I was just trying to bring a little life into this place—"

Before she could continue, the Devil grabbed the front of her vest and lifted her up.

"Don't be *stupid*."

He bored probingly into her eyes. His expression didn't change, but she saw his eyes dilate quickly.

Renate stared at him, matching his threatening gaze with her own. In truth, she had no idea where this boldness was coming from, but she liked it.

Yes. This is me.

"Normally, I would crush you and that ridiculous little device. But you don't belong to me," he grunted roughly, dropping her.

Renate reacted and landed on both feet, the impact twinging her sore muscles.

"Get this, you ignorant Elf. You might be new here, but if you get in the way of my doing my job, I will report you to Lord Pelegros."

His satisfied smirk conveyed that he believed she should be shaking with terror. Renata, feeling more stubborn than anything, said nothing, held his gaze, and shook from fury.

He snickered.

"Honestly, I pity you. You're brave now, but you're just a Mortal. If you even knew half of the trouble you're in." He sniffed the air deeply. "Aaaahh...you just arrived."

He shook his head, laughed once, and pointed a large, thick finger at her.

"It's for your own good. Remember it."

Then he stalked away.

Renata's jaw worked, trying to release the tension while tracing her fingers lovingly down her piccolo. She couldn't imagine anything happening to it. Her piccolo was the only thing that felt familiar from the very first moment she saw it in her rooms. Rooms that, themselves, felt entirely foreign.

Well, Devils officially suck.

She thought this while gently storing her treasure.

All the people had skittered away, and she was left alone in the streets.

Hitching her bag closer to her, Renata began walking towards the center of the small city, or where she believed it should be. When she finally saw someone, a female Half-Orc, sitting by a fountain in a plaza, Renata waved amicably.

The female didn't move—didn't tilt her head towards Renata. She just sat. Staring.

"Excuse me, ma'am?" Renata hesitantly came closer to the female. "Do you know where Denizan's Tower is?"

The female didn't flinch. Didn't even acknowledge Renata standing in front of her as a small droplet of drool dribbled down her haggard face.

Renata turned to look past her shoulder and towards where she was staring. In the distance, barely a few paces away, Renata saw a hanging sign.

The Denizan's Tower.

She turned back to the female whose face remained blank.

"Thank you," Renata said, hoping for some kind of response.

There was none.

She stood there a moment, feeling powerless. She couldn't even thank this poor female. Even if the Half-Orc hadn't meant to help her, she did. Money didn't seem appropriate either. How could you thank or help someone who couldn't acknowledge what was being offered?

Feeling deflated, Renata could only offer a smile and turn to walk towards her destination.

The Denizan's Tower *did* have a door, one that swung back and forth soundlessly.

The first thing she saw when she entered was a long bar extending from one wall to another, surrounded by tables. Each table was of a different height and style and was completely covered in dust. Oil lamps were lit, casting a brownish hue as the light mixed with the purple coming through the windows.

There was no music playing—there wasn't anything, or anyone, at all.

"Hello?"

Her voice did not echo. Instead, it disappeared and was absorbed into the thin stone walls.

"I was sent by the—"

She felt her voice cut off.

What the...?

She tried again.

"I was sent by the—"

Nothing.

Just then, a ragged, Elven male scrambled around the corner.

"Don't say nothing!" he hissed.

"Um...are you who I'm supposed to meet?"

"What did I jus day?"

He dashed towards her, grabbed her arm, and dragged her away from the door and deeper into the bar.

"Not too bright, are ye?" He let go of her arm. "I'm Fredrick–Fred is fine. The bar is enchanted, so the sleepers don't get in. We should be good over here."

"Sleepers? Is that what those people are?"

He nodded quickly, his greasy brown hair falling into his eyes.

"Neither living nor dead."

"How can they be alive and dead?"

"They sold their souls, didn't they? Then broke their contracts." He shook his head pityingly. "No hope for 'em now."

Broke their contracts?

Renata's mouth suddenly became unbearably dry. She didn't have hers. For all she knew, she had violated hers without even knowing. Turning into a sleeper suddenly seemed a lot worse than waking up without memories.

You're playing with fire.

He turned and walked toward the bar area and dug around underneath, producing a dusty green bottle.

"I try not to drink alone, hard to stop. But ye're here now. Care for a nip?"

"Absolutely," she responded hastily, tongue feeling like sandpaper.

Fred grabbed three glasses, all with chips, and poured two fingers each.

"Spirits for the spirits, ye know," he said without a hint of irony, a small head tilt towards the third glass.

Renata lifted hers and smelled the liquor. It smelled sweet and woody. It could be poison, but honestly, she couldn't bring herself to care.

"Leo says ye're here on something and some sort. Wouldn't tell me. And I don't want to know. That's why I have the muting magic up." He wiggled his fingers as if casting a spell. "The less ye can say, the less I get in trouble. But the least I can do for Leo is set ye up a room."

He took a long sip of his drink and continued.

"But if yer gonna stay at me place, ye gotta follow me rules." He pointed a dirty nail at her. "No bringing in any guests. I don't care if it's just a succubus or an imp. Go get your pleasures somewheres else."

Renata almost choked on her drink.

"Oh no. I don't—have an...no, I'm good."

He raised an eyebrow.

"Girl, ye're in Hell. Temptation is the name of the game here." He raised his glass to his lips, finishing it off. "Ye'll give in to something, all right. We all do."

He looked down at the empty glass as if to will the liquor back.

"Just *don't* do it here," he emphasized, gesturing to his bar.

She lifted her hands in surrender.

"And stay away from the sleepers. Ye can't help 'em, don't try."

"How did you—"

"Don't try! They made their deals. Then they reneged! Let 'em do their job and have some semblance of peace."

Suddenly curious, she said, "They have jobs?"

"They work the mines. Digging out all those gems you see everywhere."

"What do they do with it?"

"Well, they give it to their lords, don't they? Paying off the debts they still have."

Renata shivered. She couldn't think of anything worse than becoming some unseeing zombie wandering around and *still* being in total servitude.

"Leo said ye's would be going to The Forked Tongue tonight?"

Renata was struck by how matter-of-fact he was.

"Yeah, but I don't know much else. Do you...do this a lot? Help the soulless, I mean."

The Elf licked his lips, and his eyes darkened.

"Yeah, I s'pose yer could be sayin' that."

He pointed toward a precarious staircase.

"If ye're headed to the den, ye need to be getting going. Just go up to yer room. I think everything you need is there. If not, just call."

He turned around and walked towards the back of the bar.

Realizing she'd been dismissed, she drained her glass. Before standing, her eyes glanced at the third glass, still full of amber liquid, and wondered if spirits really cared about liquor. *She,* on the other hand, could definitely use more. Two fingers hadn't been nearly enough to subdue her growing nervousness.

Making her way to the stairs, she realized that none of the loose boards were making noise. Not a squeak or a moan of age, despite their movement as she walked. Renata knew now that she was an expert moving around noiselessly. This unnatural lack of noise, though, disturbed her.

After reaching the top of the stairs, Renata saw only one open door. Inside was a modest, if a bit dusty, bed atop laid a small bag and a letter addressed to her.

Renata,

If you're reading this, then that means you've made it to our safe house. We know Fredrick is a bit odd, but he is a good male and devout follower of Nainaur. Tonight, The

Forked Tongue is having a party with several Devils and their invited guests. This will be the perfect moment for you to search for the tome and ask about the contract. Be on guard. Devils are powerful beings capable of magic and trickery. If they can corrupt you, they will. Blend in. Remember your objective. Await my next correspondence.

May the Almighty smile upon you,

Leonardo
1.
P.S. I have provided you with appropriate garments for the party. They should be in the closet.

She tossed the letter on the bed, opened the small wardrobe, and gazed at what was inside.
Oh, hells no.

CHAPTER 5

She has come to me as I knew she would. Let the games begin.

The first thing Renata remembered about that night was the gleaming glass doors of the mansion. This was not the evil demonic mansion she had envisioned. Then again, it made sense why everything looked so beautiful on the outside, just as the city initially looked. But there was only death and misery behind that beautiful facade.

Never trust a Devil. Never sign a contract with a Devil. Lying is as natural to them as breathing. Temptation is their power.

Renata took stock of her feelings, making sure that she was focused and ready for her first real mission. She half expected it to trigger a response of panic or fear, but it didn't. In fact, she felt perfectly relaxed. As if this building was as familiar to her as her home. Of course, in her case, this could only be an expression. This place felt safer than home. Home meant two parents who could barely look at her and a lover whose sorrowful glances made her heart clench every time she thought back to them. It had all made her feel so powerless. But elegantly dressed, walking in a Devil's den? That was power.

Leo had picked out an exquisite piece. It was a dark gray with touches of black and had a dropped neckline.

Renata likes dresses.

She was beginning to understand that verbalizing or actively acknowledging her likes and dislikes helped her to establish who she was—who she might have been previously. She felt as if, after talking to the other citizens of

Vergessen, that opinions and beliefs were the foundation of most people's identities, whether they knew it or not.

She lifted the long skirts and approached the double doors. She didn't hesitate to push them open as self-preservation was, apparently, something somewhat unfamiliar.

She was immediately greeted by the faint smell of leather and dust coming from within, like an old store that had been collecting peculiarities for hundreds of years. The room was brightly lit with glittering glasses and decor in every corner and despite the smell, no speck of dust was found. Giant candelabras were adorned with the same otherworldly gemstones she had seen on the surface of the homes, and the tiled floor was also streaked with their exquisite beauty. The only unsettling aspect of the foyer was that it was completely empty.

The doors apparently kept the mansion incredibly insulated as they blocked out the sounds of orchestral music coming from within—a sound so welcoming to her ears. Her fingers twitched, and she had the overwhelming desire to plop down on the floor and sway gently to the music. However, she resisted her baser needs and swept her keen eyes around the room.

As if on cue, she suddenly heard a thumping noise, as if someone was stumbling down the stairs. In an instant, a thin creature landed clumsily in front of her. Renata shrank back, fingering the dagger hidden under her skirts. But the figure simply righted himself, dusted off his pants, and grinned at her wickedly. Which was made even more sinister by the Devil mask he wore. Ironic since, as his red skin, short horns, and long tail indicated, he was, undoubtedly, a Devil.

"Whooooo are youuuu?" he asked in a sing-song voice.

Renata leaned back to give herself some distance in case the stranger jumped for her, "excuse me?"

"Mmmmm. I saiiiid whoooo are yoooou?"

He batted his long eyelashes but didn't break his wide smile—teeth shining brightly, cuspids slightly pointed. His delicate black horns were adorned with rings that glittered in the candlelight, and he was wearing brightly colored pants and a black silken shirt.

"M'lady, are you lost? I don't recognize you—hmmmmm do you *belooong* to someone?" he demurred as he looked Renata up and down, seeming genuinely curious.

Renata steeled herself.

Leo said flattery worked so...

"Oh dear me." Making a show of twisting her fingers. "I had no idea this was such an intrusion. You see, I am here for someone, but I'm not entirely sure how to find him, sir. But I'm sure you're so important and can help me? I am simply positive that you know your way around."

Renata looked down at her feet coyly and attempted to feign innocence.

The Devil threw back his head and guffawed.

"You can't be serious!" He laughed, grabbing his sides. "That is the most ridiculous display I've seen in a while! Darling, I love a good compliment as much as the next ego-driven fiend, but you've got to do better than *that.* Perhaps start with complimenting my manly prowess?"

He waggled an eyebrow.

She ground her teeth together and narrowed her eyes.

"Fine, yes! I *am* looking for someone, so if you wouldn't mind!"

She tried to shove her way around the Devil.

"My myyyy dearie, don't get your tail in a knot."

She felt it pointless to mention that she didn't possess this particular appendage, unlike him.

"I'll say this for you, little lady, you are interesting. I can see why he likes you. Not many get to sign a contract with him these days. So picky picky picky."

He tsked, shaking his head with each word for emphasis.

"He?" Renata was suddenly *very* interested in talking. "You know who it is?"

"No, no. First introductions, then information. That's called decorum."

The Devil spun on his toes and flipped backward, jingling the bells on his mask. He landed flawlessly with a swish of his hand, bowing deeply.

"I am the royal jester to the High Devils, Demons, and Monstrosities here in The Hells. But you may call me...Jester!"

He smiled, obviously pleased with himself.

Renata wasn't sure she understood the joke. She also couldn't recall if she was allowed to share her name with this creature.

Was it Devils you can't tell your names to? Fairies? Gnomes? Ah. Screw it.

"I'm...Ren," she replied, remembering the nickname that Benji had given her.

Huh. Yeah. That's it. I'm Ren.

Renata felt like a stranger.

"I am here looking for the Devil I signed a contract with. I need to see him immediately. We have... important business to go over."

Jester breathed an overly dramatic sigh.

"Oh, Mortals. All the same. They sign contracts with *Devils*, which everyone warns them *not* to do, and then get all vexed when they regret it. Why is that, do you think?" he said with a pause.

It took a beat for her to realize that this wasn't rhetorical.

"Oh. Ugh, naivety? Desperation?"

At least these were the reasons she had assigned to herself.

"Yes, yesssss, that is right," he nodded enthusiastically. "You know, I *could* help you find who you need," he crooned, "but why would I do so much work for free?"

His wicked smile appeared again.

"How about we play a game? If you win, I take you directly to your master." Jester made a point of pausing for dramatic flair. "And if I win...well, then let's say you owe me a favor?"

Ren snorted.

"Absolutely not. Mortals may be naive, but I'm not stupid. I'm not making a deal with a Devil."

She made another move to walk past him but almost tumbled, stepping on her long gown.

How is it that I can leap in the air almost twice my height and can't walk in this damned thing?

Jester laughed gleefully.

"Haven't you already sold your *soul* to a Devil? A very dangerous Devil at that. What's a little *agreement* with a *Lesser* Devil going to hurt?"

He pouted his lip and blinked his eyes innocently.

Ren took a mental note of this expression to use for later.

"And obviously, nothing would be *binding.* I'm not asking for a contract. I'm just playful!"

Another grin.

She processed his words, surprised at herself for even considering.

"Wait. You're a Lesser Devil?"

She tried to recall the few details that Leo had told her.

Jester looked smug.

"I *do* love the green ones. But *you* aren't as innocent as you seem, are you?" He squinted his eyes. "You've seen death. So so much death."

Ren stepped back with a start, once again snagging her dress below her heeled boots.

The fiend didn't elaborate on the point, ignoring Ren's reaction.

"A Lesser Devil doesn't have wings for one, and our magic is a bit more, lets say, benign. I couldn't compel you to do anything you didn't *want* to do, for example."

He then purposefully walked towards her and leaned down, inches away from her face.

Ren wasn't particularly short, but she had noticed a pattern in the stature of Devils being quite imposing.

"And if I do say so myself, so much more majestic and unique with our lovely shades," he said, touching his red skin. "High Devils aren't nearly as lucky—muddy, muted skin like you *Mortals.*"

"I don't want to play your games," she said, this time successfully pushing past him and stalking off.

Great, turn your back to a Devil. Where are you even going?

Jester did not follow. He just stood in the foyer, giggling.

Her body kept moving, determinedly, not having a plan, until she realized the music was getting louder.

Of course. You can't bloody help yourself.

Going to see an orchestra was an idiotic idea. Orchestras meant people and if Jester so easily identified her as *other*, how would she not draw the attention of every Demon, Devil, or worse in this mansion?

Admonishing her instincts, she took an immediate right down a deserted hallway.

Leo made everything sound so easy as if the palace were full of other wandering soulless people looking for their contracts. But there she was, out in the open in an unfamiliar plane of existence, trying to *steal* something from a Devil.

It was the first time it hit her. She'd known that was the goal. Get the tome back. But it was only now that she had understood the consequences. What an idiotic thing to do— surely that would violate her contract. And if so, she'd become a sleeper!

She groaned.

Satisfied that she had put enough space between her and Jester, she halted her march.

Okay. Where to start? library?

The hallway was lit sparingly with torches every several feet. All the doors seemed identical except for one, which had gemstone details veining through it. She approached it cautiously. The red crystalline features ran between gaps in the wood, looking like lava running up and down from the outside. Her stomach growled.

So pretty.

She tried the handle. Locked. She grumbled in frustration.

The plate behind the metallic knob was carved with intricate floral patterns and held a large keyhole, just large enough to peek into. But no matter how hard Ren squinted, she couldn't make out anything from the other side.

She retrieved her blade, placed it into the keyhole, and jiggled. The door didn't budge, but the back plate made a clicking sound—a sound that provoked the semblance of recognition.

She scanned the hall, looking for inspiration, and silently approached the torch bracket in front of her. She suddenly felt a momentary, quick vibration from her piccolo as if in encouragement. It was the only other thing she had brought besides her gilded dagger. A small token of comfort.

Each bracket was adorned with varying sizes of glorious red gems held together with long and metallic arms and decorated with artful and delicate figures of Devils holding pikes and dancing.

Clasping with both hands on one of the miniatures, she gave a tug. The metal was strong but slightly rusted and pliable. Ren hiked up her skirts to grab at her dagger. She propped the sheathed dagger on the bottom of the bracket, supported her leg on the wall, and put all her weight on the dagger. After several seconds, she felt a give and heard the echoing clank of metal hitting a stone.

Ren, hardly believing her plan had worked. She grabbed her newly acquired lock-pick but hesitated. Her dark eyes roved over the red gems as the flames bounced through them, creating a kaleidoscope of designs on the wall. She wet her lips, reached for the largest of them, and placed the hilt of her dagger against the prongs holding it into place. It didn't take nearly as much force to free, landing gently in Ren's expectant palm.

Her breath caught. It was…a masterpiece. Something she was convinced could only exist by some otherworldly magic. Then he came.

Oh, my Renata. You delight me so very much. You greedy, greedy girl.

She whirled her dagger poised in her hand, ready to strike. But the hall was abandoned.

Ren clenched her teeth together.

"I'm not playing your games," she gritted out. "I said *no!*"

Her voice echoed through the empty halls, and the torch instantly snuffed out as waves of black smoke floated like steam off her body.

Ren spun again, swiping her dagger through the air wildly, finding no target.

She could still see as the other torches' flames danced around, flickering as the blackness moved towards them, dissipating right before it could engulf the flames.

The effect didn't last long. It never did. It rose and curled around her and soon faded as if she were a snuffed candle letting off her final smoky tendrils.

For an instant, she thought about abandoning the den, continuing to walk until she could no longer see the palace. But her stubbornness won out against her trepidation. Nothing was going to stop her from finishing what she started. She slipped her prize into her bodice and approached the door.

Delicately, she inserted the small metal piece into the lock and instinctively knew to close her eyes and...listen. She could hear small clicks, little tinkling notes telling her when to twist and when to add force, like when her fingers knew how to grip a knife or fly across the openings in her piccolo. It took about a minute, but finally, she heard a satisfying clink.

Ren smiled at herself and quietly pushed the door open.

To her great disappointment, it wasn't a library but rather a large sitting room. A fireplace on each wall was lit and burning, and several elegant cushioned chairs were placed around the room. It was positively homey.

It wasn't all a loss, however. There were several bookshelves holding old and distinguished-looking tomes and scrolls.

Trying again to be as quiet and graceful as possible, she entered the room and silently closed the door behind her. She traced her hands down each tome, inspecting the spines. Disappointingly, the majority of the books were indecipherable, their names and titles written with sharp and incomprehensible letters resembling jagged knives.

She suddenly heard the door rattle slightly after passing two of the largest bookcases.

Panicked, Ren quickly jerked her head around, hoping her instincts would show her the perfect hiding place. There it was—a small gap between two bookcases right behind the door.

As the door opened, she threw herself toward it. The only problem was that Renata apparently hadn't trained how to stuff five pounds of tulle into small hiding places.

Dammit, dammit, dammit to hell!

The door opened, snagging on her dress.

With a start, Ren realized that it was Jester who was standing at the entrance, looking amused.

He shook his head and reached out a hand to pull her from her hiding place.

"You're not very good at this."

He chuckled.

Glaring, she clasped his hand.

He gave a sharp tug and wrenched her and her now crumpled dress free from the tight space.

"Actually, I think I am very good at this. But *this*," she gestured angrily, "*monstrosity*, keeps getting in my way!"

Jester cocked his head to the side.

"My dear, I know Monstrosities. Some of them are my best friends, and that dress is *not* a Monstrosity."

Exasperated, she sighed.

"What are you even doing here?" he said, raising a delicate eyebrow. "If I didn't know any better, I'd say you were up to no good."

"I...got lost. Then I was scared that if someone found me—somewhere I wasn't supposed to be...I'd...be punished?" she said uncertainly.

Not a great liar either, Renata.

Smiling widely again, Jester's eyes sparkled.

"Lucky for you, mischief and dishonesty are two of my favorite things. But listen, you need to stay out of trouble tonight. I don't know what will happen if someone finds you, as entertaining as that would be." He paused for a moment and pursed his lips. "We might even get to see you flayyyyed." He sighed, nostalgic. "We haven't had a flaying in so long."

Not for the first time that night, Ren was struck dumb with nothing in response.

Jester then pulled off his Devil mask, revealing a young male with a handsome face.

"Let's make this interesting. *You* get to be my entertainment for the night." He smirked, revealing two dimples, and tossed her the mask.

Catching it nimbly, she stared at the red Devil.

"Other Mortals are here tonight," he continued, "but servants and Mortals are wearing masks. The lords wanted to have a masquerade or some such." He rolled his eyes. "But those Devils are too *proud* to hide their own faces." He pointed a long, clawed finger at hers. "Don't lose that. Being indebted to a Devil, even a Lesser one, has consequences. Oh. And the next time you open a locked door, you might find more than you bargained for."

And without another word, he silently slipped out.

CHAPTER 6

She worships me with her sins. How delicious it feels to defile her. To show her her true nature. Breathtaking. But I feel myself, perhaps too diverted.

Ren slipped on the mask and got to work. She went through every book in the sitting area to no avail.

Frustrated, she held up a book to throw it across the room.

No. Ren likes books.

She fought the impulse.

Instead, Ren placed it gently back on the shelf where she found it, rolling her eyes at herself.

You're ridiculous. Books can't feel.

Resigned, she approached the door, she'd locked it this time, and unlatched it carefully to avoid alerting any lurkers outside.

She peeked her head out—empty. The only change was the lantern a few feet from her, now re-lit. She tried not to think of more angry Devils walking the halls, passing only a few feet away from her.

I'm sure it was just that Jester.

She creeped out the door soundlessly, having finally got the hang of the dress.

In the hall, she could again hear the orchestra. The elegant music began to crescendo, and she felt another tug as it beckoned her, the temptation growing.

She wasn't *technically* supposed to *avoid* everyone here, was she? Leo had encouraged her to blend in, hadn't he? Sneaking through halls wasn't exactly blending in, and she'd never find out anything about her contract doing so.

She tilted her head, orienting herself towards the music. She had no trouble finding the two large double doors inside. She could hear the enticing music, talk, laugh, and occasionally swished gowns.

Well, it doesn't sound like torture and Mortal sacrifices.

Before she could talk herself out of it, she pushed one of the doors open, barely wide enough to see.

There were hundreds of partiers. Some were in groups conversing while others danced and swayed to the music. They were all dressed in immaculate gowns and dublets. The decor could only be described as opulent with glittering gemstones shining from every surface. Chandeliers, tables, classes, dinnerware, and seating were all embossed with different chromatic stones.

Looking around, it was easy to distinguish Devils from Mortals as they all wore masks of different colors, all with depictions of demons or imps.

They weren't cowering as she'd expected them to be. In fact, the majority were included in the partiers. Giggling, standing in corners, and sipping champagne. Some were Lesser Devils like Jester, skin in every hue imaginable. Pink, blue, purple, and red. Their tails swished, and horns were on full display, with only some donning masks. She supposed, as Jester had said, that the ones without masks were of a more important status.

There were also several Devils with large leathery wings cascading down their backs. Unlike the Lesser Devils with their colorful complexions, they looked perfectly Mortal except for the long black horns perched on the crowns of their heads.

One female in particular exuded divine beauty. She wore a fitted corset dress made of the finest silks and was absolutely dripping with the most alluring jewelry. All reminiscent of those found all over the city and now, in Ren's own bodice. The Devil had a haughty laugh and was sipping from a long-stemmed champagne glass as she flexed her opalescent wings.

Ren felt her stomach clench as bile threatened to rise as the female's jubilant giggle echoed off the walls. How could such effortless abandon exist mere steps away from such misery? And how could these people bask in this vulgar display of privilege when there was so much suffering on their doorstep?

Her disgust morphed to anger as a female laughed again, tossing her crystal-embossed hair over her shoulder. Ren wanted to rip it out. Wanted to scream at these people to *help*. Surely, with all of this extravagance, they could do *something*. Or—perhaps, she would *make* them.

Her hand twitched again, but not for her piccolo this time.

Then...

Indulge me, darling. Just this once. You could hurt them, you know? It wouldn't be hard. Not for you.

The phantom voice caressed her ears.

She froze. The voice was getting stronger.

No. No. Please. No!

She didn't want to send smoke signals showing her location to everyone in the room.

But nothing happened.

Still, it was worrying—being haunted by someone or something couldn't be a good sign. It hadn't previously been threatening. In fact, this was the first time she believed it had violent intentions. But not from it...*for* her. As if encouraging her to lash out.

She breathed in slowly, calming her wrath as she stepped further into the ballroom.

Stay focused. Find the contract. Find the book.

Once inside, she had a full view of the immaculate stage. She gasped. Never had Ren seen such an orchestra. Hundreds of members played both traditional and unfamiliar instruments. She didn't recognize the song that they played, but it didn't matter. She longed to join in, take the stage with the rest, and savor the song. To add it to her small memory bank.

"That certainly would *not* be blending in," she grumbled to herself. "Maybe just a listen."

She walked on the party's fringes, trying her best to be unassuming and taking glimpses out of the side of her eyes to make sure no one was watching her. She was just one of several Mortal females smattered around the room.

Once she could see the musicians clearly, her stomach clenched in craving. Yet she was disappointed to discover that the orchestra was ending their current score.

A man stood up. No—not a man. A Devil.

He was wearing a starched white shirt rolled up to his elbows and a solid black vest. It was evidently his turn to play solo because he gracefully walked to the front of the stage, his violin held tenderly in his hands.

His eyes were dark burgundy, and his white hair lay elegantly on his shoulders. His face was angular and masculine, with a long, elegant nose. But the most mesmerizing feature was his devilish horns. Smooth as his skin and dark black, they curved gracefully up from the top of his head towards his crown before ending in a sleek point. Not sinister or threatening, but rather like a crown worn by a virtuous prince.

And then, he began to play. While the orchestra surely accompanied him, he was the only thing that existed for Ren. She only heard his honeyed notes and watched as his long fingers stroked the strings deftly.

He'd completely entranced her.

His arms moved, gliding the bow across with exquisite finesse. His eyes were closed, long lashes laying gently on his pale cheeks.

An unfamiliar sensation wafted over her. While her brain tried to process the meaning, her body understood and took over. Her face heated, and her pulse skittered. She was having a hard time catching air, and her dress felt too tight.

The devilish creature swayed rhythmically with the notes, and she could see a small crease between his brow as if so moved by the arrangement he could not help but feel it in every muscle.

Too soon, and with one last pull from his bow, the music stopped. The echo of the last note ricocheted off the walls, and the male opened his eyes almost sleepily before bowing his head to the audience.

There was a throng of applause around the chamber and murmurs of approval.

But Ren couldn't move—her mouth parted and breaths shallow. She didn't even notice that she was now the only person standing by the stage.

As the male lifted his head from his bow, he locked eyes with Ren and gave the smallest smile.

Befuddled, she looked away, her cheeks hot.

Before she could return to the party—flee to hide her embarrassment, she felt a gentle touch on her elbow.

"Excuse me, my lady."

She turned. It was the violinist.

Her body, still not cooperating with her brain, stood there, transfixed, staring into his eyes, which glittered like tiny stars lived within. His smile was crooked. Sensual.

"It isn't often I find someone as captivated by music as I am."

His voice was smooth and deep, the vibration making her toes curl.

She responded, her voice finally restored. "Well, it isn't often that I have the pleasure of seeing someone— something so stunning," she blurted.

Good gods, woman. Pull it together.

She tried to give a timid smile, but she wasn't sure if it looked right on her face.

His eyes flicked for a moment at the rest of the room and then back to her. He bowed again, this time deeply, and offered his hand.

"Would you care to dance?"

While Renata certainly knew it was a *bad* idea to dance with a Devil, Ren felt a bit embarrassed at the thought of rejecting someone who was literally *bowing* to her. Plus, he could know information about contracts.

She laid her hand softly in his and noticed that his fingers were long and velvety with no calluses, odd for a consummate violin player.

Her eyes darted once more around the room as the male led her to the middle of the dance floor. No one was watching. They all seemed too involved with their own activities.

"You are new to our courts," he began. "Don't worry, my lady," he said as if reading her thoughts. "They are either not paying attention or are trying very hard not to." He gave her a wide grin, revealing two sharp fangs. "They would hate being accused of being envious. No one wants to summon Pelegros this early in the evening."

She smiled, not wanting to appear as clueless as she was.

He placed a hand on her lower back and drew her flush with his body. It was hard and muscular against her.

She gulped.

Then, a panicked thought.

Wait. Do I know how to dance?!

He smiled coyly as the music started again, and he spun her onto the dance floor. She held her breath as she willed her feet to move in time. But she needn't worry. Her body knew these steps, or enough to get by, and at least she wasn't tripping over her dress or his toes.

"Do you belong to someone?" he asked, tilting his head curiously.

As soon as he opened his mouth, she smelled the most incredible aroma of flowers. She couldn't place what they looked like, but she could feel the flicker of a memory tingle at the back of her mind. Long fields on a summer day, sweet wine next to a rippling brook. It was...enticing.

As she breathed in, her vision began to blur. She felt truly at peace for the first time. She smiled lazily, meeting the male's burgundy eyes gleaming back at her.

"You are quite lovely," he said, reaching up to caress her cheek.

It felt like the softest petals tickling her skin. It was calming. Safe. Like there was nothing in any plane of existence that could hurt her.

"You're a musician. Wind instrument, I presume," he smiled. "I can tell by your lips. Someone who knows...how to use them."

He moved his hands to her lips but did not touch them. They just hovered there.

She couldn't think—couldn't make a sound. She could only look into his eyes, completely hypnotized with every gravelly word. Her sensations began to change from slow and soft to something much warmer. Her heart thumped harder, and as he continued with every touch, pleasant ripples of sensation created throughout her body.

Ren had never been touched, not by a male and certainly not by someone so captivating.

"I find that the best musicians feel the music," he continued, ignoring Ren's lack of response. "The notes penetrate. Slip inside you and move you to ecstasy."

Finally, she found words.

"Y-yes. I feel that music has its own type of power," she stammered, trying in vain to ignore the ache forming between her thighs.

His smile widened, his fangs fully revealed.

"I am glad you understand me. Many do not recognize the power music has over people. My name is Xarek. And you are?"

"Ren."

He purred her name.

"Ren."

He seemed to like the taste of it on his tongue. He gently brushed his fingers down her back as he guided her across the dance floor.

"Stunning." He sighed, leaning close. "I admit that I am quite...curious about you."

She couldn't help but lean closer as a response. His body felt so...good. Strong and fierce, a perfect juxtaposition to his light touches.

"Wise of you to not belong to anyone," he drawled. "One should be particular about such things. Mortals deserve the best, of course. I'm sure you're not so easily...satisfied. But I could satisfy you. I would never leave you wanting."

This time, he leaned so close that his lips stroked her neck, and she could feel his warm, flowery breath tickling the small hairs there.

She couldn't breathe.

Her only response was to tremble and bite her lips, choking off a small whimper. She could feel his desire growing through her gown.

Oh my. What are you doing, my darling?

The voice. She tried to blink away the grogginess to stop the clouds from overtaking her. But her want was too great.

I see. Perhaps someone should remind you? You do not belong to him. You. Are. Mine!

His voice, harsher than she had ever heard him, snapped her out of her revelry, her mind instantly clearing right before feeling the ground tremble.

The glasses on the tables began to clink together, some crashing down, glittering the marble floor.

Xarek pulled back, startled and looking horrified.

Her right hand, still held in his, began to emit black tendrils.

He dropped her hands, and without warning, two giant bat-like wings sprang forth from between his shoulders.

The tremors stopped.

"You said you didn't belong to anyone," he hissed. "What is this, some sort of sick game? Are you trying to get us all *killed*!"

His last words echoed in the room and she could feel every face locked on them.

Ren was too stunned, immobilized with fear at the terrifying beast standing before her. Too alarmed at how captivating had suddenly changed to malevolent within seconds.

She surveyed the room nervously. All eyes watching with terrified expressions. Some clutching their partners, others covering their mouths to stifle a cry.

"I...I..."

"Go," he gritted out. "I don't know what trick you are playing." He shook his head. "But we want no part in your twisted plotting."

His voice shook with rage, his wings spreading wider.

Ren backed up. "Sorry, I really didn't—"

"I said *go*!" he bellowed.

She spun on her booted heel and ran. Running towards the double doors, feeling each set of eyes.

Crossing the threshold, she ran aimlessly. Anywhere. She needed to hide. To get a moment to untangle her thoughts and catch her breath. Hastily, she pulled open the first unadorned door she saw.

Please be a godsdamn broom closet.

The door swung open, and she flung herself inside, shutting it tightly behind her.

It wasn't a broom closet.

And she wasn't alone.

The room was dark, save for the light flickering from the mantle.

She heard it before she saw it, a deep feminine moan.

A Lesser Devil, skin pink and glistening with sweat—head flung back and mouth open. She was completely nude, and her hips were shifting rhythmically to the thrusts of her partner.

Ren couldn't completely see the male, most of his body blocked by the large armchair they were using for their stage. But she could see his face.

His head rested against the back of the chair, delicate curls tousled and lying artfully between two sinister-looking horns, both of which were larger and thicker than Xarek's, curving around his head dramatically. His fist was twisted around the Lesser Devil's tail, helping guide her body where he wanted her.

The muscles in his forearms flexed as he reached up to fondle the Devil's perfect breast.

Ren covered her mouth to stifle a gasp as, to her horror, the tendrils, still wafting from her person, floated towards the couple.

The male groaned with pleasure as he tilted his head to the side and opened his eyes, fixing them on Ren.

"My sweet, I was hoping *you* would come," he growled before throwing his head back, curls flying, a roar of rapture escaping as he climaxed.

Done. She was *done* with this.

She whirled around through the door, trying to keep her feet, urgently retracing her disoriented steps to the foyer. She threw open the stained glass doors and dashed out into the night, hearing Jester giggle as she fled.

CHAPTER 7

There are few things I hate more than being overwhelmingly curious. It's an irritation I can't quite purge. And she—well, she is the most intoxicating of curiosities.

It was completely dark inside as Ren ran up to her room in The Denizen's Tower, locking herself in.

Her chest heaved as she tried to catch her breath. She hadn't been threatened, hadn't been in danger, yet she felt desperate to escape.

She had encountered something entirely unfamiliar, in both sensation and emotion and had completely lost herself. She had lost control. A thought that terrified her.

Losing control meant losing the little part of herself that she still had—the small memories and names that she held in her mind. She was losing Renata. Doomed to be just *Ren* for whatever remained of her life.

Even now, she couldn't rid her mind of what it would feel like to be that pink Devil moaning on top of a sinfully beautiful violinist. Because in that fleeting moment, in his arms, she didn't care. Ren, Renata...they both agreed. She didn't want to think. No more war inside her mind. Only feeling. Just body taking over. Embracing pleasure.

No. Stop.

She pushed the heels of her palms into her eyes. She was more than this weak thing. They had told her that. Jamal had told her that.

He was another Half-Elf who kept bar at her favorite tavern in Vergessen. Her feet had taken her there, unbidden, after another heart-wrenching meeting with her parents.

Jamal had waved her over to the bar, and she settled in. If she was going to have another uncomfortable conversation, she was at least going to get a stiff drink out of it.

"Nothing?" he asked, pain in his eyes.

He had poured her two fingers of an amber liquid, which she didn't question. She immediately took a big swig and delighted in the rich, honeyed flavor that sent immediate relief through her.

"Nothing," she responded, swirling the remaining liquid. She was now on her second. "I woke up and had no concept of who I was. Or...not the things that matter. And everything is terrifying because everything is a first! The first taste of pastry, the first swim in a lake. You know nothing of yourself, so nothing is comforting—well, except music. I didn't forget my music."

He nodded at her, wiry hair bouncing as he did.

"Has...anyone tried to help you remember?"

She bit her lip. "A little. But it hasn't been helping. Clara and Atlas just got frustrated. Clara kept showing me things from my past—toys, pictures, the like—hoping it would jog something."

She noticed that he would not meet her eyes.

"Do *you* know anything? Any reason why this would happen?" she asked.

He sucked in some air.

"The thing is, Renata. I don't know if I'm the best person to help you with this."

She looked up at him, eyes wide. "Anything— absolutely anything you could tell me would be helpful."

He started hesitantly, "Renata. The first time I saw you, after everything that happened in the mountains, you were different. Stoic—Detached.

"You would come here and drink until you couldn't stand. Until I had to send for Nephele. But you wouldn't tell me what happened. You just...sat there. Staring off into space. The only time you seemed to even be breathing was the few times you played your piccolo, and even then, you were...somewhere else."

She considered this, wetting her lips.

"What happened...in the mountains?"

"I don't know, Renata. You wouldn't talk about it." He paused. "I know you came back a hero, everyone talking about how you saved the Mortal Plane. I heard rumors, of course, but you refused to acknowledge them—neither did Nephele. He kept telling me that you just needed time. That war was hard for everyone, but you were recovering."

She couldn't remember much else from that night, probably because she had, at some point, lost track of how much liquid amber she had consumed.

Yes, the warmth of whiskey. What a comfort it would be tonight. But getting whiskey meant wandering downstairs and seeing Fred. And honestly, she didn't think she could face anyone right now.

Feeling defeated, she threw off her dress and the infernal mask, and crawled into bed, holding her one familiar companion close to her chest but not having the energy for a comforting song.

Instead, she hummed to herself until sleep took her into oblivion.

***

The next morning, Ren was startled awake.

"Oooooghf!"

She jumped up from the bed, only wearing her underclothes, and drew her dagger—which she had hidden under her pillow—and lunged for the creature.

"Wait! Stahp!" he shouted before blinking away into invisibility.

"... Jester?"

The tall red Devil appeared again, this time sitting on her wardrobe.

"In the flesh! For now. Unless you plan to skin me alive?"

"What the hells are you doing here?" she shouted, still brandishing The Holy Transgression.

"Well, give me a moment, give me a moment."

He clumsily crawled off the wardrobe and dropped to the ground, giving a flourish despite his blundering.

"I am here to *help* you!"

She squinted at him, trying to make sure she wasn't dreaming. "I told you. No more games, no more deals with Devils!"

"Yeah, yeah, you told me." He groaned. "I'm not here to make a deal! Your patron sent me. He knows you're here and wants to talk."

She gaped at him.

"How? How could he know that I'm here?"

"Oh, how could he *not*?" He snorted. "You weren't exactly subtle last night, and besides, he owns your *soul.* You're connected!"

She groaned again.

So much for blend in.

"How do I know you're not trying to trick me or send me off to my death?"

He shrugged.

"Any other leads, missy? It's just a meeting, and it *will* be with your patron. He won't be able to hurt you while your contract is still valid."

Ren cautiously lowered her dagger.

"Who is he? I don't know anything about this...patron."

"Sure you do! I'm sure he's been talking to you. Quite chatty, that one."

"The voice?"

Well that explains that.

"What are you getting out of this? Don't Devils always want something?"

He smiled. "You're catching on. I like it! But no, I'm just here to watch. You were *incredibly* entertaining last night, and I find myself a bit...bored with the revelry of *nobles*, and the sleepers aren't great conversationalists."

He snapped his fingers and disappeared again, only reappearing laying on her bed, leaning on one arm, his tail whipping back and forth.

"So what?" she said, trying to keep the anoyance out of her voice. "Do I just...make an appointment?"

"My dear, he is waiting now! You shouldn't keep him waiting." He waggled his finger at her. "Of his many attributes, patience isn't one of them."

Suddenly anxious, Ren grabbed her tunic and trousers, dressing hurriedly. This meeting could finally mean answers. She slung her satchel over her shoulder and reached for the doorknob.

"Wait...where am I going?"

Jester gave her a pointed look. "You're not *going* anywhere. You just go *to* him!"

"Do you plan to explain the difference?" she retorted.

He hopped up and made a small jump on the bed before dismounting.

"I just need an amulet, something to tether you with him."

"But I thought you said we were already connected?"

He rolled his eyes, losing patience.

"Sheesh, I hate working with virgins. The transportation link is stronger if you have a *tether*. He'll be able to summon you whenever he needs you. Where's your contract?"

"Oh. About that. I actually don't know."

"What do you mean you *don't know?*" His eyes widened. "You have to have your contract on you at all times, or it's void! And since you haven't died or become a sleeper, you *must* have it somewhere."

Ren ground her teeth together.

"Look, I don't have it. Search me!"

Ren threw her satchel at his feet and pulled up her shirt to show her waistband.

Jester made a disgusted face.

"Um...no thanks. Soulless female Half-Elves aren't really my type.

Ren glared.

Sure, and Devils with long nails are so much more attractive.

An image of the pink Devil flashed through her mind.

Fair enough, Renata.

Jester pinched the bridge of his nose.

"What about an item? Something that you have that might connect you to his voice?"

She thought momentarily, and then her hand involuntarily moved to her pocket. The red stone tucked safely inside.

"I have a...gem. One of those that they use for decoration. He spoke when I...found it."

Jester responded with a wicked smile.

"Oh, yes, he likes to speak when you...*find* things. But sure, that will do just fine," he said, clearing his throat and holding his hand out for it.

Ren felt a tightening in her stomach. She didn't want to give this creature her stone. It was so...special. What if she couldn't find another? Couldn't show it to everyone so they could bask in its beauty and wonder how Ren could possess something so matchless?

My sweet. People will be in awe of you, with or without the vurmite.

"Did you hear that?" she entreated, looking closely at her hands as they emitted the now-familiar smoke.

Jester giggled and clapped his hands.

"Oh, I do love this part! Ahem. The gem, my dear?"

Reluctantly, Ren retrieved her stone, vurmite, and handed it to Jester.

The Devil twirled it in his hand and sneered. "Oh, dear, you *must* have pleased him with your little *discovery.*"

He emphasized the last with a wink.

Ren glared at him.

He cupped the vurmite in his hands and blew on it, a glow emanating.

She hadn't thought her little stone could be any more beautiful than it already was, but as his breath touched it, the cuts of the gem seemed to move and reshape. Her eyes widened, and her fingers itched to grab it.

Then the glow was gone.

"There," he said, handing it back to her.

She tried not to snatch it out of his hands greedily.

"Just whisper his name into the stone, and it will take you to him."

She felt the smooth, glassy surface in her hand. "What? Like now?"

He made a shooing sign with his hands.

"I don't have all day. I have other assignments, you know?"

"No wait," she blurted, "I still don't know his name!"

Jester slapped his forehead.

"I take it back. I *don't* understand why he likes you. His name is Azur," he said cheerily before snapping his fingers and disappearing.

But despite vanishing, Ren still heard the shuffle of his feet and saw the door swing open and close again.

She rolled her eyes.

"Yes, very sneaky, Jester."

She pulled her satchel back onto her shoulders and secured the dagger.

Here goes nothing.

She delicately fondled the stone before tentatively raising it to her lips, and in the tiniest of whispers, Ren said his name for the first time.

CHAPTER 8

So eager. She is different this time—re-made, in my image. Pity. She lost so much more than her soul that night. I smell her ambition—her desire. It feeds me. It excites me.

Unlike the portal, it was only a blink before Ren was in a different room. It was large and imposing, with vaulted ceilings and a window that looked out onto darkened mountains at the far end. Bookshelves lined the walls, and under normal circumstances, Ren would have been overcome with the overwhelming urge to search them all for her prize.

Now, she was too thunderstruck by the male in front of her, sitting demurely behind a large mahogany desk, legs crossed, and hands threaded together.

It was him.

Flashes of images from the night before raced through her brain. A head flung back, curls tousled, moans of ecstasy, and glistening muscles.

But today, he was nothing if not the perfect image of composure. Hair sleekly styled, not a curl out of place, he smirked at her as if he knew they shared a secret.

He was treacherously handsome, his horns curving gracefully, accentuating the sharp angles of his face. He wore a solid black ensemble that matched his onyx hair and made his red eyes glow even more imposingly in the purple light.

"Good morning, Renata. I was expecting you." With the subtlest flick of his finger, a chair appeared before his desk. "Please, have a seat."

"You...you have my contract!" she said with as much confidence as she could muster while simultaneously trying to banish the thought of how his skin might feel against hers.

The Devil steepled his fingers.

"Yes, I am the author of your contract."

She had half expected him to deny it. Now, she wasn't sure where to start. "Well, sir—"

"Please," he purred. "Call me Azur," he said with a grin and a wink. "And do sit," he gestured to the chair. "You look uncomfortable, and we simply can't have that."

Ren mentally cursed herself for having involuntarily shifted.

As she moved to sit, she noticed books, documents, and envelopes, all written in harsh script, were stacked haphazardly on his desk.

Are all of these contracts?

"Azur. I am here to inquire about my contract."

She paused, testing the waters.

He raised an eyebrow. "I thought the terms of our agreement were quite explicit."

She licked her lips nervously. "Well, you see, I can't find—"

"Contracts must stay with the bearer at all times." Azur's eyes became menacing. "Don't tell me you have misplaced yours."

The purple room darkened at his words.

Ren set her jaw. *She* didn't cower. No matter how much his eyes made her want to melt into her chair.

She lifted her chin and stared back at him.

"Well, I wouldn't have misplaced it if you hadn't taken all of my memories. I'm sure that if I had a few—"

Suddenly, Azur began to laugh, a belly laugh that sounded too jovial for such an imposing creature.

"No, no, I'm sorry, my dear." He wiped a fake tear away from his eyes. "Don't worry. I knew you'd forget where you put your contract so I ensured you wouldn't lose it. I'm quite clever that way."

He flashed her self-satisfied grin.

Ren breathed out, releasing the knot in her chest.

"That's—that's great! Where is it?"

Azur stood up and walked to stand in front of Ren, casually leaning back on his desk with crossed legs.

"I'm a little disappointed you didn't figure it out."

Azur's eyes, still glowing, hypnotically sparkled, and his face regained its serious intensity. The power radiating off of him felt like she was the opposite side of a magnet. She blinked rapidly, afraid that this might be some Devil trickery to seduce her—or whatever it was they did.

"Enough of your games. Just tell me where it is," she bit out.

He bent down close to her, and for the second time in less than a day, she was face to face with a High Devil. She could feel his breath. It smelled like roses suddenly ignited by fire.

"Why do you Devils get so close?" she managed to stammer out despite the heat rising in her chest, visions of the Devil's writhing still present in her mind.

"My dear. I truly don't know what you mean," he drawled, slowly reaching his hand towards her, grazing her thigh.

Ren gasped, too shocked to recoil.

But he jerked his hand back, plucking the piccolo from her waistband.

She came to herself, wrath appearing suddenly.

Azur's face, still so close to hers, smiled twistedly.

"Give. That. Back," she gritted out through clenched teeth.

He gave a deep-throated chuckle.

"My dear, please don't feed my sin. At least not now. I may not be able to control myself if you do," he said as he ran his fingers delicately across the dimples of her piccolo.

"Mortals are so temperamental—it is quite delightful, really. You more than most."

Ren's whole body tightened. Hating the idea that he knew more about her than she did.

"Play it," he suddenly demanded, offering her piccolo back to her.

Her anger turned to confusion.

"What? You want a performance *now*?"

"Yes, actually," he crooned, checking his perfect nails.

She had to admit, a comforting song felt like the only thing that made sense right now. The only thing that always made sense to her.

"What...should I play?" she asked, retrieving the piccolo, which did, in fact, feel warmer.

He shrugged. "Whatever you want."

Still skeptical, she raised her piccolo cautiously to her lips, keeping her eyes on the Devil lest he snatch her precious instrument away again.

When it reached the seam of her lips, her whole body contracted for a moment, pushing air through her lungs.

She began to play. But no—she wasn't playing. The piccolo seemed to be taking over—forcing the air out from her.

The song was dark. Sinister. She couldn't remember hearing or playing something so menacing. It sent tremors of fear through her.

She wanted to pull the piccolo away. Her music was not like this, should *never* be like this. These notes were threatening, monstrous—not as comforting as they should be. Music should express feeling, not incite fear!

Her body began to tremble as she tried with all her strength to wrench the piccolo from her lips. She met Azur's eyes entreatingly, but he only looked pleased.

"Calm down, my dear. It will be over soon," he said, lips curling.

At his words, Ren felt her body relax, and the piccolo give way. The change was so drastic that she almost flung it from her.

She looked down at her constant companion, feeling betrayed. But there—swirling from her arms, was the familiar black smoke. But this time, they formed into those same jagged symbols across her skin.

She opened and closed her hands, watching the letters shift.

"On my body? The contract was on me the whole time?"

The Devil was still smiling.

"Why, of course, I didn't want you to lose it. Where else would I put it?"

He stood motioning to the letters still glowing with black light.

"That piccolo never leaves your side. Not then. Not now. I knew that no matter what memories were stricken from you, you would remember your music. It's too much of you. More than your soul was, anyway."

"But...I can't read it."

"That *is* a problem, isn't it?" he said, cocking his head to the side. "Well, maybe with some practice and a tutor, you will be able to figure that out in a few years."

He turned around and returned to sit behind his desk.

She gaped at him. "That's not fair! Le—the other Devils told me that you have to understand the contract!"

He picked up a long quill, dipping it in an ink that was suspiciously red.

"Yes, you're right, darling, but you see, you *did* understand the contract when you signed it." He looked at her again with false pity in his eyes. "I can't help it if your memories, which *you* signed away," he said, pointing his quill at her for emphasis, "faded."

He returned his eyes back to his papers, apparently done with the conversation. He waved a long finger in the air, opening the door behind her.

"That's not fair!" she blurted again, realizing too late how childish she sounded.

There again was his pitying look.

Of course, it was a trick. He was a Devil. This was what he did. This was what he *lived* for.

"No," he said firmly as if reading her thoughts. "I do not trick people with my contracts. You *agreed*. Begged even. Right here on your knees." He pointed his quill to the carpeted section in front of his desk. "It was quite the sight, if I remember correctly. You were *very* convincing."

Ren refused to let him get a rise out of her with his implication.

He's lying.

"I only ever gave you *exactly* what you asked for. Did you ever stop and think that maybe you made this deal for a *reason?*" he asked, tone suddenly becoming hard. "Did you even consider that, perhaps, this was the best course of action for you?

"Of course you didn't. You are Mortal. You are impulsive and prone to folly." His deep voice was like gravel, and his red eyes narrowed menacingly. "I am sorry this happened to you, my dear, but it can't be helped, but do *not* blame me."

He waved his hand, dismissing her again.

But Ren wasn't done. She jumped up from her seat.

"You could at least tell me what it says!" she shouted, glaring back.

A ping in the back of her mind warned her to not lose her temper. This was an Immortal she was dealing with.

"Actually, I can't," he said, frowning slightly. This time, it seemed oddly genuine. "Renata, you signed your memories away. If I were to reveal a lost memory, even the memory of your contract, I would be violating the terms we both agreed upon.".

She deflated and looked again at her hands. The writing had vanished. But—surely there was something that could be done. She couldn't continue this way. Couldn't keep living a half-life. Angry tears started to well in her eyes, but she wiped them away quickly, refusing to act the damsel. She would meet her fate head-on.

"There has to be *something* I can do! I'll figure it out. Even if you can't help me."

She looked up and met his eyes, trying to demonstrate her resolve.

Azur sighed, setting down the quill.

"Renata—"

"Ren," she corrected sternly.

He raised an eyebrow, and his smile tilted, revealing a sharp fang.

"Ren. Just because you don't have your memories doesn't mean you don't have purpose. I," he placed his hand on his chest, "could give you that purpose. You are *mine,* and well, I haven't used my resources in a long while. My followers—"

"I'm not yours, and I'm *not* your follower," Ren spat.

"And there she is. This famed *defender* I've missed so terribly."

Ren stood there staring him down, her chest continuing to pulse and vibrate with anger.

"Do you want to hear my offer or not?" he asked, raising an eyebrow.

She remained silent, glaring daggers.

"I cannot restore all of your memories or even most of them. But I can *tell* you a few…anecdotes."

Ren's throat tightened. "Anecdotes? You mean like stories?"

"Perhaps stories, clarify information, give instruction..." He leaned back in his chair, crossing his hands behind his head.

"I'm assuming this isn't out of the kindness of your heart?"

"My dear, there is no kindness in my heart. I can genuinely tell you that I am incapable of kindness." He scoffed. "You will retrieve something for me. Then, and only then, will I give you what you need."

"And why me?"

"You're The Defender of The Planes and need someone with experience for this task. It's really that simple."

Ren considered. This is another one of those moral quandaries. A deal with a Devil. She heard Leo's voice banging around in her head. But despite this, she couldn't for the life of her find a reason not to continue this conversation. "What is it that you want?"

He looked her up and down with excruciating slowness, his eyes gliding across every inch of her.

"So many things, Ren. So very *many* things. But for the purposes of this conversation, I need you to find a document. It contains important contractual information."

"A document? That's it?" Ren squinted at Azur skeptically. "I know how this works. What's the catch?"

"There is *no* catch. And honestly, if there were, I wouldn't tell you." Again, he flicked his hand dismissively. "But I didn't say it would be easy. You'll have to infiltrate the house of a very powerful High Devil. If he finds you, he *will* kill you."

"Oh, is that all?" She guffawed.

"Lord Wyvryn has collected many souls over the years. Signed many contracts and collected many powerful artifacts. His gluttony for influence is...concerning. I need you to find one of these and bring it here."

She thought for a moment about his proposal. The potential risk to her life didn't provoke fear. Actually, she felt rather capable—confident that this would be something she could accomplish.

Besides, she didn't have another lead, and the Wyvryn Devil apparently had artifacts. She could potentially find the tome and get more information about her life in one fell swoop.

"His castle," Azur continued, "is in the city of Dementiz. I will provide you with all the resources you will need."

She felt Renata's voice in the back of her head, spurring her on.

Now or never, Ren.

"Okay, I'll do it!" she blurted before her brain could catch up.

"Very good."

Azur nodded with a broad smile, his long fangs fully visible. He looked down and retrieved a fresh piece of parchment. As he did, the intense smell of dust, books, and fiery roses filled her nose.

He silently dipped his quill in the inkwell and hovered it over the paper. Words, in the same elegant script as that on her body, appeared on the paper. He signed the contract with a flourish and stood to lean over his desk, offering the paper to her.

She walked closer. "You know I can't read this, I'm not signing anything that—"

Then suddenly, the text changed, perfectly legible.

I, Ren, The Defender of The Planes, will retrieve the document marked with sigil of His Lordship Azur Pelegros and forthwith, deliver it to His Lordship, the most esteemed, Azur Pelegros. By doing so, Ren will be permitted three questions to be revealed in a manner permittance to her contract. His Lordship, the most esteemed and handsome,

Azur Pelegros, will truthfully, and without malice, give her the subsequent answers.

Ren choked a laugh at the ridiculousness of his flattery.

The contract was short and to the point. She glanced over it several times, trying to decipher where a trick might be placed within its wording, but could find nothing. She glanced towards Azur, a wry smile on his lips waiting expectantly.

"That's it? I just sign?"

He reached into his desk and pulled out a small dagger.

"Oh *hells,* no!" Ren said, backing away. "Look, I get it, demon lord Devil or whatever, but I'm not signing a contract with my *blood*."

Azur just blinked at her.

"Ren, please, don't be so dramatic. You will barely feel anything, and besides." He paused to trace his fingers up and down the sharp edges of the blade. "You have already done this. If I recall, you didn't even flinch. We were at it for a while, in fact. You particularly enjoyed it when I helped you with the more *sensitive* areas."

Ren successfully stopped her thighs from clenching together, trying not to imagine his head between them.

This is such a mistake.

However, the words in her head didn't sound as convincing as they should have been.

She held out her arms and leaned across the desk, closing the distance.

"No, no, *I'm* not going to cut you. You have to do it yourself. This needs to be your decision."

He offered the blade to her.

She snatched it from him and looked down at her pale Elven skin, observing the purple veins underneath. She positioned the dagger to her forearm right under where her scar was and, before she could hesitate, made a long cut. She winced at the immediate pain—but as soon as it arrived—it was gone. Her arm bled freely, but her blood took on an iridescent hue.

She held it over the contract and met the Devil's eyes questioningly. He simply nodded in encouragement and handed her his quill.

She dipped the quill into her blood, watched as it seeped into the tip, and signed her name. **Ren, The Defender of The Planes,** because she didn't remember her surname. A question she hadn't even thought to ask back in Vergessen.

When finished, she placed the quill on the table and looked up expectantly.

"Now what?"

"Now go be a good girl. I'll send instructions and anything else you might need."

Ren bit back a retort. She turned, surrendering to her fate and still a little dizzy from the entire encounter.

"Oh, and Ren," he called before she could escape. "Next time, please don't hesitate to join in on the fun. Zelaia and I were most disappointed last night, and if I recall correctly, you did *so* enjoy it last time we all were together."

Ren's breath hitched and her treasonous body flushed in want. She had no idea how to respond. She wanted to object. To call him out on his disgusting lies.

But you don't know, though...do you?

He only smirked wickedly at her.

So she turned and marched out the door with as much dignity as she could muster.

CHAPTER 9

It was not hard to convince her. She is desperate. But so am I.

A blink and Ren was back in her dusty room. Jester was waiting for her, sitting on the floor crossed-legged, reading a book.

"Well, you took long enough!" he said, throwing the book behind him before it vanished.

Ren reached up to feel her forehead. It was clammy with sweat.

"Was I really there? Or was it just a dream?"

"Well, that depends," he said, shrugging, "did you see a handsome Devil who talked to you about your contract?"

"Yes."

"Then it wasn't a dream."

Ren could have sworn she heard him murmur *dummy* under his breath.

"Why are you still here?" she snapped, shuffling around the room.

"I am here to help you!"

He held out his hand and, with a flick of his wrist, produced flame. It smoldered for a moment before forming into an elegant black envelope.

"You seem to be *veeeeery* important, Ren. My lord already trusts you with an assignment."

Ren flicked her eyes to the envelope but didn't approach.

"My Lord? So you sold your soul to him too?"

He smiled slightly less gleefully.

"I guess we are in this game together, aren't we?"

"I still don't trust you," she grumbled, walking forward to snatch the envelope.

The words on the front were a sophisticated script—red with a dripping wax seal on the back that was still damp.

"To my beautiful muse," it said.

God, enough with the dramatics.

God? Did you summon me, my sweet?

Are you always in my head? Because I'm definitely not okay with that.

Oh no, no, no. I can only be in your head when you summon me.

I didn't summon you!

Oh, but darling, you most certainly did.

Out! Now!

And with a chuckle, she felt a coldness and knew he'd left.

"You should really work on that."

Jester pointed at the smoky substance lingering on her skin.

"Ughh. I don't know why he does it!"

"Oh, that's easy. He wants to make sure that you know that he's watching. If he isn't in your head, the smoke won't appear. He has to get consent before accessing your thoughts," he finished matter-of-factly.

"But I didn't *give* consent!" she ground out.

He looked thoughtful.

"Well, have you indulged in any sins lately? Greed? Gluttony...Lust?" he emphasized the last with a waggle of his eyebrows. "You know...the seven deadly sins?"

"I—of course not!"

"Weeeeeell, that would summon Azur. It's like calling to him. But don't worry, you can learn to control it. And anyway, if you ever want him to leave you alone, just sever the connection. He can't *spy* on you."

"She felt a bit of the tension leave her shoulders before turning her attention back to the letter.

"Ren," it began. *"I have sent Jester to accompany you into Castle Valdrock. He is very resourceful if a bit maddening at times. You can trust him as your objectives are aligned.*

The contract you are searching for will likely be located in Wyvryn's study and marked with my holy symbol,"

An example was drawn under the words. It was a splash of black paint, which evidently was supposed to be a face, yet it looked more monster than man, with two sinister horns emerging from its head.

*"I have given Jester a set of magical lock pics that you'll be able to use to infiltrate rooms even with the strongest of wards. **Do not get caught**."*

The last sentence was underlined several times.

"We discussed the risks of being discovered, but do not underestimate the wrath you will face if you disappoint me."

It was signed.

His Lordship, most esteemed and handsome Devil of your dream, Azur Pelegros.

"Ridiculous," Renata muttered.

As she lowered the letter, she saw a flash. Holding her hands up, she caught something.

"Apparently, you're really good at being sneaky. Despite your pathetic display the other night."

He showed her one of his playful grins.

She rolled her eyes, hiding her own grin as she looked down at the lock-picking kit.

"Yeah. apparently, I did it a lot...before."

They both let the words hang in the air.

But Jester, never one to allow a moment to go by before a snide remark, broke the silence.

"Okay, Elf girl! Put on your sneakiest shoes, and let's get going!" he said, jumping up.

"Wait, wait, slow down! How do we even get there? Do we, like, hop in a portal and sneak into the castle?"

Jester leaned back and kicked his feet, laughing. "Nooooo, silly girl. We can't just *appear* in the domain of a High Devil! They can detect magic—then they will find us! Then they will tie us up or make our skin into leather for their couches!"

Ren ran her fingers through her hair, exasperated.

"Fine! Then how do we get there? Do you know the way?"

He jumped up and down.

"Of *course*, I know the way. You didn't think Azur would send us all the way to Castle Valdrock without a way to get there! But!" He put one finger in the air to stress his next words. "We will have to walk! Don't worry though, it's only about a day—"

"*Walk?*"

Renata balked.

"Yes, walk. It's like a slower run—"

"I *know* what it is, Jester!"

Her legs were no longer hurting from her back alley encounter, but she wasn't looking forward to striding through The Hells with a Devil that she had only just met.

"Be careful, Ren! You might accidentally summon a *certain* Devil with such sloth." He giggled and winked at her. "Azur would give us a carriage, but there aren't really any *roads* there. I can get us closer, but Azur says the wards start somewhere in the forest."

"Wards?"

"Sure! All lords have them in their domains. They will alert them if any unwanted guests arrive. Getting out is easier. I'll leave an open portal here for a quick escape."

He floated his long fingers through the air. A barely noticeable ripple opened near the window.

"Portaling and teleportation are quite different. I can portal to a known area, usually. But it takes a great deal of magic unless you've prepared the portal beforehand. Teleporting can only be done over short distances.

That should just about do it," he said, dusting off his hands as if he had finished some kind of manual labor. "Meet you outside!"

In a puff of red smoke, he was gone.

Ren massaged her temples.

"No one said anything about a hike," she grumbled, gathering her few belongings in her satchel and descending the stairs.

Fred was sitting at the bar, staring off into space.

"No luck last night?" he said, snapping back into reality.

Ren gave a grimace. "It uh...didn't go as well as I had hoped."

He scratched the scruff on his chin. "Well, yer look like ye still breathing. So that's something."

"Yeah." She looked around, wondering if Jester was watching from a corner.

Fred cleared his throat.

"For the spirits."

He slowly pushed the glass, the same from the night before, toward her, making sure to catch her eyes as she did. He put one finger over his mouth.

Ren tried to act naturally, taking the glass in her hand. It was still filled with liquid, but it no longer looked amber. It looked exactly like—but it couldn't be. She lifted it to her lips, her confidence momentarily faltering.

Fred's eyes widened and gave the smallest movement of his head.

She drank. When the iron taste hit her throat, she almost spewed it out. Fred reached across the bar and slapped a hand roughly across her mouth.

"Drink!" he half-whispered, half-shouted.

Her entire body convulsed in disgust as she swallowed the revolting liquid. It *was* blood. Then she heard him—Leo—in her head.

"Renata! Oh, I am glad to see that you are okay!"

In front of her eyes appeared the incorporeal version of Leonardo. He was wearing his white robes, looking a bit more haggard than when she had last seen him.

"Leo! What the hell was that?!" she spluttered, wiping the remaining blood off her mouth.

Leo smiled sheepishly. "I am sorry, Renata. I always forget to warn people of the holy water. A pure liquid gifted freely to Nainaur, which can be blessed. For now, we can use it for communication."

"Leo. I'm really getting tired of surprises."

"Oh yes, well. Everything is likely to surprise you these days. I won't insult you by treating you as a child."

Ren pursed her lips.

"Am I to assume you didn't make any progress with the relic last night?"

Ren smiled sheepishly.

"Actually, no. I looked—but it was a bit...complicated. It's just that—I wasn't fully prepared."

Leo gave her a pitying look.

"That's not surprising. While we hoped that you could retrieve The Vutar'ka Zhartun on your first night, we knew that it was unlikely."

"I plan to look in...another area soon. I think I have a lead."

Leo's image shifted, taken aback. "I must say that I am relieved at this unexpected news."

Ren paused, considering. "Yeah, I...heard some Devils talking of a large collection of artifacts collected somewhere close by."

It technically wasn't a lie.

Leo furrowed his brow.

"Really? I haven't heard of any collections in Ogriazeth, but then again, I have never visited the city myself. Very well. We will contact you in a few days. Fred knows what to do."

Ren looked back at the barman, and he lifted his own glass to Leo, "Good ter see ye, Lee.

Leo bowed his head. "May The Almighty protect you."

Without waiting for Ren to respond, he disappeared.

Ren squinted her eyes and tried not to heave at the lingering metallic taste.

Reading her expression, Fred said, "Yeah, it's not the most enjoyable flavor, is it? It is useful, though."

"What about your mute wards? How was I able to talk to Leo?" she asked.

"Oh, you were still muted. I couldn't hear nothing yous was sayin'."

Fred reached behind the counter and produced a small brown bag.

"Some rations for ye. The sleepers don't eat much food, so I wanted to make sure ye had something."

As he passed the small parcel, Ren felt a strong twinge of guilt about Jester before giving him a tight handshake and slipping out the door.

Outside, she saw the same Half-Orc female sitting motionless on the fountain edge. Momentarily distracted, Ren hadn't felt the tug on her bag.

"Pssst. Elf lady. Reeeen."

It wasn't until a still-invisible Jester gave her a push that she came back to attention.

"Sorry, yeah, I'm here. Hey, Jester. Do the sleepers know what's happening? Or do they just stay like that?"

Jester did not reveal himself.

"Hmm, that depends. Some sleepers can communicate, but others just work. I really don't know why. I try not to think about it." he said, voice becoming grave.

Ren didn't push. This was the first time she had heard Jester be serious about anything.

She felt another tug as Jester led her through the street.

"I know a way to avoid the big bad Devils around here," he whispered.

"Jester, why are you staying invisible?" she asked after walking a distance from the bar, "Fred can't see you from here."

Tugging Ren along, Jester didn't respond.

It wasn't until they arrived at the outskirts of the city, the same area where Ren had appeared the day before, that Jester popped back into existence.

"The forest of Nahmir," he said, gesturing around with a little turn.

Ren stopped and crossed her arms.

"Are you going to explain what that was about back there?"

Jester did not stop walking, but his tail lashed around nervously.

"Nope."

Ren started following again before Jester could get too far ahead.

"Are you wanted or something?"

No response.

"Sorry, I didn't mean to pry," she said, remembering how uncomfortable she became when people brought up her past.

Jester stopped walking and turned around, a smile that didn't look quite as genuine plastered on his face.

"Yes, you did. But don't you worry, little Elf. I just didn't sleep so well. Not with you snooooring the whole night!"

"W-you were watching me sleep?!" she exclaimed. Ren ran up to Jester, trying to grab onto his tunic. "Wait! You can't just—"

Jester disappeared, reappearing in a tree a few feet away.

"But Reeeeeen, you looked so cuuuuute," he teased.

"No. More. Watching! It's creepy. What if I was…doing private…things!"

Jester gawked for a second. "Private things?" he mocked. "What sort of private things could you possibly be doing?"

Jester poofed out again, transporting himself to another tree further ahead.

Ren clenched her jaw, stomping towards him. "I don't know! Things! Like—things that women do alone!"

Jester hung upside down from a branch.

"Thiiiings. Ren. You can't fool me. We both know you've never even been kissed!"

Gaping at him, she halted.

"W–I *have* been kissed! I… had a boyfriend! His name was Nephele, and he was very nice!"

"Ohhh, liar! Azur told me that you lost all your memories. That when you woke up, you couldn't remember *anything.*"

Ren finally reached the tree where Jester was slowly swinging back and forth.

"I *can* remember things…just…not everything."

"So you remember your first kiss? You remember Nepheeeele. Tell me, did he like it rough? Or was he the boring, gentle type?

Ren blushed deeply. "I'm not talking to you about this."

She huffed, stomping forward.

Jester jumped down beside her.

"See? We all have things we don't talk about. Ready to go? I can portal us closer to the Dementiz."

She squinted at the Devil. "Don't try anything tricky!"

He gasped and put a hand on his chest.

"Why, Ren! I am *insulted* that you'd even suggest such a thing."

She moaned and grabbed onto his expectant palm, and they zipped through space before skidding to a halt among dark, barren trees. Ren had to blink several times for her brain to process the sudden change.

Ren finally became oriented, Jester was several feet away, having already started marching ahead. He was walking leisurely, occasionally kicking up ash playfully.

They walked in silence for a while, but Jester's words spun round and round in her head. He was right. Ren had no experience with intimacy save for the other night. She thought of the violinist, Xarek. How much desire she had felt. Surely, it had been some type of devilish cunning.

And then Azur—his red eyes, piercing and hot, looking at her as his hips moved. That image was branded into her mind. Thinking of his moans made her whole body shiver. But she couldn't picture herself in that scene—uninhibited like his partner had been, throwing her head back in pure ecstasy.

She wished she could purge the whole experience. It was better to just stay focused. Maybe Renata was like that. Maybe Renata had known love. And maybe Nephele had been the one to show it to her—but not Ren. She flushed at the thought.

She tried to distract herself by looking at the trees. The deeper they went into the forest, the larger the trees became, but there was still no greenery to be found. At first, Ren assumed it had been a fire that had devastated this area, but now she was starting to wonder if they just grew that way.

"It's time to stop for the day," Jester said, breaking the tense silence.

"Really? It doesn't feel like we've walked that long."

Truthfully, Ren hadn't been paying attention, and the unfamiliar streaking in the sky gave no indication of what time it was.

"Better to stop now, build a camp while it's light than to wait. This isn't a particularly safe place."

"Don't people walk through here? To get to Dementiz?"

Jester shook his head, stopping.

"No, Devils mostly portal. *We* just can't because the portals are watched. No one who wants to live travels these roads."

That's encouraging.

Jester walked around a few trees, looking for something.

"Mmm hmm, I think here will be just fine. These trees will block us from view in case anything comes searching." He plopped down onto the ashen floor and stretched out. "Did you bring anything to eat? I'm staaaarving," he said, grabbing his stomach dramatically.

She produced the small bag that Fred had given her. Inside was a block of cheese, some dried meats, and a few pieces of fruit. After eating in another awkward silence, Ren was surprised when Jester spoke.

"So you lost your memories as payment to Azur?" he asked, looking down and tracing his fingers through the ash.

She furrowed her brow. She hadn't thought that her memories might have been the *payment* for something. She had assumed that she had wanted to get rid of them.

"I...think that I, my past self, wanted to forget."

Jester looked up at her. "Why would you want to forget everything?"

"That's exactly what I've been asking myself. Azur hinted that there was a good reason for me to want to forget. That I should... respect that decision."

He nodded, thoughtful.

"You can't trust Azur, Ren. He is...evil. He will do anything to have souls..."

She bit her lip, suddenly conflicted.

"I know, Jester, but what other choice do I have? I have nothing now. Maybe Renata—maybe *I* made a mistake. I couldn't have known the real consequences. Why would anyone want to forget their whole life? Everyone and everything they've ever known. I'm just... I'm so..."

"Confused," he finished.

"Yes," she muttered, calming herself before she could spiral.

Jester continued to doodle in the ash, suddenly solemn, then murmured, "There are things I want to forget. I would...leave it all behind. Everything. If I could just forget," he said, voice growing softer. "Ren, you got to start over. Be whoever you want to be. You're *free.* No one to hold you back or remind you of the mistakes you've made. The people you've hurt. The people you've...lost."

Ren looked down at her hands.

"But even if that were true, I would still have hurt them. I mean, any mistakes I made in the past are still my mistakes, whether I remember them or not. Jester, trust me, this is awful. You wouldn't want this. People talk to you like you're not even there, telling you what you should believe—should do. What about what *I* want to do!"

She paused, suddenly realizing that panic was rising in her chest.

"Ren, you are you. It's the same person."

"No, Jester, you don't understand. I feel like I don't have a choice. I feel like Renata made my choices. She told me who to love, where to live, how to dress! But I don't even understand why she—I—made those decisions, and if I change them and decide I don't want them anymore, am I betraying myself?"

Renata grabbed her head, a sharp pain starting to form behind her eyes. Ren inhaled and exhaled slowly.

It was a time before Jester spoke.

"Ren, I hope you escaped whatever you were running from." He stood up, wiped his pants off, and said, "I'm going to check the perimeter."

Then he vanished.

Renata knew what he was doing, but she was glad for the privacy all the same.

He returned several minutes after Ren had calmed down.

"We shouldn't light a fire tonight. Stay as inconspicuous as possible. I haven't seen anything—but just to be safe," he said with a thumbs up.

That was perfectly fine with her. It wasn't cold. In fact, it was positively muggy.

The dark was upon them faster than Ren expected. Night there apparently only meant that the strips of lightning disappeared behind dark clouds, which only took minutes.

Jester bedded down, curling his red tail around his leg, before turning his back to her, "Night night, Elfy," he said softly.

"Good night, Jester," she whispered back automatically.

In less time than it took the light to vanish, Jester was snoring softly, twitching every so often in his sleep.

Sleep didn't come easy to Ren. Her body, usually so reliable, refused to get comfortable.

I'm not an outside girl, she thought irritably.

After several hours trying and failing to sleep, she sat up and dug into her satchel, which she was using as a pillow, and felt around for her piccolo.

Not wanting to wake Jester, she made her way past several trees soundlessly. She perked her ears and listened, trying to make out any sounds to indicate creatures or beasts nearby. With Elf blood, her hearing tended to be better than most other beings.

She looked at her piccolo.

"No more playing evil music. Okay?"

The piccolo remained cold in her hands.

Satisfied, she brought her piccolo to her lips and softly played. The song was low and quiet, something new for her new adventure. She thought of her new companion and decided that, though she probably couldn't trust him, she was glad to not be alone.

The melodic notes about him were lighter—more lively to show his spirit and sharp wit. She surveyed her mind for more inspiration for her song, but try as she might, her mind kept fixating on Azur. It wasn't shocking—he owned her soul. But was it just this that kept her thoughts returning?

He truly was devastatingly handsome. *How unfair.* Evil things shouldn't be so spectacular. They should be gross, oozing with slime.

But, being as it was, she felt that a song about him wouldn't be gross or macabre, but instead, she felt that it would be deep and moving. Mysterious. Notes hidden under layers of notes.

Ren.

She felt the voice before she heard it. She stopped playing.

Azur! I didn't summon you!

Ren. You must stop.

No! I want to be alone!

She mentally shouted the words, recalling what Jester had told her about severing the connection.

The last thing she heard was a rumble of frustration before. Sweet, blissful silence.

Relief. Finally, some semblance of control. She sighed, once again lifting her piccolo to her lips but suddenly, it vibrated, and her ears perked. A low guttural growl came from her right. She twisted around to gain her bearings, reaching slowly for her dagger. Her heart began to pound.

"Ren! Run!"
And then black.

CHAPTER 10

Would that I could start over.

Ren slammed back into consciousness as she felt a sharp pain in her chest.

"Ren, run!" Jester screamed.

She saw nothing. It was too dark. She sat up—clutching the wound on her chest, feeling the sticky blood seep out.

She heard a high screech before the air became unbearably cold.

"Jester! Where are you?" she screamed, trying to scramble to her feet.

With a start, Ren drew her dagger and realized that it was glowing with golden light. It cast a reflection in the dark, and she could see Jester crouched down menacingly, his fangs barred, tail swishing.

"Ren, do you see it?" he shouted, not shifting his eyes in her direction.

She swung around, brandishing The Holy Transgression, and there, in the shadow of its light, she saw a beast. Nine feet tall with a hunched back and one eye. Its mouth was open, dripping with saliva through its serrated teeth.

"Oh, hells."

From the light of her dagger, the creature's eye dilated. It stopped and roared so loud that Renata's teeth chattered, and Jester covered his ears before vanishing.

With no other target, the massive creature lunged for her, using the momentum from its long spindly legs.

Ren's instincts took over, and she dodged out of the way, her wound throbbing. She spun around, trying to gain her bearings, but if the monster wasn't in the glow of her light, It was impossible to see.

This time, she caught the sound of shuffling before the shrill screech, and, in a split-second decision, she jolted to the right. She felt the ash from the ground kick up as the beast missed her by inches.

Having lept too far, the beast slammed into the tree. Long blackened twigs fell to the ground, and Ren had to throw her hands up to avoid the onslaught.

"Hey, beasty!" Jester shouted from a few feet away. "I thought Ren was the ugliest thing in the forest! Turns out I was wrong!"

She heard the beast shift and run towards the sound.

Jester, what the hell are you doing?

She scrambled around, trying to catch both creature and companion in the dim light. Finally, her light reflected off the beast's giant eye as it lunged for her.

"Arrgh!" she bellowed as she vaulted and grabbed onto a hanging tree branch.

The beast snapped at her heels as she kicked out, flailing her legs to knock it back.

While the beast swatted his long claws at Ren, Jester threw himself towards the pair and clawed at its face.

With little effort, the beast shook Jester off, flinging him away. Jester's thin body flew across the clearing with a momentum that would make any impact potentially deadly. But instantly, the Devil disappeared, only to reappear on his feet.

The creature turned around, eye focusing once again on Ren, believing she, dangling from a tree, was the easiest target.

He wasn't wrong. Ren's grip on the branch was precarious, especially considering that she was still holding the dagger. She tried to adjust, pull herself up, but the beast was slashing at her feet, scraping bloody gashes into her legs.

She swung her body forward, kicking the beast squarely in the eye. The creature hissed in pain. Ren used the instant to swing herself and latch her legs onto the branch and began to shimmy towards the tree's massive trunk, the friction of which made every injury smart.

The beast began to toss its head from side to side, searching for its prey. Once spotted, it clawed at Ren, who was now upright and balanced on the thick branch. It lashed out but overreached, giving her the perfect opportunity to graze the side of its abdomen with the dagger.

It roared with pain, its flesh sizzling an angry red where her dagger struck. The scent of the melting flesh assaulted her nostrils.

Before Ren could stab the creature again, she saw a rock fly towards it.

"Come this way, you big brute," she heard Jester's voice from the thicket.

"No don't—"

But Ren couldn't finish her sentence. The creature turned its body and barreled towards Jester.

Ren lost sight as it launched itself away from her light.

Dammit. I need a better vantage.

Maybe if she brought the dagger higher, she thought, she could shed more light. She lifted the light over her head and found angled branches above. She reached up, trying to ignore the pain in her abdomen, and pulled herself to the next branch. She repeated the movement until she was several feet higher. She crouched on the branch, still able to hear the crawling and shrieking, but luckily, there were no painful yells from Jester.

Her tunic was soaked with blood, and she could feel it dribbling down to wet her trousers. Renata knew that she would lose consciousness soon if she didn't get the wound closed.

She lifted the dagger in front of her, desperately trying to adjust her eyes to the dark. As she did, she saw Jester walking backward as if to lure the creature toward her tree.

It was Ren's turn to smirk.

Clever.

"Come here, big boy. That's it, get you some tasty Devil meat."

The creature lunged, and Jester twirled to vanish—expecting the creature to aim for him. Instead, the creature, who had caught sight of Ren, swung a thrashing arm towards the tree.

Jester, unaware of the change in trajectory, lost his balance as the creature swung back for a second blow and sliced him across the stomach. The Devil wailed in agony—and vanished.

"Jester!" Ren screamed, matching the volume of the frustrated creature snarling angrily, maw dripping with fresh blood.

She brandished the dagger frantically, trying to see where Jester had appeared, but all she could see was a dark puddle of blood on the ground.

Swinging its head toward her light, the grotesque thing bored its knife-like nails into the trunk of Ren's tree and climbed.

She looked up, desperate to give herself more distance, but there was nowhere else to go—no way the next few branches could take her weight. The creature, with its gargantuan claws, didn't need to balance on branches as Renata did. It only needed to slam his dagger-like talons into the trunk.

She shimmied herself to the edge of the branch, hoping it would hold and praying that there was another tree close enough to jump to.

Then she heard him. A low moan from below the tree.

"Ren. Please."

A gurgle and an unmistakable choking sound.

That sound—it was so familiar to her. The music of death and suffering that Ren had heard so often that it was seared into her mind. The echo of words that would eventually turn garbled before...silence.

Ren turned, eyes burning with fury. She didn't feel fear. Didn't feel pain. Only the red-hot wrath to *kill.*

The creature was only a few feet away now, pulling itself up by its talons, and as it reached Ren's branch, she charged, leaping with her dagger clutched in one hand, the other used to grab onto the beast's skull before thrusting the blade fully into its eye.

With a terrible shriek, it thrashed and roared as black pus streamed down its jaws. Ren felt herself slip. She reached up—and tried to grab the low-hanging branches, but her fingers, slick with blood, couldn't clasp.

She fell.

Ren screamed, closed her eyes, and felt the air on her skin as she plummeted to what would surely be death. Release after the inevitable impact and crunching of bone.

Instead, she felt a jerk on her torso as pain shot through her open wound, and a fresh gush of blood dribbled down her stomach.

Fighting through the pain, she opened her eyes and saw that she was not falling but flying. Held by two arms that ended in nightmarish claws.

His face—his monstrous face. Hair flying, he was no longer stoic and regal. This creature was all Devil.

Azur.

He pulsed with power. Every emotion emanating off his body in a tornado of passionate fury.

And his wings. She had never seen anything so terrifying. Massive and black, ending in harsh points, accentuated with monstrous barbs.

When he landed, the entire forest rumbled.

He set her down gently, but she collapsed, unable to stand. He looked momentarily as if he would reach for her but decided better and pushed off the ground into the air.

The creature was still wailing in the tree, writhing in pain as it slowly slid to the ground.

When Azur reached it, he drove his two razor-sharp claws into its side so deep that they disappeared within its insides. In one quick jerk, he shredded the creature into pieces, and Ren had to cover her head as viscera rained down upon her.

He was heaving, chest rising and falling with his rasping breaths. He was shirtless, muscles soaked in sweat and blood, wings having apparently shredded any remnants of his tunic. They were stretched wide in a glorious and terrifying show of dominance and power. His eyes were wild, and his hair whipped about him despite the lack of wind. His sharp features looked as if they were smoldering, cheeks like coal that emanated smoke. The smoke was absorbing all the light from her dagger, which he held firmly in his right hand. He tossed it aside unceremoniously and landed beside her.

"Nice trinket," he remarked in a voice even deeper than the one she was used to hearing.

"Jester! What happened to Jester?" was her stammering response.

The Devil bent down to eye level, and a chill of fear raced through her body. His face, now close, was beastlike and radiating fiery tendrils.

"You're in shock. I need to take you with me. Wyvryn will have to wait," he grunted, moving to pick her up.

She swiped him away.

"Stop, no! Don't touch me! I won't leave without Jester!"

He froze, dropping his arms.

"Jester will be fine. He has the power to teleport and has already returned to my domain. Devils heal more quickly than Mortals, even ones who are Half-Elven. You need immediate medical magic, which I can't do here."

She reached for her chest and made a sharp inhale. Renata knew that she would die from her wounds if she wasn't immediately tended to, but Ren remained motionless.

"So, may I take you now?" he asked, an eyebrow raised impatiently and a voice like gravel.

She nodded, swallowing.

"I need you to say it, Ren. Azur, you can take me."

She looked him over, perplexed. This Devil *owned* her. And now he was asking to save her?

"Azur, you can take me," she whispered.

He gave a nod and gingerly lifted her to cradle in his arms. With a start, she realized that she felt safe there as her whole body instantly relaxed.

Must be the shock.

He pulled her closer.

Despite the ichor and gore, he smelled amazingly like parchment and roses. As he took off, she could feel his strong arms adjust to her comfort, avoiding her tender wound. She drifted off to her first restful sleep in The Hells.

***

Ren woke up with a start. Sitting up in what turned out to be a small bed, she found herself in a modest room under the softest sheets she had ever felt. Her body hummed with contentment, demanding that she lay back down.

She pulled at the neck of a silk nightshirt to examine the deep wound underneath.

When did I put this on?

But the wound was gone. All that remained was a thin red line, evidence of her failed adventure with Jester. This scar, unlike the one on her arm, was a memory, a new one.

"Pa-leaaase don't undress in front of me. You know how much it makes me uncomfortable."

Her head shot up.

"Jester, you're all right!"

The Devil was sitting beside her bed, another book in hand. She could have sworn she saw a small change in the color of his red cheeks.

"They fixed me up good, that's for sure. I do have a question for you, though."

Ren breathed out, relieved.

"Sure, I'm just glad you're not dead."

"Of that, we can agree on," he nodded excitedly. "But Ren, how is it that," his tone changed, "you could be so incredibly *dense* as to play *music* in the forest of Nahmir!"

Ren was shocked. "I...didn't think I was playing very loud and—I couldn't sleep—"

"Do you *know* what happens to people if they die before fulfilling their contracts? Hmm? They turn into sleepers!" he yelled.

She clamped her mouth shut, embarrassed. It was her turn to flush deep red.

"Jester...I'm sorry. But look, no one *tells* me anything! I'm floundering here! I barely have memories, and my sense of danger is part of that, I think."

The Devil breathed out slowly, calming himself.

"You have to be more careful! I'm too pretty to be an emotionless husk! And I'm sure Azur wouldn't be wild about the idea—at least not before we finish our errand. Just use that brain of yours next time," he said, pointing to his temple and crossing his eyes. "Maybe keep that instrument stored for a while."

Ren felt her disappointment manifest.

Wait.

"Where is it? Where's my piccolo?" she sputtered, panicked.

Jester pointed to her side table. Whole and uninjured lay her precious piccolo.

"Calm down, Elfy. It's your contract, remember? It can never be away from you, and it can *never* be broken."

A twinge of discomfort. She hadn't even thought about how breaking her contract might *also* mean breaking her piccolo. Ren opened her mouth to say something but was interrupted by a groan from Jester.

Tendrils of smoke were rising from his palms and from behind his head.

"Gotta run, buddy. I'm being summoned."

And with that, he vanished, but not before the smokey substance began rising off of her own body.

Ren, we need to talk.

Well, that isn't foreboding.

In truth, Lord Azur, such-and-such of handsome stupid-land, wasn't who she wanted to see, but she supposed she owed him at least a conversation after last night.

Before she could respond to him, she was, once again, standing in front of Azur's desk.

She shivered as she was still only in a thin, silken nightdress, the sensitive buds of her chest pebbling. Ren stubbornly didn't move to cover herself.

"Geez, can't you give a girl two minutes to get dressed?"

Azur, sitting behind his desk, gave a momentary start before regaining his composure. He was again the symbol of poise—wings stored and immaculately dressed.

"Pity about your injury," he said lazily, "a scar down your chest? And they were so perfect before."

He returned his attention to a paper on his desk.

Despite herself, she crossed her arms, finally feeling exposed at his shameless reference.

"Did you need something? Or am I to stand here all day freezing my ass off?"

He gave a wry smile.

"As much as I'd love to discuss your *ass,* we have business to attend to. Now that you are healed, I need you and Jester to return to the forest of Nahmir and complete your mission. But first, what is *that?*"

His eyes moved to The Holy Transgression, which was lying on his desk amongst the piles of papers.

Ren's throat became very dry.

"It's just a weapon—"

"Don't *lie* to *me.*"

He stood up from his desk and leaned in, fangs bared, threatening.

"Fine." She steadied herself. "It was given to me as a defense against *Devils* who might try to harm me. Nothing more."

His red eyes locked on her face as if trying to read her. He reached for the dagger and clutched it in one hand. His eyes darkened, and his hand slowly changed into a monstrous talon. He squeezed, and with what looked like very little effort, the dagger shattered, pieces littering the floor.

"You will *never* bring a holy relic of Nainaur into my presence again," he growled.

She just stood, stupefied. He had just destroyed what she thought was a gift from a *god.*

"Well, now you've done it!" she barked, exasperated. "How am I going to protect myself!"

He moved in a flash, stopping right in front of her and looking down through long black eyelashes.

"Oh, my sweet Ren, haven't you realized it yet? The King of The Hells would never let anything happen to you. You are too precious to me," he stroked a menacing claw slowly down her cheek, a gentle caress.

"The King of The Hells? Why does he care about *me?*"

This time, Azur opened his mouth, shocked. He bellowed a laugh.

"Sweet innocent, Ren! Did you not know who I was? I am your king."

Ren took a step back.

"*You're* the King of The Hells?"

She put the pieces together. Xarek terrified of her and mentioning the risk of summoning Pelegros.

"You not only belong to a Devil, but you belong to the lord of *all* Devils," he said, spreading his arms wide. "The *most* egregious and sinful of them all. Congratulations."

I am so fucked. What did you do, Renata?

"I usually demand my charges to bow to me, but I find disingenuous loyalty bothersome. I'd rather bask in your proud stubbornness—Your lust, your wrath. It does delight me so."

He winked.

"I do *not* lust after you!" she fumbled.

Another laugh.

"Ren, you reveal too much of yourself. I never mentioned *me.*" He cocked his head to the side. "But it isn't surprising. Most females can't contain themselves. I am the *god* of lust. I *created* it."

Suddenly breathless, she searched her mind for a way to change the subject.

"A...*god?*"

"Yes, your Mortal god hides away, only getting involved when they feel like it. I, on the other hand, prefer a more...intimate approach."

"Well, *Your Highness*," she barreled on in an attempt to not think about the consequences of talking back to a god, "as safe as I feel about you jumping to my rescue every time, you've told me you can't enter Wyvryn's domain, and you've broken my only means of protection. Not to mention that if I hadn't had it, I would have been long dead before you *honored* us with your presence."

His eyes flashed threateningly, but his smirk remained. He stood at his full height and adjusted his silk vest.

"You make a good point, my dear."

A clank and two daggers fell at her feet.

"*These* are real weapons. They won't just burn a creature of The Hells. They will incapacitate it. While you could kill it, I know your expertise is more in hiding and sneaking. Whoever gave you that other plaything was an *imbecile.*"

She bent to pick them up.

"Now that's what I want. Willing submission at my feet. Though I'd much prefer you on your knees."

She grumbled, righting herself. "Absolutely *not.* Don't flatter yourself."

Azur shrugged his shoulders coyly and returned to his desk.

"Darling, I'm the king of pride and lust. Self-congratulation is literally in the job title. Now run along, Ren. I have a great deal of work to do, and you have something of mine to recover."

And before she could retort, she was standing in a clearing in the Forest of Nahmir.

CHAPTER 11

I thought that this organ in my chest had long died until it was stricken with anxiety. It was—unpleasant. I continue with my aims, heart notwithstanding.

Thankfully, Ren was fully clothed when she appeared in the clearing with Jester. She didn't think she could deal with any more snide remarks from Devils this morning.

Jester was in a much better mood today and babbled ceaselessly about different pranks he'd pulled the other Lords.

"Lord Wyvryn is definitely not my biggest fan. One time, I stole all his hair products and replaced them with glue. He was *so* mad. You'd think that a Lord of The Hells would be able to re-grow their hair in a snap, but actually, it just grows like the rest of us."

Jester flipped his own silky black hair.

Ren couldn't help but chuckle. She learned that stories were almost like music. Wonderful little productions of things from someone's heart. It encouraged her ever so slightly to think that even though she didn't have stories or memories to share, she could share her music.

Their walk remained uneventful as the daytime apparently wasn't conducive for giant Monstrosities to go hunting. Jester even asked her to play a song on her piccolo before he interrupted to give another account of one of his famous exploits.

"And Lord Evernight tried to throw a sword at me, but—"

He paused, pointed ears perking.

"We are close, Ren."

She tilted her head, and indeed, she could hear the murmurs of voices in the distance.

Jester crouched down and slowly approached a clearing.

They stood on the peak of a tall hill overlooking a valley of ash. A massive castle sat in the distance, right at the bottom of the hill.

Unlike The Forked Tongue, this castle was everything a malevolent castle should be. It rose high with black spires that disappeared into the purple clouds. The windows were tinged with green grime, and every corner screamed macabre.

"Gods above," she murmured. "You've been in there?"

"Yeah. a few times, actually. It's not hard to get in. Wyvryn is a dumb twat and keeps his back door unguarded."

Jester snorted at his own joke.

Ren was unamused.

"Now we just wait until nightfall and then sneak in! Easy peasy!"

The two settled, night still being a few hours off. They shared some rations and tried to catch a few moments of sleep.

When she noticed that Jester was, just as she was, unable to find sleep, she broke the silence. She had tried to ask for days now, but she couldn't find the right space between almost being killed and Jester's relentless joking.

"How long have you known Azur? Or—been with him?"

He turned over and propped himself up on his arm, grim.

"A long time, Ren. A very, *very* long time."

"And he's evil? Truly evil?"

He didn't immediately reply.

"Yes, Ren. He might act like he is noble, protecting you. But for some people, some *things* can't be redeemed. He's...done a lot of evil throughout the planes."

She bit her lip. This was not what she wanted to hear. She couldn't quite reason it out, but she wanted him to be good. Or at least capable of good. Maybe it was just her treacherous emotions from the night before, how safe she felt in his arms.

But there was another feeling too, one that confused her when she looked at him and saw the small stars in his eyes like novas of pain.

"It's his fault, you know," Jester continued, "all of this. The ash, the destroyed lands, slavery, the sleepers. It's all because of him. He created this society—signed the first contracts, and cursed the first Devils. He is sin incarnate. The worst things you can think of, the worst deeds a being can think of, all originated with him."

"If we knew why he's so horrible, why did we sign contracts with him? Why do people keep doing it?"

Jester stared past her, distant.

"People get desperate, Ren. They can't see a way forward except to make a deal with a Devil. The Devils take that desperation, the lowest moment of someone's life, and exploit it. Azur, being the most powerful Devil, has the most magic. The most desperate seek him out. But as powerful as his magic is, his malevolence gulfs even that."

He paused.

"I knew a Lesser Devil, Ahdan. He was beautiful, eyes the color of the night sky before the lightning blinks out. He sold his soul to Azur. He was my constant companion. Two lost Devils against The Hells." A small laugh. "Our affection for each other grew and despite the hopelessness we found ourselves in, we fell in love. I cherished every moment with every part of my soulless body. He was perfect."

The dark was upon them, so Ren could only hear Jester's shaky breaths.

"His mother got sick, you see. A disease that was affecting the Lesser Devils. It was horribly slow and took every inch of dignity from its victims. In his desperation, he sought out a Devil. He found Azur. He agreed to give Azur his soul in exchange for his mother's life—for a cure for the disease.

"Azur used his magic, and his mother was cured, only to die two years later from an accident in the mines. Ahdan was...inconsolable.

"Azur did *nothing*. The contract had been signed and fulfilled on both sides. But Ahdan was soulless, an orphan with nothing left to bargain with.

"I tried to love the pain away. To give him enough reason to...stay. Support him and remind him that, soul or not, we still had each other. We still had a life to live and could even have a family one day. That there was hope. But my love wasn't enough for Ahdan."

Silence filled the night as he finished.

"Jester, I—I am so very sorry."

What else could she say to him?

This memory. I wish he didn't have this one.

But forgetting the painful memory would also mean forgetting Ahdan and what they had together.

"It is because of this that you *must* understand, Ren. Azur is cruel. He is vengeful and manipulative. He lives and thrives off the souls of others, not because it gives him power, but because he *enjoys* it." His voice shook. "Just be careful."

Their conversation died there in the silence of the night.

Once the castle was cloaked in darkness and the lights in the windows began to wink out, they moved.

Their first challenge was climbing down the steep slope. It wasn't as hard as Ren had anticipated since Renata was so nimble, and Jester could just teleport. They barely made a sound as they dismounted onto the soft earth.

Jester put a finger on his lips and gestured for her to follow him down and around a thin gravel path.

As they approached the castle proper, she saw six or seven guards, all Devils, at the front gate. They were all dressed in gold and black uniforms.

The back of the castle, however, as Jester had claimed, had only one guard. A Lesser Devil with light blue skin, was walking around a fountain sulking, and tail swishing impatiently.

"They also put the new guys back here," Jester whispered.

The Devil was too busy muttering to himself to see the pair as they snuck behind a thorny hedge and ascended onto a wall that encircled a large garden, long since withered. Ren followed Jester close behind several feet until he paused, pointed down, and vanished. Even though it was dark, Jester's red face and tail were not hard to spot beneath the overhang.

As for herself, Renata tested the footholds with her fingers and nimbly climbed up. Her grip was strong, and she felt safe hanging there despite the mossy surface, which would cause even some experienced climbers to lose footing.

Ren was back on her feet in a few seconds, staring at an iron grating inserted into the castle's foundation.

"You can't teleport other people?" she grumbled, wiping her dirty hands on her tunic.

"Of course! But it's much more entertaining to watch you struggle. Sadly for me, you're just a bit too agile," he said, giving her a feigned, disappointed look.

Ren responded very maturely with sticking out her tongue.

The iron grate was relatively large and, to Wyvryn's credit, looked well-maintained and reinforced.

"Your turn!" Jester said, poking her side, where she had stored the lock-pick set.

Rolling her eyes, she removed two long picks, one flat, the other slightly curved, and located the small key indention. But she stopped—frozen in place, ears buzzing, picks turning ice cold.

"What are you doing?" Jester hissed.

She didn't know. She could feel the discomfort in the back of her head.

"There is something wrong with this grate."

Jester furrowed his brows and looked back.

"Like what?"

She closed her eyes, thinking.

"I think it's trapped. An alert or—something?"

Jester's eyes glanced around the curved frame and began to gingerly feel the stone. As Ren followed suit, she noticed that this was the first stone building that hadn't been reinforced with vurmite. She thought of the small gem in her pocket. She had been afraid to leave it and had convinced herself that it was for emergency purposes, to communicate with Azur, and *not* that she couldn't bear to part with it.

Suddenly, a change in texture, a shift from stone to metal. Ren pushed, and she heard a small hum from the picks.

Jester jerked his head to her.

"You did it! I think?" he said, trying to look encouraging.

Ren bent down again, adjusting the angles of her tools before gingerly inserting them into the fissure—

Nothing happened, but she heard Jester release a breath.

"Honestly, I was only half sure that had worked."

"Great. thanks for that vote of confidence," she murmured. "Now, shush!"

Leaning her ear close to her hands, she held her breath, trying to listen for the perfect clicks of the lock. The picks gradually began to warm in her hands. She almost reeled back at the unexpected sensation, but her piccolo vibrated reassuringly. Finally, she heard the small chink, and the door swung open.

"I thought you said getting in was *easy,* Jester?" she said, wiping small droplets of sweat off her forehead. "I'm pretty sure that lock was magicked shut!"

He responded with a guilty look.

"I guess when you mess with a fops shampoo, they strengthen their wards?" He gave a small, awkward laugh. "But it worked, didn't it?"

Ren grumbled, striding forward.

The tunnel was barely tall enough for Ren, and Jester had to stoop to make his way through. Humidity was thick in the air, and small dripping sounds echoed at intervals.

"There should be a hole in the wall not too far from here," Jester whispered.

Ren felt a brush against her leg and jumped back, almost crying out.

"What in the nine hells was that?"

Jester paused his march, almost causing Ren to run into his back.

"That was just my *tail.* Why are you so jumpy? It's like you haven't broken into the castle of a magical Devil lord before!"

"First of all, I'm pretty sure I *haven't* done this before, and second, I can't see a bloody thing!" Ren spat.

A pause.

"You can't see in the dark?"

She gaped.

"No, Jester! I'm completely blind in here!"

"Oh. Well, that's inconvenient. I'm going to touch your shoulder and lead you there, okay?"

He gently placed his long fingers on her shoulders and guided her.

"Mortals are so weird," he muttered.

At that moment, Jester reminded Ren so much of Benji. His stories—his good humor—and how he didn't mind helping Ren, even when she was a bit bumbling and clueless, though she'd never admit it to Jester, and he'd likely never admit it in turn.

"Here we are!" he said, squeezing her.

They arrived at a large crevice in the wall, which she could only see because there was a light shining from another grate further down.

Leading the way, Jester crept silently towards the light, ears twitching slightly.

The two arrived at the second grate above their heads. This one was round, and there was an identical grate directly below it.

Jester signaled to Ren to check for traps and then pick the lock. Ren reached around but couldn't feel anything.

"I don't think this one is locked," she said, leaning to whisper into his ear. "I think it's some kind of drain."

He waved his hands silently, communicating, *hurry up and open it then*!

She narrowed her eyes and pointed her fingers at him, *no way. You touch it first.*

Pursing his lips, he looked up and placed the smallest tip of his sharp nail on the iron.

Nothing.

They breathed out in unison. No traps.

"Transport us up there. This thing will make too much noise if we try to move it."

"I can't transport through walls or solid objects, Elfy! We'll just have to risk it."

Ren screwed up her face in exasperation but grabbed the grate with Jester, regardless.

"On three," she mouthed. "One...two..."

Jester pushed hard against the bars.

"I said *three*," Ren blurted, trying to maintain a whisper while pushing her weight up.

The metal made a high-pitched scraping sound that echoed down the halls.

"I *went* on three," he hissed back.

They stood underground, motionless, listening for guards.

"I think we are in the clear," Jester said, way too soon for Ren's taste, and pulled himself up before offering her a hand.

Emerging from the hole, a putrid scent hit her nose, sharp and stale. She slapped a hand over her mouth, struggling not to wretch.

The chamber itself was large and rectangular. Sharp instruments–hooks, shackles, and knives–lined the walls. In the center of the room were a table and a chair still coated in fresh blood.

"This is a fucking torture chamber!"

She gasped.

Jester gave a blasé shrug.

"Yeah, well. It's the easiest way in, and if anyone were here, we'd know it! They'd be screeeeeeaming. If you work for Azur long enough, I'm sure you'll see a few tortures yourself, maybe even perform one!"

Jester quietly skipped to the door, pleased with Ren's discomfort.

The door was large and metal but wasn't closed.

Makes sense—why bother locking an empty torture chamber?

They sidled out of the chamber into a long hallway with various cell doors on each side, ending with a spiral stone staircase.

Before they could move closer, they simultaneously saw black boots appear on the stairs.

A guard.

Jester grabbed Ren roughly and blinked away. Both landed hard on the floor of a nearby cell. It, like the chamber, was filthy and stained with blood. There was no cot or chair, only shackles, and a soiled bucket. Between the teleport and the smell, Ren felt like her insides were going to spill out.

Jester, who must have spotted the open door, climbed to his feet and peeked out, Ren close at his heels.

The smacking of boots against stone still echoed, but it was calm, unhurried, and getting further away each second.

Agreeing silently that the guard was far enough away, the pair slipped out of the cell and crept to the staircase. Jester surged to the top in a second to check the next level while Ren's silent feet scampered up.

Appearing at the top, Ren almost choked. The halls were decorated with the most incredible collection of curios imaginable. While several aligned display cases were filled with antiques, gems, and trinkets of all types, she couldn't take her eyes off the most glorious. A stunning array of musical instruments framed by paintings with colors, mixes, and blends of pigments that crashed together.

This was it. The perfect visual for how Ren felt when she played her piccolo. It was completely breathtaking. If Jester hadn't grabbed her arm, she would have likely stood there, captivated, for hours.

"Speed it up, Elfy!" he said, yanking her forcefully.

The castle was asleep. It was easy to avoid anyone in the halls since most people's footsteps echoed on the marbled tiles, and it was more than easy to conceal oneself behind the giant cabinets of trinkets. It was only when Jester almost got his tail stuck in a door, letting out a shocked squeal, that Ren thought they'd be discovered.

After making their way up several stories and around six or seven endless hallways, Jester materialized once more several feet in front of her at an ornate wooden door, making a *ta-da* flourish.

With silent footsteps, Ren slunk over to him.

Unlike the rest of the castle, the door was glittering with vurmite and gold. Ren found it irritatingly distracting as she tried to concentrate on checking the door for traps.

Jester paced anxiously behind her, darting his eyes around the hall.

Ren took a full minute to find the switches—there were two—and pick the lock, but they entered without incident.

This empty room was even more spectacular than the hall. It was an elegant office, every wall covered in shelves upon shelves of vestiges, relics, and books of all shapes and sizes. The only surface uninhabited was the large window on the far end.

"Don't get all doe-eyed, Elfy. Get in, get out! That's the plan!" he said as he ran over to the first set of books, pulling them off the shelves and discarding them roughly.

Ren fully gasped now.

"Jester, what are you doing!? These things could be thousands of years old!"

She dashed to pick them up gingerly and return them to their rightful place.

He didn't pause his rummaging.

"Leave the junk! Azur said that lives were on the line here! And say what you want about that *prick*, but he isn't prone to lying!"

Then, something caught Ren's eye, lying on a polished stone desk.

A violin.

I know that violin.

Memories of Xarek's breath, too close to her skin, sent an involuntary chill through her body.

Ignoring the thumps of books hitting the carpet, she walked, almost floating, to the violin.

It was lacquered and shining, the bow laying delicately astride it. It looked ethereal, god-like in its perfection.

I need it.

"What are you *doing?*" Jester grumbled from the other side of the room.

Ren quickly busied herself with the papers lying on the desk.

"Looking! Not all of us throw things around like a banshee on a bender!"

Most were written in the now-familiar, sharp script. She picked one up, examined it, and returned it to the desk. She repeated this motion several times searching for Azur's mark until she spotted a small scratch of writing that she could read—written with such twisted letters that she almost didn't recognize it.

Only two words.

Renata Eldanuer.

CHAPTER 12

Alas, I am incapable of good or selflessness. Trying only leads to the inevitable pain and tragedy I wrought upon The Planes. I cannot deny that it is a part of every cell in my Immortal body.

Spots appeared in her vision. Renata Eldanuer.
My name.

She clutched the letter in her hands, wrinkling the edges slightly. Another Devil, Xarek, knew about her. More than *she* knew about her. Knew her name—had been writing about her.

Hands sweating, Renata shoved the page into her pocket.

I have to get out of here.

Plonk! Plonk! Plonk went the heavy tomes as they hit the floor.

Find the document and run.

Mind reeling, Ren continued her clumsy search and, barely thinking, grabbed the pristine violin from the table.

A shot of anxiety went through her as she saw that underneath lay a thinly bound book with a black symbol of a Devil on it.

Azur's symbol.

She grabbed it, one hand still holding the violin.

"Jester, I–"

A tremor shocked the room as more tomes tumbled from their resting places and antiques clinked against glass.

Jester whipped his head towards his companion.

"What did you do this time?" he barked.

The tremor got stronger, and it was all Ren could do to avoid dropping the instrument.

"Damn it all!" Jester bellowed, disappearing before the study door slammed open, four guards running in with swords and spears.

Reacting swiftly, Ren ducked under the desk as two spears were hurled at her head.

"I'm sorry I can't take you with my gorgeous friend," she whispered to the violin as she moved it deeper under the stonework and shoved the marked document into the back of her pants.

The guards rounded on her as she sprang up, landing on the desk smoothly and grabbing a dagger out of her belt.

The desk separated her and two of the guards, who were swinging their short swords wildly. Ren was right out of their reach, but needed to move fast.

The other two guards, now spearless, were engaged with Jester as he jumped from each of their shoulders, disappearing before they could grab hold. They slipped and fell toward their counterparts as they tried desperately to grapple him.

"Arrrrgh," bellowed the guard closest to Ren—a red-skinned female Lesser Devil—as she threw herself on the desk, her black armor clanking loudly.

Ren shuffled back, avoiding her lunge, but she had no more space to move. On one side of the desk was a wall, and on the other, a back window that looked out on a ten-story drop to the courtyard.

"Jester, a little help!" she shouted as the red Devil closed in, sword aimed at her chest.

"Xarek is gonna have so much fun with you, pretty thing," she chuckled darkly.

The shock of emotion that wasn't exclusively fear went all the way to her feet at the mention of his name.

Ren steadied herself, trying to time her next move, when the second Devil, a male, skidded to the other side of the desk. She had no space to dodge as he threw himself at her, successfully wrapping two large arms around her waist and knocking her off her feet.

To her horror, she felt the small booklet slip from her waistband as her body slammed into the stone. The male held her tightly as the red Devil approached, a short sword raised to strike. But as she struck down with the sword, her movement shifted.

Jester had appeared just in time to give a hard shove. This slight loss of equilibrium caused her to miss Ren's head and jam her sword into the stone desk, sparks flying. The male, with his powerful grapple, averted his eyes. A brief disruption gave Ren the perfect opening to bring her leg up hard against his crotch, loosening his grip as he doubled up in pain.

Ren spun out from under him right as the red Devil jumped forward, dismounting the desk, and thrust her weapon in her direction. Ren, now with more space to move, was able to easily dodge the advances, but she knew that her distance moved her further and further away from her quarry.

Jester, now behind Ren, was still engaged with the other two weaponless guards. But as his giggles indicated, they were mostly trying to unsuccessfully subdue the trickster.

Her combatants had recovered themselves and were closing in on where she stood, giving a few test swipes with their swords—Ren batting them away with her dagger.

As the male guard's arm pulled back from a swing, Ren spotted the marked booklet lying crumpled behind his heel.

Ren darted low towards her prize, hoping the male would believe she was trying to tackle him to the ground. The male did swing at her but, as she'd hoped, miscalculated his aim. She slid across the floor, grabbed the document, and re-secured it in her trousers.

Still crouched on the floor, she whirled around, trying to ensure that her back never faced her attackers. But the mistake had already been made: the sword of the red-skinned female was coming down upon her.

Ren rolled once more, dodging and hitting the bookshelf, but not before the female's sword cut a long slice along Ren's right leg. Hissing, she struggled to a stand and brandished her dagger threateningly. She saw the male fighting with a constantly vanishing Jester, who somehow had managed to incapacitate the others.

"It's been a while since we've gotten a Mortal," she crooned, backing Ren into the wall. "Mortals scream so much louder. Such delicate skin. Makes a nice ripple when—"

Ren didn't let her finish. She was done listening to Devils. She lashed out swiftly with her dagger, piercing the female's neck. The Devil, eyes wide, dropped her sword but didn't reach for her throat. The dagger, as Azur had claimed, froze her in place.

Ren twisted the dagger and bared her teeth as she felt the gush of black blood trickle down her hand before yanking the serrated weapon out. The female Devil collapsed, mouth open as if trying to speak, but could only bring forth the familiar gurgling sounds of blood as it made its way up her windpipe.

Time stopped for Ren. She watched as life faded from the female's eyes, and she waited. Waited in that timeless spot for shame to hit her. For the feelings of remorse overwhelm her senses, causing her to stumble before regaining herself. Forcing her to compartmentalize this moment of survival before, eventually, the ever-growing knowledge of taking a life assaulted her waking hours with regret.

But it did not come. Instead, she felt...sated. Almost proud of cutting the creature's life short.

"Time to go, Elfy!" Jester yelled, appearing before her as he shoved her out of the way from the guard to her right.

"I can get us back, but I can't portal in here—he had some sort of ward! We need to get outside!" he yelled.

Renata glanced back at the final guard. His eyes were wild and a little fearful as he menacingly descended upon the two.

In a flash, Ren shoved Jester to the side, sending him crashing through the window before she flung herself out. The wind lashed against her face as she plummeted through the air, hair whipping, eyes watering. But before she could blink them away, she felt a hard tug on her waist and slammed hard into a wooden surface.

Ren and Jester were back at the Denizen's tower, gasping for air.

Jester was huffing, bleeding from a large wound to his forehead, and trying to prop himself up.

"Don't cry, Ren," he said between gasps, "I know my...heroics are spectacular—but."

"Oh, shove it!" she said, rolling onto her side, breathless. "Tell the *master* that we got his damned document."

"Oh, *never* call him that. I'd hate to see the glee on his dumb, smug face. He definitely prefers Royal Panty Dropper Supreme!"

The two caught each other's eyes and smiled. A little delirious from the whole experience—they burst out laughing.

However, the laughter was short-lived, as Renata's hands and feet started to smoke.

"Ugh. Lord Luscious Lips is calling. Someday, you'll have to teach me how to do that teleport thing," she said with a wink.

"First of all, it takes a lot of magic, something *you* wouldn't know anything about, Elfy girl," he teased.

But before Ren could retort, she appeared once more in the cold study of Azur Pelegros.

Azur was leaning forward on his chair, face propped on his knuckles, one eyebrow perked.

"I hear that you think my lips are...luscious?" he said with a crooked smile.

"I thought you weren't supposed to spy!" she said, narrowing her eyes.

"She doesn't deny it, I see."

She tossed the papers on his desk irreverently.

"I barely made it out with these. Sorry if they're a little blood-stained."

But he wasn't listening; his body went rigid, his eyes were wide, and his jaw was working.

"Did you just throw a relic marked with my unholy symbol?"

It was Ren's turn to raise an eyebrow.

"Did you *hear* what I said? We almost got captured! Then you wouldn't have your *unholy* relic!"

Azur breathed in slowly, trying to regain composure. He ran his hands delicately across his silken hair and cleared his throat before gently shifting the pages and stacking them into a perfect pile. He raised two long fingers and snapped. A scroll appeared, floating by his head.

"Service rendered, you are allowed your three questions."

Ren steadied herself.

This was it. The moment that could change the trajectory of her life. But what to ask?

Her mind was overloaded—there were just too many questions. It was the same reason she hadn't asked about her surname. Some questions just didn't occur to her until the subject was broached, and all she found was blackness where a memory should be.

The questions couldn't be too direct. She's learned enough about Devils to know that she would not get another chance if she wasted a question. They couldn't be explicitly related to her life but needed to be broad enough to give her insight.

"Why," she started cautiously, "would *someone* have wanted to join The Great Fae War?"

Azur sat back, crossing his arms, thinking.

"The Fae Wars were a culmination of centuries of tension between the two Fae courts. The Seelie and Unseelie—

"But—"

He shushed her.

"Ren, do not waste your second question before I can finish the first. I will not warn you again. Historical context is important, darling."

She glared at being shushed but let him continue.

"The two courts are not so different in many ways, but the same cannot be said for the ideologies. The Seelie believe in the father of the Fae, Faydir, while the Unseelie believe he abandoned them to famine and destruction.

"The Unseelie, land decimated, have been trying to invade the Seelie for not only these ideological differences but also to seize their resources. While the Seelie also struggle with their own land, their court is near the rivers, making the land fertile enough for their citizens to grow crops. The Seelie have refused, however, to trade with the Unseelie for the last several centuries.

"In recent years, information began to circulate that the Unseelie had given up on their plans for the Seelie and had, instead, set their sights on The Mortal Plane. Your plane.

"The Seelie and the Mortals joined together to defend their lands against the Unseelie invasion and did so successfully.

"Coming to your question. In a war such as this, there are a litany of reasons an individual might join—glory, adventure, riches—just to name a few. And then there are the rare beings who do it because it is right."

Ren kept her gaze on Azur, searching his face for more details. But as always, he gave nothing away.

She had heard small details of the origins of the war during her time in Vergessen. But many citizens refused to give her any specifics, while others told her to be careful who she talked to lest she upset someone with her perplexing queries about a painful time in their history. Clara—Mom—just pursed her lips and shook her head when Ren had brought it up, dismissing the conversation altogether.

She knew that they called her Defender of The Planes, and that meant something. Not only had she been involved in the war, but she had probably been some type of important figure. It wasn't surprising—her skills couldn't have just appeared. They had to be attached to some echo of her former self. Apparently, that self was a female who fought in wars.

Yet this had its own set of complications—wars meant death. She recalled the familiar gurgling of the Devil female and the pained noises of Jester from the night before. At how the discordant sounds were so familiar to her ears. Music that she had learned by heart and could play to perfection at any given moment.

This familiar song meant that she had likely killed many Fae during the war as she refused to allow herself to think about prior. It had been easy for her to rationalize up until that point. Defender hadn't technically meant she was doing any killing. Her gut clenched. But killing that female had been so easy—so quick. Her body reacted, and it felt...right. And that disgusted her.

"I've done...bad things."

"Is that a question?" he arched an eyebrow in warning.

"No! No—just a statement." She bit her lower lip. "This is my question. Can a person... be redeemed? If they've done evil? Even if...they can't remember it?"

Something changed. A pained expression appeared on his face. He wasn't hiding this time. He swallowed, throat bobbing.

"I'm sorry, Ren. I do not know. Thus, I cannot answer your question. Question three?"

Her mouth fell open, stunned.

"No, that's—not fair!"

Her cheeks heated in anger.

The Devil stood, black mist swirling around him, eyes darkening.

"Ren, our agreement was that I answer the questions to the best of my ability. I have done that. I have warned you to be prudent with your questions—"

"But you are a *god*. Isn't redemption one of the things that you *do?*"

A vein twitched in his neck.

"I'm not that kind of god, Ren. I am the god of damnation—not redemption. If you want those answers, take it up with Nainaur."

He sat down again and, with a strained expression, continued.

"Ren, after so many bad things, even if you can't remember them, you are tainted. Stained. Irredeemable. In some moment, after so many sins, there is no turning back."

Pieces fell into place. She must be evil—that is why she was so quick to sin. She had killed Fae in the wars, and no matter what the reason, she had blood on her hands. So much blood. People in Vergessen thought her a hero, but all she felt was shame. Shame only compounded by the lack of shame for killing that very night.

"Even if I'm sorry—repentant? I can't...be better?"

"Technically, that is another question, but," he paused, "my brother Nainaur says that once violence has entered your heart and your soul has been lost to it, you cannot be saved."

Ren started.

"Nainaur is your brother?"

Azur clenched his jaw.

"All of us gods are siblings. We are bonded through our very essence. All with our own special blessings and powers."

"And you? Nainaur says I can't be saved. And what do you think?" she asked, surprising herself. Why would it matter what the god of all evil thought about redemption?

Maybe she had asked because she was desperate. As Jester said, no one comes to Azur unless they have no other choice. And this must be the reason why she abandoned everything. She couldn't live with herself and what she'd done. It was the only explanation that made sense. She had forced herself to forget—to rid herself of the bonds of shame and trauma. Hers and everyone else's who lost family and friends to her hand.

"My opinion on the matter is irrelevant."

It was all the confirmation that she needed. She was truly lost—truly damned, and she deserved it. She deserved to be a mindless husk—a sleeper.

So, it was this knowledge that she knew what she wanted her last question to be. She heard Jester's taunting voice in her ears. *"You can't fool me!"*

She cleared her throat, hoping it would mean that her voice wouldn't shake from embarrassment.

"What I want is...something you took from me."

His eyes flashed in warning.

"I cannot restore your memories."

"I know the rules," she said with more confidence than she felt.

To smother her nerves, she let Ren the Performer take over—she let this be her stage.

"I want something you took. But not a memory."

His eyebrow raised in question. She had piqued his curiosity.

"Go on."

"An experience I would very much like back and that, I feel, I very much deserve to have. As a woman of such great accomplishment, as you've said."

Her heart skipped.

This could end in two ways. He would either be so fascinated by the idea, an opportunity to toy with her, or he would show his full wrath as king for even suggesting it.

But this was what she wanted, as frivolous as it might seem to him. To reclaim this one moment. To have a real Mortal experience and, perhaps, lose herself for a time. Quench the pain in her heart.

He remained motionless, like a snake ready to strike.

"I want...my first kiss back." She paused, unsure if she could even finish her sentence. "And... I want you...to give it to me. So will you—give...it to me?"

It fell out of her mouth a little less elegantly than she had hoped, and she had to look away.

Azur, however, remained unmoving behind his desk.

She let the words hover in the air as one of the most powerful beings in the cosmos stared at her unblinkingly.

No. There is definitely something worse than seeing his wrath. He could laugh at me.

The idea of kissing had plagued her after Jester's teasing. It was cruel that she had never felt wanted. Intimacy. Surely, it wasn't so ridiculous. She needed this. If her fate was to be a soulless zombie, she needed to know what it felt like.

After several long seconds, his face changed. But before Ren could process its significance, he had crossed the room, grabbing her face—an insidious fiend devouring its prey. She only just saw a flash of wickedness in his eyes before he descended upon her. There was no softness, only primal hunger.

He traced his tongue over her lips, spreading them apart before claiming a swollen lip between his teeth and biting.

Renata gasped into the perfect bow of his mouth as the sharp pain sent a thrill racing through her. Every thought disappeared from her mind, and her instincts took over, as did her craving. She knew this. No, this wasn't her first time. She reached up and clutched his hair, his soft curls feeling like satin between her fingers as they coiled through.

Azur chuckled at her boldness before a hand began to move down her back, fondling the softness above her thighs gently before giving a possessive squeeze.

Yes, don't stop.

His kiss became more forceful as his hand continued its descent from her face to her neck as he gradually curled his fingers provocatively around her throat. He did not squeeze, but the message was clear. He could if he so desired—she was at his mercy. The gesture only increased Ren's desperation—a moan escaped her, and an ache between her legs began to grow.

Pulling her closer, he offered up the slightest growl deep in his throat, and it was all Ren could do not to gasp with delight between fast kisses.

His hand moved again—this time tracing a line from the backs of her thighs and up her torso, deepening his kiss as he went.

Yes, yes, oh god.

With a throaty laugh, he gave a teasing squeeze to her throat.

Ren's entire body quivered with pleasure.

She knew then, without a doubt, would have bet her soul again on it that this was the closest to paradise that she had ever, would ever come. She could die here and be content. At peace. All thoughts of redemption were lost to this blissful moment. Then—

He broke their embrace, taking a full step back.

Ren could only gasp for air, blinking herself back to consciousness, her lips still slightly parted.

He was looking down at her, expression unreadable. The only evidence they had been clinging passionately to each other was one small curl lying gently on his forehead.

"Was there anything else you needed?" he asked clinically.

She gazed, mind muddled. She had a million things she wanted to say—wanted to ask. But her brain couldn't seem to string anything together.

"Since you seem to have lost your tongue," he said with a knowing grin, "I guess we are done here. That *was,* after all, three questions."

He adjusted his vest and walked leisurely back to his desk.

"If you are planning to stay in my domain, I may call upon you again. You seem to have your...uses."

Every emotion crashed into Ren at once, the strongest of which was embarrassment. The moment, the kiss so pivotal to her, meant nothing to him.

"Don't worry, darling." he said, sitting, "It's just business."

And she vanished.

CHAPTER 13

I knew it would happen again. If I touched her.

She was alone in the tavern bedroom, trying to drown her racing thoughts in a bottle of mysterious liquid. She was self-destructing—from pleasure and from pain. The irony of the amalgamation was not lost on her. That was what he was—the ultimate pleasure and the ultimate pain.

Her heart felt like it would be ripped out of her chest. She was coming down off the blissful high that his lips had given her. That temporary reprieve from the growing certainty in her mind that she was not a good person. No matter what decisions she made from now on, she could never erase the agony she had caused, even if she was still not certain of the magnitude of her sins. It didn't matter. Unseelie were living creatures. Like her, like Benji, like Jester. They had family and friends.

Family and friends like Renata had.

Ren turned over on her bed, it was still night, and she realized how exhausted she was. She stared out at the starless sky and wished for a simpler time—stealing coins with Benji on the ship. Another pang of guilt.

It was so blatant now. She simply couldn't run from her sin. Her greed, her lust, her wrath—the evidence was always there. She'd hardly questioned Benji when he told her to take from the other passengers. If she were honest, the pilfering gifted her a small thrill. A stroke of excitement.

She squeezed her eyes closed and willed herself to focus on the meager goodness of her life. Benji's smile as he listened to her play, Jester's taunting and ceaseless stories. It wasn't much, but it sustained her, if just for a moment. Then, inevitably, his face came. King of The Hells. Stony and penetrating.

She recalled how his angular face glowed like coals when he unleashed his wrath. How unbridled it was—ripping, tearing, and mauling, all in an effort to save her. To protect her. No matter the motives, his selfish desire to retrieve his prize, he was still the first person to fight for her. Make her feel safe. Irony again—feeling safe in his monstrous arms. And as his hands explored her body, she felt entirely protected. Nothing in the cosmos, The Planes known and unknown, would dare hurt her there. No more swords could pierce through this being's protective embrace. No emotion could pierce through. And though she knew it was entirely one-sided, she would linger on these feelings. Take comfort in the, perhaps, misplaced relief before, finally, sleep.

***

She woke up with a start. Someone was knocking at her door.

"Miss! Another message for ye!" Fred's voice said.

Groaning, she turned towards the door.

"Coming."

Meeting with The Gilded Triangle was not something she was looking forward to after making out with the most powerful sinner alive. The guilt rippled through her.

She rolled lazily off the bed and dressed, braiding her long, silvery hair to disguise its knots. It had been a while since she'd bathed.

Tromping down the stairs, she saw the small glass tumbler waiting for her, but no Fred. She picked up the glass and swirled the viscous red liquid inside, watching as it coated the sides and slid down thickly.

She pinched her nose and drank, chills forming on her skin at the offensive metallic taste.

With a swirl, Leo appeared, dust wafting up from the floor. His hands were clasped in front of his robes with a concerned look on his face.

Ren felt absurdly awkward as if she were being admonished for her sins by a parent. Not knowing what to do with her hands, she decided the best course of action was to follow his lead and cross them in front of her, standing at attention. More discomfort. The stance, reminiscent of something from her past.

She didn't like it.

"Renata. It is good to see you," his words hurried, "did your intel bear fruit? Are you closer to locating Vutar'ka Zhartun? Nainaur has become increasingly impatient."

Taking a page from Azur's book, Ren kept her face impassive.

"I'm sure you realize that this will take time, Leo. This is an entire plane of existence with many locations to search. But I believe I'm getting close."

Liar, her inner voice quipped.

Leo nodded.

"Yes, of course." He looked down at his hands. "Renata, this is a bit unorthodox, even for me, but Nainaur would like to speak with you. Alone."

Ren's eyes widened. An all-knowing god wanted to talk to *her.*

I'm completely fucked. He knows.

Kisses from The King of Devils suddenly no longer seemed safe. Could The Almighty punish her for such a transgression?

"Do you...know what he wants?" she asked sheepishly.

Leo's eyes became hard.

"No, Renata. My Lord and The Almighty Savior of Mortals has asked for an audience with you. I dare not question his supreme wisdom."

"Yes, of course. It's just that—I wanted to make sure I was prepared. Seeing a...god...must be an intimidating experience. Some might say a unique one," she hedged, trying to see what he knew if he'd discovered that her patron was Azur.

He nodded reverently, calmer than before.

"This will truly be an inspirational moment for you. I have no doubt that once you are in the presence of The Almighty, you will recognize the urgency to recover your soul and turn to him. Nainaur will call upon you soon. Await his summons here at the tower."

"Yes, all right. Of course," she said, trying to sound as cooperative as possible.

"We will be in touch, Renata."

With the slightest blurring in the room, he left.

Relieved, Ren sank into the nearest seat, rubbing her forehead with two fingers. With only the slightest change in temperature, she noticed that her hands were seeping the smoky substance.

"For the love of all that is holy and evil! Could you give me a *second*!" she bellowed before vanishing once more.

The room changed, and Ren appeared mere inches from the form of Azur, who was standing poised in front of her—so close that she had to look up to see him.

He looked expectant. Annoyed even, without a hint, that he was at all affected by their tryst the previous evening.

"Ren, I again have need of your services," he stated, plainly.

She backed up a few inches.

"Of course you do," she grumbled.

He slid his hands into his pocket.

"Testy this morning, are we?" he asked in mocked concern. "Did you...get enough sleep? Or was there something or some*one* that...occupied your mind?"

Her hands clenched into tight fists.

"No, nothing *occupied* my mind. Nothing too *interesting* has happened to me as of late. I slept like a baby, actually."

Hiding a smile, the Devil made a disbelieving sound through closed lips.

"I'm very glad to hear it. One mustn't lose sleep. It leaves one wanting, don't you think?"

"Look, what do you need? I'm a bit preoccupied right now."

He slid the booklet out of his pocket.

"I need your help with this," he said, casually.

Ren let herself smirk in response, feeling a bit gleeful.

"Well, well. Mr. All Powerful Devil God. You need myyyyy help?"

She batted her eyelashes, a move she'd recently learned from Jester.

"Yes, in fact, I do," he said, his words laced with boredom. "Did you look at this document before you delivered it to me?"

She hadn't. She hadn't even thought to pry.

"No. I didn't."

He nodded and opened the small book, which showed her the first page. But it wasn't a book at all—it was music—handwritten in dark sharp scrawl.

Unable to control herself, she seized the pages, holding them in her hands with urgent desire. It had been ever so long since she had seen the gorgeous writing of sheet music. Most musicians couldn't read it, making it painfully uncommon.

"You can read it?" he asked.

Speechless, she nodded, caught up in her own trance.

He spoke purposefully.

"I need you to play it for me."

Tearing her eyes away from the pages, she responded, "Play it? I can. But—why?"

He lifted his chin.

"As much as I admire your curious spirit, it is a private matter."

She looked back down at the music, craving. Oh yes, this is what she wanted to play—she wanted to discover the secrets within those notes. What feelings had the composer hidden within?

Wait.

"It's a message isn't it. A letter? You need me to play it to find out the meaning."

There was the subtlest change in his face.

"Yes, in fact. It is. So would you help me?" He cleared his throat. "Please."

She gaped. The Lord of Hells just said *please.*

Nothing makes sense anymore.

And an idea.

When in hell, do as the Devils do.

"Of coooourse, I'll help you, Azur," she crooned, matching his normal patronizing tone. "But as you know, I don't work for free."

She smiled mischievously.

Azur gifted her his own wide smile.

"You are *truly* remarkable, my darling. Indeed, I am intrigued. What would you like in exchange?"

Ren felt for the crumpled paper still in her trouser pocket and produced it.

"What does this say?"

He took the page and straightened it, taking a beat to read. As he did, Ren noticed that his breathing began to deepen, and his eyes flashed.

"I agree," he said without glancing up from the script. "I will reveal what this says if you play me the music."

The ritual began. The contract appeared, arm cut, and line signed.

"Now play," he ordered.

She plucked her piccolo from her side and settled the music on his desk. It was a complicated jumble of unstructured notes. She brought her companion to her lips and began the song. She played the first line, a heavy cadence of minor and staccato sounds, but as she moved along, she felt herself lose grip. Lose the time of the song as the pages alighted in fire. Smoke filled the room.

Ren jumped back, yanking her piccolo from her lips, choking and gasping for air.

Azur didn't move, he only stared into the smoke, jaw tightly clenched.

The smoke began to take shape, and a form made entirely of black webbing appeared and spoke.

"Xarek Wyvryn does hereby agree to uncover the weakness of Lord Azur Pelegros and vows to surrender this information for the exclusive employ of the designated party to use as they see fit. If this information serves to subdue Lord Azur Pelegros, Xarek Wyvryn will thusly take over Lord Azur Pelegros' position as King of The Hells for the rest of his Immortal life."

As the words echoed off the stone walls, the webbing shattered and floated to the carpet before melting like snowflakes.

"It was...a contract," Ren murmured under her breath.

She looked up to Lord Azur, his hand frozen in the air in front of him as if reaching for something.

His eyes wavered.

Ren didn't know what to say, so she waited as Azur looked through her.

He finally lowered his hand and swallowed.

"It seems," his voice was steady despite the change in his eyes, "that my dear friend Xarek is trying to do away with me."

"But...you're a god, right? You can't be killed," she offered.

Finally turning his attention towards her, his eyes set back to their serious tone.

"You are right, my dear. The trouble is, Xarek Wyvryn is not an idiot. Whoever he signed this contract with has plans for me. It didn't say kill, after all."

He lifted his hand to run it through his hair, a curl falling free. He looked flustered—actually flustered.

"Wow. A god is scared of a little violin player," she said coyly.

He walked towards her torturously slow.

"Oh my darling Ren," his face pained, "do you know what this says?"

He held up the paper with her name on it.

"Xarek knows about you—knows your name. He has plans for you, my pet. He plans to try to *use* you. *Control* you."

Ren suddenly felt very small and very afraid. She had felt Xarek's power that night. It wasn't as overwhelming as Azur's, but something about Xarek's power, his type of power, was irresistible to her. Ren recalled the fog in her head. Her mind flooded with desire and lust as she danced. The smell of his breath made her numb to everything. Everything except Azur's voice.

"He can't do that. Right? He can't control me—"

"Oh, but he *can,* my darling. He does what Devils do best!"

"Have *you* tried to control me?" she spat more from fear than anger.

"No, Ren. I cannot compel you. I cannot control you," he said, "we have a contract."

It wasn't an explicit revelation of truth, but she understood nonetheless.

"It's in my contract? That you can't control me?"

His chest barely moved as he breathed.

"One might say that there have been contracts signed by myself and other parties in the past to ensure that every interaction between the two parties must be...consensual. However, other Devils," he proceeded, "are not bound by such constraints. Devils, especially those that are lords within The Hells, like Xarek, have influence over Mortals. Powerful influence."

Her throat closed. She tried to suck in air, but it wouldn't come. This was happening again. The loss of control—the complete inability to grasp any certainty in her life. Her unknown past haunted her, the unknown path ahead, and now the knowledge that she could be utterly manipulated and controlled by another entity. She felt her legs shake, and she looked around wildly.

"Ren. Ren!" a voice came.

She started to lose her footing and fall, but as she did, Azur reached out to steady her, scooping her up in his arms.

"Godsdammit, Ren!" he said as he crossed the room quickly, pushed the giant stacks of documents off his table, and laid her there.

She was gasping now, eyes beginning to blur, struggling to suck even the tiniest amount of oxygen into her burning lungs.

Azur had one arm wrapped around her, and the other pushed silver hair from her sweating face, cupping her cheek.

"Look at me, Ren. Just look at me."

She did. His eyes were fire, the color of the flame before blue and yellow met.

"You're safe here with me, Ren. You will *not* be used by Xarek."

Her eyes were unfocused. She was losing herself again. She was going to fall deeper into a black hole that she didn't even know if she wanted to crawl out of.

"I have you, Ren." He placed one large hand in between her breast bone. "Just stay with me."

But she couldn't. There was nothing else for her to stay for. Her eyes streamed salty tears that landed in her open mouth, still futilely fighting for snatches of air.

"Let me help you," he said softly. "You have to *let* me help you. But it's your choice. This doesn't have to be the end of your story."

He was right, wasn't he? She wasn't sure if she was a good person. She knew whatever she had been couldn't be forgiven. But that didn't mean life had to stop for her. She got to decide who she was, didn't she? Didn't *Ren* have the right to make her own choices?

She grabbed him by his vest and pleaded with her eyes.

Don't let me die here, Azur.

He blinked. His hand was still on her breastbone, which started to glow with warm magic. Black wisps curled around his fingers and flowed into her chest. Her throat instantly began to loosen, small fragments of air finally making their way into her lungs. She sputtered and gasped as tears streamed down her face.

Azur leaned his forehead to hers.

"That's it, just breathe. A little at a time."

She obeyed until her rigid body loosened and her watery vision cleared. She realized she was still clutching him, and he still had her locked in an embrace.

"You're okay now," he said, releasing her and straightening.

"W-what the hell was that?" she croaked.

The Devil looked at her pityingly.

"You had a panic attack, Ren."

"A panic attack? But...I've never had that before. Why-what happened?"

Azur shoved his hands in his pockets.

"Wait. H*ave* I had these before?" she asked.

He did not respond.

She pushed herself up and stumbled down from the desk.

"I'm *fine*," she barked as Azur reached to steady her. "It's just a shit ton of shit to process and I can't—what does this mean for me?"

Her breath was still uneven.

"That depends entirely on you," he said, his voice quiet. "I won't let him touch you. You're under my protection."

She nodded small, processing. "But he could, potentially?"

Azur's nostrils flared.

"Does he have the power? Yes. Would he have the opportunity, *fuck* no. I will not let him use you."

She scoffed. "When did you start to care so much?"

His sharp ears pinkened.

"Because you're *mine*, Ren," he replied sharply, nostrils flaring, eyes flashing.

She didn't know how to respond. She was too surprised at his abrupt loss of composure.

He cleared his throat.

"But there is something else, darling." His voice still maintained its sharp edge. "Something that perplexes me. The document you found? Xarek plans to use *you* to take down my kingdom."

CHAPTER 14

Xarek does not know the hell I will rain down upon him.

Ren felt lightheaded again.

"This is why he wants to compel me? To get some sort of advantage—information about you?"

Azur rolled his neck, releasing the tension there.

"That is what the documents seem to imply."

Her mind spun. "What do we do?"

He stopped, tilted his head.

"Ren, *we* don't do anything. This isn't your fight—"

"It most certainly *is* my fight! This Devil prick wants to *control* me! I won't let anyone control me. Not him, not anyone. I'm done with people telling me what I should do and who I should be."

Though the words surprised her, she realized they were true. She didn't want to be Renata anymore. She wanted to be *Ren*. To get to decide who she wanted to be, that's what mattered. What *had* to matter if she was going to keep living.

Azur eyed her skeptically.

"I told you I wouldn't let anything befall you. Now you want me to let you run headlong into a war between some of the most powerful creatures alive?"

"Can't you...do both?" she asked, a crease appearing between her eyes.

"Not as well as I would like," he huffed, exasperated. He lifted his hands to massage his temples. "I want you to stay here, at my safe house for a day or two while I figure out what we can do. I am sure Xarek will not strike out in the open, especially not now that we know their plan, but it would be more *convenient* if you were close."

Her first impulse was to reject the offer, she was too involved with him and she still had the tome to think about.

"I have guest rooms for the others. You can occupy one for the time being. Jester will make sure you know your way around."

"Jester is here?"

Strangely, the idea of the little red Devil being close comforted her.

"Yes, he lives in private quarters. I'm sure he's told you that he has been with me for some time."

Her stomach lurched.

She didn't like thinking of Azur as someone who possessed Jester's soul. The story of Ahdan came back to her and she felt sick.

"Are you ever going to let him go?" she asked, quietly.

He looked down at his nails.

"No," he said with finality. "Come with me."

He walked past her towards the back door. This time, when he opened them, he did not use his magic as he crossed the threshold usually used to teleport them into the tavern.

She hesitated before following, wanting to protest and keep talking about Jester. But she got the impression that Jester didn't need—or want, anyone to stand up for him.

And then there was the small voice buzzing in her head.

Leo said wait in the tavern! You can't just skip a meeting with The Almighty!

Ren desperately wanted to shush Renata again. But she knew that her voice was right. Then again, staying in Azur's safe house might be the *exact* thing that Nainaur would want. For a sacred relic, the house of the king of Devils was the perfect place to investigate.

She scrambled to follow him down a brightly lit hallway adorned with paintings of Devils in different settings. Some were standing, wings unfurled in combative stances, fighting creatures unknown to her, while others were engaged in intimate encounters, fangs bared, lust in their eyes. She tried not to picture Azur as one of these and hoped he couldn't feel her wandering thoughts.

They stopped at the end of the long hallway, and he gestured to the door.

"All yours, my dear."

She pushed past to look inside.

This might have been the most surprising incident that had happened all day. This was *not* the modest room she had been in previously. Inside was a massive four-poster decorated with elegant pillows and a plush comforter. A fire was flickering in the hearth, and two chairs sat before it. Chairs that, unfortunately, reminded Ren too much of the one she had seen Azur reclined on her first night.

"You are technically a guest in my home for now, and I am nothing if not accommodating to my guests. Us Devils are very hospitable creatures as a rule."

She snorted. "Tell that to Xarek."

The smallest smirk appeared on Azur's face.

"Just don't break anything. I'd hate for you to accrue any debt while you're here. Paying off Devils can be quite challenging, I hear."

She gave him a poisonous look.

He ignored it.

"Now, if you don't mind. I have a lot of work to do. Plans to murder lords of The Hells don't devise themselves! Make yourself at home."

With a nod, he walked leisurely back down the hallway, and Ren cursed herself for darting her eyes toward his backside.

A thorough inspection of the room was even more spectacular than her view from the hall. Each surface was encrusted with vurmite and glittering in the purple light from the two large windows. There was a terrace overlooking an ashy valley and a vanity holding several books—unsurprisingly, none were Vutar'ka Zhartun.

Suddenly, there was a slight change in temperature.

"I know that's you, Jester," she said, turning and crossing her arms.

Jester was paused in a sneaking position, evidently trying to grab and scare her.

"It's been quite a day," she said with a huff, "can we drop with the tomfoolery for a bit?"

Jester looked offended.

"Absolutely *not*! I *live* for this Ren! You wouldn't rob a soulless Devil of his one joy, would you?"

He pouted.

She grumbled under her breath while examining the baubles on the vanity.

"You're only here to annoy me then? Or did you *miss* me?"

It was her turn to sound coy.

"Ick, no! I'm just here because Lord Azur Stuffy Pants wants to invite you to dinner." He waggled an eyebrow at her. "What have you *done* to earn such an *honor*, my dear Ren?"

Another grumble.

"The last guest Azur invited to dinner was a little pink Devil. Perhaps you've met her? Zelaia?"

Ren choked on her own spit.

"What?!"

Jester wrinkled her nose.

"Ew. If you plan to get anywhere with Azur, don't make that noise."

"Oh. No. Surely, he doesn't expect me to *do* anything?"

Jester shrugged.

"Who knows? He's the lord of lust and lechery. What did you expect?"

She suddenly felt very hot, air again hard to capture but for a wholly new reason.

"I didn't think about it."

But if she were being honest, she had thought about it.

A lot.

"I'm only here to tell you that he has stocked the wardrobe full of appropriate clothes and anything else you might need. He does like his gluttonous dinners to be fabulously lavish," he drawled.

"You're not coming?" she rasped.

He narrowed his eyes.

"Azur wouldn't deign to eat with a soulless Lesser Devil. And besides, thanks to someooooone we know, I apparently have to do some reconnaissance."

"Sorry about that," she said, feeling slightly guilty.

He shrugged. "Part of the job when you can turn invisible. I'm used to it, Elfy."

"Is that not something common with Lesser Devils?"

He shook his head.

"Nope, thanks to Azur, I'm speeciiiial." Another eyebrow waggle. "Have fun tonight, little Elfy! Don't let Azur have all the fun! I hear his cock is *huge,* but I bet he's selfish in the bedroom—"

Ren lunged at him, but he *poofed* away, giggles echoing until they finally disappeared down the hallway.

"Menace," she grumbled.

Opening the wardrobe, she found it to be full of a variety of dresses in different colors. Her breath caught as she delicately removed the first of them.

The dress was made of the softest velvet black—low cut and patterned with sheer mesh that draped across long elegant sleeves embellished with patterns like tree branches. It was almost completely backless but crisscrossed near the rear and cascaded into a short train. It was breathtaking. She wanted to put it on and never take it off.

She almost vibrated with excitement as she draped it across the vanity. Only then did a shining necklace catch her eyes. It wasn't adorned. It was a simple silvery chain with a dangling empty bracket like something had been removed. With a start, she withdrew the vurmite from her pocket and placed it in the brackets. It was a perfect fit. She would be the most beautiful Half-Elf in the realm with this, she was certain.

I can't wait to see you, came his low, gravelly voice.

She swatted away the gathering smoke to dismiss him and went straight for the washroom. The tub was already filled, and soft red petals floated on the surface.

Ren clenched her teeth, wanting to disapprove but also incredibly excited for this little indulgence.

After washing every surface of her body and adding a little of the scented oils to some more intimate areas.

Not for him, obviously.

She slid on her perfect slinky dress and adorned her neck with her gem. Ren discovered she wasn't much for hair styling, so she let her silver hair fall in flowy waves on her shoulders.

Rotating primly in the mirror, Ren heard a knock on her door. When she opened it, she had to stop herself from falling over. Azur was dressed in all black but wasn't business attire that night. His ensemble was elegant and refined. His hair wasn't slicked back, hiding his curls. Instead, he had allowed them to wind freely around his sleek horns, a couple falling down his forehead. His lips were slightly parted as he looked her up and down.

Realizing that this stunning male was staring at her, Ren could feel her chest flush and she hoped she didn't look splotchy pink.

He held out his hand.

"Lady Ren, would you please join me for dinner in my sitting room?"

Sitting Room?

That seemed quite a bit more intimate than she was expecting. In her mind, she'd imagined a grand ballroom with an entire table between them.

Ren struggled to hide her anxiety as she placed her hand in his.

"Yes, sure."

This was the first time they had touched since their kiss, and the sensation sent her head spinning as she thought back to where his hands had been.

He led her down the hall to two double doors that he opened for her, allowing her to walk first.

"Are you always so gentlemanly to your victims?" she asked, sweeping past him.

"Only the ones I need," he said matter-of-factly.

"I see, you just *need* me, is that it?"

She huffed.

"As I've mentioned, my *need* is quite insatiable."

Unmentionable areas in her body clenched at this statement.

He walked across the room and beckoned her to a small table in front of a roaring fire. The table was set, and food was plated with several types of meats and cheese, with an elegant bottle of red wine poised to be poured.

Azur pulled out her chair for her and, despite herself, sat primly, feeling increasingly like royalty.

"Please, help yourself. I know rations aren't the most filling," Azur said, smiling politely.

She looked down and, unable to control her growing hunger, did indeed tuck in, hoping Renata remembered table manners. It turned out she knew some formalities, and could get by, even remembering to place the napkin on her lap.

Azur reached across the table and poured her a generous glass of wine.

Ren's mouth watered as she extended her hand and took the delicate glass. Lifting it to her lips, she noticed that Azur was frozen, not blinking.

She tasted the first sip—

It was incredible. The flavor was deep and full, like fresh red fruit, ripe on a summer evening. She smiled to herself, knowing this unique flavor would be a memory she could come back to. She took another generous sip and couldn't help the slight moan of culinary pleasure that escaped her.

"My my. I didn't think I'd be hearing that sound so soon," Azur quipped from across the table.

Ren almost spit out her wine.

"Excuse me, *sir*. I don't remember much about table manners, but I know this isn't a polite conversation!"

He laughed fully.

"I'm sorry, Ren. I didn't mean to offend."

He took a small sip from his own glass, licking a small drip from his supple mouth. Ren had to stop herself from shivering.

"I have no bad intentions, I can assure you. I don't make it a habit of mixing business and pleasure."

"Oh," was her only response as the forbidden emotion of disappointment crept in.

"I just don't see you that way, Ren," he stated, swirling his wine in its glass. "I understand your silly little game with this kiss. You're not the first to be curious, and I hate to disappoint you, for you obviously crave something more, but I really don't have the time for such frivolous matters. You do understand, darling?"

Ren's mouth was fully agape.

"*Excuse* me?" she burst out, "that's *quite* the ego you have on you, *Lord Pelegros,* but while I *was* curious last night, I decided after such a *disappointing* performance on your part that if I wanted to have a mediocre kiss and conversation, I'd take it up with Jester."

His mouth tilted flirtatiously. "Is that so?"

"It *is* so!" She stood up and tossed her napkin on the table. "If you knew anything about me, then you would know the thing I hate most is when people *tell* me how I feel. Only I get to decide that!"

She spun on her heel and stormed out the door, stomping towards her rooms. He didn't follow.

Of all the preposterous...of all the egotistical things he could have said! Lord of Pride indeed!

She kicked her dress off and threw herself on the bed, wearing her borrowed silken underclothes, and screamed into her pillow.

She knew that the kiss had likely meant very little to him, but the confirmation was deflating. Despite what she might tell herself, it had been important to her. It was her first kiss, and it was undeniably plane-shattering.

He hadn't needed to kiss me, so like—whatever that was! It could have been a little peck! He was clearly teasing her. That lustful beast was trying to gain the upper hand in some sort of contest of wills.

Then, an idea.

A deliciously *awful* idea.

An idea completely *devilish*.

Ren settled her head gently in her pillow. She slid her hand down her chest to her stomach and leisurely drew slow circles around her navel. The sensation sent small, pleasant electric shocks down her body. She stopped for a moment before she let her fingers wander. When she reached the lining of her silken undergarment, she paused and let out a nervous breath. This would be another first. She continued her journey down, delicately touching the tender, soft skin between her legs. This feeling, this exploration, was altogether new, and it filled her with excitement and anticipation.

She began delicately testing the sensations of herself. The textures of different layers and lips, each responding and soon slick with desire. She found that certain rhythms made her blood rush and her legs clench. After a few practiced strokes, she whimpered in lustful satisfaction.

My myyyyy. Did you summon me, darling?

His voice.

She smirked to herself as she dipped her fingers lower and spread herself wide, feeling her own desire. The warmth that had pooled and ached for friction.

She could feel his voice hovering close as the phantom smoke swirled around her. She could almost feel his breath on her neck.

Ren.

Renata.

I know what you're doing.

She ignored him. It was *her* turn to stroke his sin. To see why he was the Lord of Envy as well as the Lord of Lust.

She circled around herself, teasing, stoking her fire as well as his.

If you do this. There is no going back for you.

His voice was stern with warning, but he couldn't hide the slight groan hidden beneath.

"I know," she whispered before gradually sliding one finger gently into her wetness and gasping at the new feeling. She heard a husky sound close to her ears, breath blowing gently on her neck.

You wicked little thing.

A chuckle was followed by a strained sound, as if he was trying and failing to control himself.

Ren closed her eyes, pleased with herself, as she moved her second finger to her small opening, pulsing from anticipation. She permitted a zealous moan, and it slid easily inside. She began to shift her hips forward and back—testing.

Do you like that, Ren? Who are you thinking about?

She gasped, feeling his presence in the room. The mist pulsed as she ground against her fingers ever so steadily. Dragging them in and out and beginning to writhe as she felt the rough exterior of her palm graze her sensitivity.

Why are you doing this to me?

His voice was strangled.

He could have severed the connection—he didn't. He wouldn't. Of that, she was confident. He could sit there before her, in his domain, and act stoic, the perfect face of reserved calm, but right now, she was in control, and she would crack that perfect facade.

She could feel the pressure of ecstasy rising as the friction of her hand grazed against her. Ren began to pant, her body taking over—knowing exactly what to do. She began to grind and buck, completely at the mercy of her desire.

Ren could feel Azur's heavy breathing as if he was lying next to her, his breaths shallow and moans now unconcealed. She knew that he was also seeking his own pleasure by watching her. Perhaps he was in that same chair, across from hers, before the flames of the fireplace, which cast shadows down his perfect face. With her eyes closed, she could imagine him stroking himself there, fixing his eyes on her, and growling with villainous longing.

My darling...you might be as evil as I am.

He groaned.

She was so close, cresting the waves of her ecstasy— she cried out, letting herself briefly delight in her sinful yearning. But the control was gone, and this moment was only about release. Writhing with pleasure, she clasped her free hand around her throat and squeezed, imagining Azur's strong hands grasping there threateningly.

Such a good girl. Show me exactly what you love to do to yourself.

She felt herself falling, falling over the peak of bliss. Her cries of release caused her whole body to quiver and her core to flutter with aftershocks of pleasure. And with these shockwaves, she felt his release, heard echoes of his voice as the stroke of black flame licked her body, roving as he gave in to his own ecstasy.

She bit her lips, whimpering, her body spent and content, reveling in the sound of Azur's hard breaths. Even now, she could hear a low grumble emanating from his throat.

Her chest heaved as she gulped in air, head dizzy from the euphoria.

His voice finally spoke, sounding breathless.

Ren, you are exquisite. Come to me, darling. I will show you true pleasure. As only a god of lust can.

She breathed out, still tingling with want.

Poor Azur, I hate to disappoint you, for you obviously crave something more, but I really don't have the time for such frivolous matters.

She responded—then cut their connection.

CHAPTER 15

She is toying with me. Monster. She is truly despicable and stunningly clever. Too clever. Somehow, Xarek knew. She might destroy me if she doesn't destroy herself first.

Ren slept exceedingly well in the huge four-poster bed. Though with what she had pulled the night before, she doubted it would be a repeat occurrence.

Azur hadn't tried to call upon her again that night, which suited her just fine. She knew she had the upper hand and assumed the Devil was just licking the wounds he'd sustained to his insurmountable ego.

She lay in the plush bed, soaking up every ounce of comfort, knowing she'd soon return to a lumpy bed at the tower, when she heard a knock.

"Come in!" she grumbled, assuming it was Jester.

Instead, a pink Devil with matching pink hair walked in. Zelaia. She was carrying a tray of breakfast food and locked eyes on Ren, giving a knowing grin.

Well played, Azur.

She strolled over and placed the tray on her bed.

"You must be veeeery important for Lord Azur to let you sleep in here." She looked Ren up and down.

Suddenly feeling both frustrated and insecure, Ren tried to flatten her bed-head and pull the sheets up to cover her half-naked body.

Zelaia touched her tail and wound it through her hand, reminiscent of how Azur had clasped onto her as they moved in unison.

"You're not really Azur's type," she said, tilting her head as if confused. "He typically likes his lovers bigger-breasted or perhaps a male with long hair, but I guess everyone gets adventurous sometimes."

"Did you *need* something?" Ren snapped. "I assume you're here to wait on me. I'm sure Azur wouldn't want to know how subpar a job you've been doing."

Zelaia ran her tongue across her sharp fangs.

"Oh, little girl. I am not here on Azur's orders. I was just curious."

She turned with the elegance only achievable by a Devil and sauntered out.

Ren clenched her teeth but tried to keep her feelings in check. She didn't want to give him the satisfaction of knowing she was envious.

She kicked off the sheets and searched for her tunic and trousers, stubbornly refusing to wear the new ones Azur provided. But to her dismay, Zelaia had brought them newly laundered. She pulled them on, grumbling angrily to herself.

She settled next to the tray and popped a few pieces of fruit in her mouth, surveying the rest. There was a small bottle on the spread with red liquid and a note.

"Of all the things you finished last night, it turns out your wine wasn't one of them. Make sure to drink it where I can hear that lovely moan again."

All in his familiar handwriting.

She wanted to throw the damned thing across the room but knew he'd notice this wrathful action. Besides, the beautiful carpet didn't deserve such an offense.

"Wake up caaaaaall!!" she heard Jester yell before her door banged open and a presumably invisible Jester barged in.

She saw the sheets shift on her bed, and when he finally became visible, he was a mere inch from her face.

"Accck!" she yelped, almost tipping off the bed.

"Reeeeen. You have a secret, don't you?" he said in a hushed voice, dark eyes mischievous.

Her pale cheeks turned red, and her eyes widened, horror-struck.

He smiled wickedly.

"Oh, settle down! I know you weren't with Azur last night. He was positively grouchy this morning! He's never that way when he's had a tussle in the sheets. Unless! Unless you were very, *very* bad." He tilted his head, feigning curiosity and pity. "Oh, my lovely Ren! Were you very, very bad?"

She shoved his shoulder. "No! I left his pompous ass before dinner was even over."

He surveyed her for a moment.

"Yes...I think I believe you. You're also way too moody to have been with sexy Devil-daddy."

"Jester," she said, a thought occurring. "Have you and Azur ever—"

"Ew, yuck! No way! Whyyyy would you even ask that?!" he bellowed, rolling around on the bed dramatically.

"I don't know. Zelaia was in here, and I just thought that maybe—"

"Listen, Ren. Zelaia is a special lady. She is a good friend, and I think Azur sought comfort there. But, say what you want about Azur, he doesn't make it a habit of sleeping with his minions, okay?"

After their previous night, Ren wasn't convinced. Then again, so far, she had been the one to initiate all of their intimate contact.

"But we're getting off-topic!" The devil said, in a serious whisper. "Your secret is that you've been *summoned* by someone in the tower. They're all panicking, looking for you. It's quite funny, actually."

Her food felt like it was about to make a reappearance.

"Oh, hells. Yeah, I was...expecting someone," she said, trying to swallow her panic.

Jester narrowed his eyes.

"Hmm. So you need to get back to the tavern, yes? I *could* send you there," he said, tapping a long nail on his chin. "But you'll have to do something for *meeeeeee!*"

She pursed her lips. "Nothing binding, right?"

He raised his hand in a swearing gesture.

"Not binding! Why, Ren? Are you planning on *betraying* me?" he swooned.

She ignored the comment. "What do you need?"

He bit his lip, and despite being so close to her, he whispered, "I'm helping a friend. A Lesser Devil named Gabriela. Do you remember that guy, Lord Evernight, that I mentioned? A fan of sword throwing? Thing is, Gabriela recently fulfilled her contract. But Evernight won't let her leave! He locked her away until she agreed to sign another contract and indebt herself to him."

"That's awful! Can they do that?"

Jester looked sorrowful. "They can do whatever they want. She's free from obligations to serve Evernight contractually. But that doesn't mean she's free."

"Of course, I'll help you Jester." she said decisively. One of the first decisions she was absolutely sure about.

The Devil smiled ear-to-ear, his dimples alight on his cheeks.

"Thanks, Ren. I don't think I'd be able to do it without your sneaky tricks. I'll fill you in on my plan after your mysterioooooous meeting."

He stood up on the bed, giving it a few test jumps, before somersaulting to the ground. He clapped his hands twice and made a complex form with his arms and fingers before a large fiery portal appeared.

"Show off."

With mock annoyance, Ren stomped to the portal and jumped in.

After appearing in her familiar room, she suddenly felt anxious. How much did The Gilded Triangle know? She scrambled to the door and bounded down the stairs lest the God of The Heaven wait longer for a Mortal Half-Elf to appear.

"I'm sorry, Fred! I was just going out for a bite!"

As she dismounted the last stair, she saw a figure sitting in a dusty chair. The first patron she'd ever seen in the Denizen's tower. His face was old and creased with deep wrinkles.

"Excuse me, sir. I heard someone was looking for me?"

"Renata Eldanuer," he said politely, standing. "My name is Nainaur. I am glad to finally meet you."

If Ren hadn't been holding onto the railing, she would have fallen over. The Lord of The Heavens looked nothing like she had imagined and even less like his brother.

The god had cheery cheeks and a wide nose with wispy white hair that struggled to cover his balding head. His eyes sparkled like Azur's, but were an otherworldly blue instead of red. His voice was gentle, almost a whisper, but looking again, he was still imposing. Not in the way that Azur was. Azur sucked the air out of the very room, threatening to choke anyone who opposed him. Nainaur had a calm power.

"My followers have told me that you have taken up the mantle to find Vutar'ka Zhartun. I hope you can appreciate the magnitude of this task, my child."

Ren was dumbstruck. It was strange to her that this being, appearing so unassuming and meek, could intimidate her to speechlessness. She felt that if she said something wrong and provoked his ire, it would be the soft ire of a disappointed father rather than the fiery anger she had come to know from Azur. In some ways, so much more painful.

"Yes, Leo told me this task was of utmost importance to you."

The god pinched his brow together.

"It is indeed. The recovery of this tome could help millions of people, Ren. It will even help you."

"Me?"

"Without question. If you recover the relic Vutar'ka Zhartun, I will be able to restore some of your memories."

Her heart skipped a beat.

"I know that you have doubts, my child," he continued, seeing through her in the uncanny way gods did. "You exchanged your memories, and now you fear their recovery." He shook his head solemnly. "But do not fear, Renata. I am The Almighty. I can protect you. Restore you. *Redeem* you."

Her breath caught.

"You can...redeem me?"

He smiled. "Yes, even you, Renata, if you serve my holy purpose."

Her throat bobbed. She thought of Azur. Of the fragile trust they were starting to build. But her relationship with the male, notwithstanding, he was evil. He was a torturer and a killer. He trapped people and took their souls. Why should she ever put her faith in such barbarity?

Nainaur, in contrast, was the God of The Heavens. The Almighty God of Forgiveness and Mercy spoke of the importance of helping people. That's what she wanted—to help people. The decisions should be so easy, yet somehow...

"Perhaps I should show you, Renata. I know that your time in The Hells has been difficult. It is almost impossible, even for the most devout creatures, to resist its temptations. I was able to capture some memories of yours, and I can give them to you."

Ren stared, confused.

"How can you have my memories?"

His eyes sparkled kindly. "To be more precise, they are another's memories. But they're shared. You'll be able to see them as if you were remembering them yourself."

Perhaps Nainaur thought she would jump at this chance. But she couldn't. She was terrified. Now that it came down to it, by living through Renata's memories, she would have to admit they were one and the same. Before, she could pretend Renata was some severed appendage—painfully cut but no longer relevant to her current, albeit at times more complicated, life.

At the same time, she couldn't deny the temptation for a glimpse. As the god had said, resisting temptation was not something she was currently succeeding at.

"Take my hand, Renata. I will show you."

Letting her body lead, she obeyed and took his hand. It was soft, like landing on a safe cloud, before she looked into those ethereal blue eyes.

"This might be a bit disorienting at first," he said right as her body was flung across time.

She saw flashes—images of different moments— blurs of colors blended together in a cacophony of unintelligible scenes. She tried to focus—to capture any single time to identify. Then she saw him—

Nephele.

His face was bright, blue eyes shining. He tilted his head back in unabashed laughter and threaded his fingers through hers. She saw herself—Renata—beaming at him, blissful. Her face looked almost unrecognizable with so much joy painted upon it. They were sitting together under a bright yellow sun, talking and smiling—unable to look away from the other lest they lose even one second of time together.

The image melted into another, this time in the lively bar in her hometown of Vergessen. She was standing on a table playing her piccolo, and Nephele was next to her, singing and dancing. They circled each other playfully as the patrons clapped and cheered. She saw him nudge her teasingly, making them almost topple off the table. They both had to stop their performance to laugh at their clumsiness, and the crowd joined in their laughter and toasted the two musicians. Nephele wrapped a strong arm around her waist, pulled her in, and kissed her. It was a beautiful kiss. Tender but passionate.

Another scene appeared.

"Nephele, I have to go," she heard herself say.

"Why, though, Renata? Why does it have to be you? Stay here, stay with me. You don't have to fight! This isn't our battle."

She saw herself clench her fists.

"I'm not *special*, Nephele! They are taking citizens from our city to fight in a war, and I can't just sit in the tavern playing songs night after night, knowing that I could do something to help!"

She saw Nephele's face pinch with distress.

"Then we will go together."

"Nephele, no, I—"

"Renata, I'm coming. I can lend medical aid, work in the field hospital. I can help. If you go, I go. That was our promise to each other. That we would never leave the other behind or alone. I'm coming."

Ren was whipped back into the ether and then landed hard on her feet, standing once more before Nainaur in the dusty tavern.

"Nephele. You took these memories from Nephele."

The god nodded sadly. "He loves you, Renata. He still waits for you to return to him."

She was so dizzy. Through Nephele's memories, she could feel his love. How honored he felt to be a part of Renata's life. She felt the want in his heart when he kissed her and his determination to follow her even into war. That was everything, wasn't it? A love like that.

"I broke my promise," she said, almost whispering, voice cracking, "I broke my promise to Nephele. I left him alone. I left him behind."

Nainaur set his hand on Ren's shoulder.

"It wasn't your fault, Renata. I know you've been running. Running from your memories and your fears. I want to help you. I want to send you back to your family. I want you to recover those moments of happiness and live your life the way you are supposed to be living it. In the sun. Not trapped and groping for meaning in The Hells."

Renata felt her eyes prickle.

"You can do that? You can send me back? Break my contract?"

His kind eyes surveyed her once more.

"I can, my child. But only if you recover the Vutar'ka Zhartun. And I know where you can start. Azur, your patron, knows of its location. Find out where it is, and seek it out. Only then will I be able to restore your memories and return you back home."

There it is, then—the way forward. But then why did she still have doubts? Was she standing in her own way, determined not to be happy? In the end, this was why she was here. To follow this through. What was the alternative? That she would live in The Hells, trapped like Jester, fulfilling deed after deed for Azur?

Jester...

"If you can break my contract, could you break someone else's?" she blurted.

He gave her a concerned look.

"I try to stay out of my brother's machinations."

"I have a friend—Jester. He has been a slave to Azur for a long time, and maybe, if I get you the tome, you can free him too?"

the god responded, sounding almost proud.

"You are truly a kind person. Yes. I think I might be able to make an exception for Jester."

Ren let out a long breath.

"Okay. I'll get the information from Azur."

The god kept his smile.

"I will leave you now, Renata. Please find Vutar'ka Zhartun. The longer you terry, the more people will suffer. Remember, Nephele is waiting."

He vanished.

CHAPTER 16

I know it has to be me. I'm the only one who deserves it. I will annihilate anyone who dares challenge my power. My birthright.

Unsurprisingly, Jester, her now shadow, was waiting for her in the small tavern bedroom.

"What would happen if Fred came in here and saw you?" she asked, shutting the door quickly behind her.

Jester jumped towards her, putting up fits.

"I ain't scared of no soulless barkeep!" he said, pretending to throw punches.

"Fred doesn't have a soul?"

"Nope! I mean, he wouldn't be here if he did, would he? That dumb-dumb sold his soul to Xarek for a *magical bar.* Ridiculous! He thought it would make him rich. Xarek gave it to him, all right. But the only residents here are sleepers, who don't drink and don't pay! So he's basically stuck here waiting around for the occasional Mortal to wander in. More importantly! Are you gonna tell me what your super secret meeting was about?" he asked, crossing his arms.

Ren paused. "Jester. I think I might know a way to free you from your contract."

The Devil looked taken aback.

"What are you talking about, Ren? I can't be freed."

She bit her lip.

"I think you can, Jester. The same people who sent me here told me that they would help—"

"No, Ren," he said sternly. "Listen to me. Whatever you are doing, stop. Don't worry about me."

"Jester, it isn't right! I know you've been with Azur a long time, but—"

"I said no! I don't need your help, and I don't *want* your help. I've made my choices. So drop it."

An uncomfortable silence befell the room, and they stood, not moving or speaking for longer than was comfortable.

"Sorry," she said quietly. "I won't bring it up again if you don't want to talk about it."

He nodded, crossing the room and unpacking a few things from a satchel he had laid on her bed.

That was her first plan out the window. She had hoped that Jester, having a rapport with Azur, would be able to ask about the location of the Vutar'ka Zhartun. Now, Ren would have to figure out how to ask Azur herself and she hadn't seen him since their tense dinner.

True to his nature, Jester never stayed down long. He twirled like a ballerina and leaped, landing in front of her.

"You didn't let me explain my plaaaaan! We go tonight! To get Gabriela! Lord Tight Tushy is going somewhere. Maybe damage control from Wyvryn?"

"Definitely!" Ren said, trying to show enthusiasm. In truth, she needed to feel like she was doing something good for someone. Being in The Hells was, well, hell. It was oppressive in its emotional heaviness, and she craved a bit of positivity.

Her mind began to wander.

You want to do something nice to feel better? That's so selfish!

The smile on her face faltered.

"Hey, Ren? You in there?" Jester asked, waving a clawed hand in front of her.

She snapped back from her thoughts.

"Sorry, yeah. What's the plan?"

Jester's brow furrowed.

"I need you to be at the top of your game tonight. You seem distracted."

She smiled, changed, apologetic.

"I'm good! Just give me the details."

He bobbed his head, smile returning.

"Right! But first!" He reached into the pocket of his black trousers, taking hold of Ren's hand. "I have to ask you something. From the first time I saw you, I knew that you were something special." He bent down on one knee and let out a shaky breath. "Ren—"

"*Jester*! What the hells are you doing?"

"Let a male *finish*," he bellowed. "No wonder Azur wouldn't have sex with you," he muttered under his breath. "Ahem...will you do me the honor of—going on an adventure with me?" he said, producing a polished ring that twisted like vines, a small orange vurmite set in the center.

Ren cackled. "What even is that, Jester?" she asked, taking the elegant piece.

"It's to help with where we are going. I hear Mortals are a little less tolerant of the elements."

A genuine smile pulled at her lips.

"Thanks, Jester. That was thoughtful."

"Not thoughtful at all, actually. If you didn't have it, you'd probably die. It's purely selfish."

Ren turned the small ring on her finger gently. It was exquisite. The vurmite, though small, seemed to produce its own light.

"It's a loaner, Ren. Don't get any ideas," he said, raising a sculpted brow.

Ren couldn't stop the disappointed expression that crossed her face.

Ren, darling. Are you missing me? Seems like you're having a craving.

She bit her tongue and banished Azur from her mind.

"Wow. You really *do* like jewelry," Jester commented, watching Ren swipe away black smoke with an annoyed expression. "I guess I know what to get you for your birthday," he chuckled.

"Just tell me where we're going," she groaned.

"Right! Evernight lives pretty far. We will portal there. He isn't as paranoid as Xarek. He puts his wards closer. Plus, he has people portaling in and out of his mines every day. We'll just be two more."

"The mines? We are going to the mines?"

"One of them. Not one of the very active ones. The volcano sort of mucks that up. But Evernight still uses it as a prison for non-cooperative servants, sleepers, and slaves."

The ring was starting to make more sense.

As she slipped it on her finger, she could feel a warm vibration from the band.

"When do we head out?" she asked.

Jester pulled out her two daggers and lock-pick kit from his satchel.

"Now?"

***

When they appeared at their new location, Ren had to blink several times to let her eyes adjust. Jester had been right, the heat was oppressive, and she immediately started to perspire.

The two were standing in what looked like a small cave with a lone lantern for light

There were three entrances to their part of the cave, but Jester didn't hesitate to walk toward the closest one. He stopped before crossing the threshold and held up a hand to signal for Ren to stop.

Standing on her toes to see over Jester's tall form, Ren could see that the next room was littered with chairs, mostly broken or tilted in some fashion. There were several sleepers walking around aimlessly while others sat staring off into the space, some sleeping on the floor.

"The sleepers won't report us if we're seen," Jester whispered. "They'll just think we work here. It's everyone else we have to avoid."

Ren tilted her head to indicate she understood.

Jester motioned for her to follow as they entered the large sitting room. The sleepers barely glanced at them as they casually strolled to the other side, an open doorway leading to what appeared to be someone's study. Papers and scrolls littered the floor.

"Hells, Evander. Clean your damned space," Jester murmured, stepping over several fallen pieces of parchment and quills. "The only thing more evil than imprisoning an innocent Devil is being disorganized."

Jester shuffled around the room, opening drawers and looking under papers.

"We need to find a map or something that says where he might keep Gabriela."

"What about the sleepers?" Ren whispered.

"What about them?" he said, continuing to push papers around.

"We could ask them."

He stopped.

"They can't communicate, Ren," he said with a frown. "I wish they could, but they're all...blank."

Ren thought back to the Half-Orc female who was sitting outside the tavern. It was true that she hadn't *directly* talked to her or even really acknowledged her, yet there seemed to still be an understanding behind her eyes.

Leaving her companion to search, Ren returned to the room of broken chairs. The closest sleeper was a bald Gnomish male with a large nose and even larger green eyes—piercing in their color.

She cleared her throat.

"Excuse me, sir? Would you happen to know where Lord Evernight keeps his prisoners?"

You sound ridiculous.

The male did not meet her eyes.

"We are trying to help a friend, you see. If you could aid us in any way, we'd really appreciate it."

He said nothing, head lulling to the side.

Ren felt a hand on her shoulder.

"I know it's hard, Elfy girl. But they're not there. Not anymore."

Feeling defeated, Ren turned and followed Jester who had apparently abandoned his search of the office. He instead hunkered into a crouch to walk down a nearby cavernous hallway.

Ren could feel the beads of sweat drip down her face, heat emanating off the stone below her booted feet.

As they turned the corner, the small hallway opened up into a large cavernous hollow. The ceilings were tall, and stalactites dripped from overhead like devilish fangs.

Jester slapped a hand over Ren's mouth right before she let out a squeal of delight. Each and every surface of the cavern was dotted with different sizes and colors of vurmite. Ren's insides growled with desire as the meager light bounced off the jewels, creating a rainbow of color.

Darling girl, you must stop being so greedy if you don't want to hear my voice in your pointy little ears.

Can we just assume if I'm feeling greedy that I'm not *calling you?*

She mentally gritted the words out.

I can't do that. Greed is a part of what I am. You can't expect me to ignore you if you're screaming my name, can you?

I'm busy!

Fair enough, pet. I'd rather hear you screaming my name under different circumstances, anyway.

"You are so predictable," Jester hissed, swatting the air in front of his face to keep the smoke away.

The large space was almost completely abandoned, save for two Lesser Devils patrolling a large pool of water. A sheen of steam languidly swirled around its surface. The effect enhanced the vurmite's already wondrous glimmer.

"You need to incapacitate one of them," Jester whispered matter-of-factly.

"Sorry—I need to *what* them?"

Jester made a strangling motion with his hands and then stuck his tongue out. "Incapacitate!"

Ren just blinked at him.

"Jester, I'm not sure I even know how to *do* that."

Jester put his hands on his hips, "I can't take them both down without alerting every guard in this place. So figure it out, Elfy!"

He vanished, appearing several feet from the pool of water, and ducked behind a stalagmite.

Crouched down and unmoving, Ren wracked her brain.

Incapacitate—not kill.

She felt something—a small prod of encouragement from near her waistband. Without thinking, she reached down and touched her piccolo—it was warm under her fingers. She slid it out of its holster to examine it, still not understanding its mysterious language.

She cautiously raised it to her mouth, hoping that it would give her another signal as to her next steps. The old piccolo seemed to sigh as it grazed her lips softly. Ren heard it—a melody ringing in her ears, pushing to be released.

Lost in her contemplation, she hadn't at first noticed the loud *crack* of rock from where Jester was hiding. It was only when the two Lessers spun on their heels that the echo ricocheted back to her.

"Fuuuuck," she heard Jester groan as the two hulking guards barreled toward him.

She fumbled with her piccolo, almost dropping it. Her memory haunted her with the images of an injured Jester in the forest of Nahmir and the sounds of him gasping for air.

Not him, no. Come for me.

Shaking from panic, she lifted her piccolo to her lips, hoping the distraction would give Jester some time. While Ren's heart felt urgent, the song came out as hushed, barely audible as it sang sweetly through the cavern.

Three sets of eyes shot in her direction, Jester's face twisted in disbelief.

"What are you doing over there!" a gray-skinned Lesser bellowed, altering his course.

The other, teal-skinned, continued toward Jester.

Ren didn't stop playing. While her mind raced with ways to escape, her body remained relaxed, begging her to stay calm and *play*. To keep her breath *steady.*

She watched as Jester leaped over the stalagmite, readying himself for a fight as the teal Lesser sprinted forward. And then, he tripped, falling to one knee, cursing. The gray one also faltered, wavering on his feet before falling face-first into the rocky ground with a *thud*. They both clambered to regain their footing but were unable to lift their heavy bodies.

The teal Lesser put his hand on his forehead, blinking rapidly, while the other leaned for support on a protruding boulder.

Jester stood unmoving in the corner of the room, eyes wide.

Ren, just as confused, kept playing, afraid that any pause in her efforts would halt the piccolo's mysterious effects. So the melody continued, rebounding off the walls, sounding as if she was playing her own duet.

The two Lessers grunted with strain before falling utterly prone, unable to regain their stance. Their movements became slower. The gray Lesser was still fighting the effects, reaching his arms forward to drag himself in a desperate attempt to reach Ren and stop her playing, but his arms weren't cooperating. With every note played, their movements became less and less noticeable—

a finger twitch here, a head tilt there, until eventually, they ceased altogether.

Seeing her two victims completely subdued and with a slight thrum of satisfaction from her instrument, Ren felt safe enough to finish her song. She paused as the last notes sang through the cavern, waiting anxiously for any recovery from the Devils.

Jester, less concerned, immediately walked over, stepping over the two snoring Devils, his mouth hanging open.

"You're certainly full of surprises, little Elfy!" he said, placing his hands on his hips and looking at her proudly.

She smiled warily. "Another thing I forgot I could do, I suppose."

"Right! Your music has the power to bore people to sleep. Truly inspiring!"

"Shut it, Jester," she said, pushing past him playfully. "I was only trying to create a distraction...it just happened."

"Hmm," he said, scratching behind a red pointed ear. "Might come in handy later, but for now, we're alone."

Jester motioned around the completely quiet cavern.

"The sleepers only work during the day," Jester explained. "It isn't kindness, though. The lordlings learned that if you work them too much, they just plop down and refuse to move. No matter how much you whip them."

She gasped. "That's...disgusting."

"It's The Hells. Nothing more, nothing less."

They both kept a slow pace, stopping every few feet to listen for patrols or other approaching creatures.

After two or three curves in the tunnel, the cavern dipped down, makeshift stairs carved into the rocky walls. If they hadn't already been going slow, their pace would have surely lessened on the precarious steps.

As they descended, the smell of sulfur grew.

"Ah! Why does Hell have to smell so bad?" Ren murmured.

Jester paused.

"That's not my home's normal smell," he huffed. "That's waste. We might be near where they keep prisoners."

Jester tumbled a few steps, losing his bearings, and poofed away to land on his feet.

"Damnit, Jester, *no*! I can't keep up with you!" she hissed, sliding.

When her feet finally hit the plateaued ground, she swiftly crept down the hallway and turned the corner.

Jester was standing in front of a stone door with a large bar lock. The only way to see what was on the other side of the door was a small opening at the bottom.

Ren scurried over as Jester bent down, his tail in the air.

"Gabriela! Is that you?" he whispered.

At first, there was no reply.

"Gabriela, we are here to help you!" Ren offered.

They then heard a small shuffling behind the door as Ren bent down. She saw two bare yellow feet walking towards them and then two yellow eyes on the round face.

"Who are you?" she asked, voice wavering.

Jester licked his lips nervously.

"We were sent by some friends. We've come to get you out."

Ren eyed her companion, confused. She could have sworn he said that Gabriela knew him.

Gabriela's cat-like eyes filled with tears.

"Oh, thank The Almighty."

"Get your lock-pick, Elfy!" Jester said as he stood up, shaking the locking mechanism.

Ren straightened and pulled out her picks, expertly inserting them into the cylinder. This lock, not magical and therefore more primitive, unlatched almost immediately.

Jester lifted the bar lock and pushed on the door as it stiffly opened.

Gabriela was clasping her hands in front of her in thanks, yellow skin stained with ash and blood. She threw herself on Jester and broke into shaky sobs.

Jester immediately wrapped his arms around her.

"It's okay, Gabriela. We are getting you out of here."

Unsure of their next move, Ren sidled up to Jester.

"What now? Do we just portal away?"

Jester shook his head, stroking the female's hair which was as yellow as her skin.

"We have to be outside of the wards. Like at Xarek's. This one has wards up until past where the sleepers are."

"I'm sorry, Miss Gabriela, but we must get going," Jester said gently, pulling her away and looking kindly into the female's eyes.

Gabriela bobbed her head and hiccupped. She seemed so much younger than Jester despite his childlike disposition.

The two led a trembling Gabriela up the clumsy stairs and through the cavernous room where the two Lesser Devils still snoozed peacefully. Finally arriving in the small sitting room, Ren noticed several more sleepers had joined the depressing gathering.

With the final room in sight, the three walked gingerly around any sleepers in their way.

"I'll go to the next room first," Jester said, still in a whisper. "I can open the portal, and then you two can run in."

Ren tilted her head in approval before Jester blinked out and came to view in the doorway in the middle of the next room, barely visible from their position.

"*Aaaaaaah!*"

Ren whipped her head around. Towering over her, was a giant beast of a Devil—wings unfurled and clutching Gabriela by the arm, lifting her high off the ground.

"Who do you think you are?" he growled. "Trying to steal my personal *property!*" he bellowed at Ren.

His voice was gruff and grating like a hammer slamming against a stone.

"Oh, I see. Little Mortal came to save her friend? Even better. I get two wenches for the price of one." He trailed his tongue across jagged yellowed teeth. "I've never fucked an Elf before. I wonder if they scream for mercy like Devils do?" He grabbed Ren's upper arm painfully. "I hope you enjoyed your little outing, Gabs! I'll be taking the time out of your perky little ass."

Ren unsheathed a dagger with her second hand and thrust it towards the Devil's arm. The dagger glanced off—a spark of light emanating off Evernight's body.

"Let. Them. Go," she heard a thunderous voice rumble from the room.

All their heads, and even some singers, turned towards the imposing sound.

The previously scorching atmosphere suddenly turned cold.

Jester stood in the doorway, eyes black, fangs bared. His dark hair was floating around his head as a sudden torment of wind blasted through the room. Veins of smoke were pulsing from every pore of his tall, red body.

Ren watched the lord's face drop, panic overtaking every feature. Ren felt the Devil release her arm, and Gabriela landed with an, "uff," on wobbly legs.

The Devil hit his knees, shaking.

"Please. I didn't know," he said, putting up his hands in supplication.

The entire room was darkening, and even the sleepers were beginning to cower in Jester's presence.

In a flash, Jester was upon the lord, grasping his neck with one hand, lifting the massive Devil off of his knees.

"I've never liked you, Evander. I should thank you for finally giving me a reason to eradicate your presence from this plane."

Jester's horns seemed to grow momentarily longer as he squeezed his sharp nails into Evander Evernight's neck.

Tears streamed down the Devil's face as he choked out a few more sad wheezes of apology. "Please don't do this, I'll repent! Just let me live!"

Jester was unmoved and, with one more flex of his forearm, caved in his windpipe with a low crunch. He tossed the Devil's corpse irreverently. It slapped the ashy floor, blood gushing from his crushed jugular.

The creature, Jester, walked steadily over to the two females and offered Gabriela his hand, eyes still seeping black tendrils.

"Evernight won't be bothering you again, Gabriela. Please come with me."

The golden Devil, eyes wet and shaking, laid her hand meekly in Jester's.

"Let's go, Ren," he said, voice emotionless as he turned calmly, striding with Gabriela to the exit, a fiery portal awaiting.

CHAPTER 17

I see reverberations of myself in her more and more with every passing day.

The three staggered to a halt as they were spat out on the outskirts of the forest of Nahmir. Ren was reeling, confused, and disoriented.

Gabriela was on all fours, sputtering and retching. Ren bent down to rub her back.

"It's okay now, Gabriela. You're free."

Jester surveyed the area, checking behind trees and rocks to ensure they hadn't been followed. But who would have dared follow after that performance?

Gabriela finally calmed a little, sitting cross-legged on the ground.

"I can't begin to thank you enough," she stammered, wiping her eyes. "I know The Almighty sent you to save me—you must be one of his faithful."

Ren heard an almost imperceptible growl from her friend.

"Don't thank The Almighty, Gabriela. He didn't do *shit* for you. We did."

Gabriela made a whimpering sound, and Ren inhaled sharply, surprised by his pointed words. Jester joined the two females on the ground. He reached into his pocket and pulled out a small coin purse.

"You're on your own from here. This should be enough to get you anywhere you want to go."

She took the bag timidly.

"But, sir, if you're indebted to a Devil, you'll need this money," she said, sensing his possession as other Devils had previously.

"Don't worry about me. You just get yourself to safety. Do you have family or friends you can stay with?"

"Yes, a few towns over, but it's a long walk."

"I can portal you, no problem!" he said with a smile before Gabriela threw her arms around his neck, giving him a peck on the cheek.

Ren scooted a bit back, feeling awkward.

Jester helped the Devil to her feet and summoned a portal. With a look back at her two rescuers, she blew a kiss and disappeared.

"That was fun!" Jester said, stretching.

"Are...we going to talk about what happened back there? What happened to Lesser Devils having *benign* powers?"

Jester ignored her and began walking towards the city.

"Jester, wait. You can tell me. I won't judge you," she said, taking his hand and halting his movement. "I just want to help," she tried to inject as much care into her voice as possible.

A long breath marked his surrender.

"There are a lot of things you don't understand about The Hells. Even more, there are a lot of things you don't— *can't* understand about me. My relationship with Azur is complicated. But it has its benefits, too. I have the power to help people, but that's really all I can say. I hope you can respect that."

She realized at that moment that Jester was being as truthful as he was capable of being. She could see the discomfort in his expression, and she knew if he could tell her more, he would. Yet she, with all her demands of honesty, hadn't been truthful with Jester. He had saved her more than once, and she hadn't done him this courtesy.

"What you said about The Almighty, why did you say it?" she asked.

Jester's expression turned cold.

"*That* is something I cannot speak of without violating my contract."

"I see. There is something I want to tell you about The Almighty."

Jester furrowed his brow as she spoke. She noticed a faint uptick in the pulse at his neck—fear in this creature that she now knew was capable of destroying an Immortal.

"I am working for him. He's looking for something called Vutar'ka Zhartun. Have you heard of it?"

Jester's lips parted slightly. He didn't look like he was breathing.

"Ren, what have you done?" he said, almost inaudibly.

"If I find it, I could restore my memories!" she said quickly. "He said that he could release you from your contract..."

The second part trailed off, and she hoped he wouldn't shut down again.

Jester scrubbed his face in his hands.

"He said..." she continued, hoping to ease his anxiety, "he told me that Azur would know where it is."

His eyes shot to her. They were wild and piercing.

"He? You talked to Nainaur?"

His tone was becoming increasingly aggressive, and she officially regretted her decision to tell him.

"Yes. I've met with several gods recently, as you know," she said defensively.

One of Jester's eyes twitched as they widened in disbelief.

"Nainaur is the sworn enemy of Azur. How could you even consider that I might get involved with this? I have to tell Azur. I can't—won't keep this from him."

"That was actually what I was hoping for. Maybe he can help us—"

"You don't understand! Vutar'ka Zhartun is an ancient relic given to Azur by his brother, Faydir, before his death!"

Jester snapped his mouth shut.

"Faydir? The Fae god? He *did* abandon the Fae?"

Jester's jaw tightened.

"I don't know. But that's...what I think. Regardless, Nainaur *cannot* possess the tome. I'm sorry, I have to go. Can you make your way back to the tavern alone?"

Before she could respond, he disappeared.

***

Ren sat alone in her room, which was starting to feel homey, and played her piccolo. She knew she should probably be trying to decipher the piccolo's secrets, but she couldn't help getting caught up in the trance of beautiful notes.

She was trying to create something new, something that reflected her fractured and contradictory feelings, but the playing was rough going. She struggled to hit satisfying pitches. Even so, the process brought a semblance of contentment.

Abruptly, she stopped playing as she noticed her fingers slowed over the openings of the piccolo and began to release dark, smoky curls.

Ren moaned in acquiescence at his summons and materialized in the familiar office.

The door behind her slammed open, and she spun around, startled.

Azur walked in and pushed past her—his clothes slightly disheveled and his curls tousled. Her mind went to inappropriate places until she saw that he was soaked with blood.

Azur sat behind his desk and pushed his curls back into their proper place, smearing a small amount of black blood on his forehead. His eyes were hard as he glared at her from across the room.

Her stomach flipped.

If she didn't know that he couldn't harm her, she believed he would launch himself across the room to rip out her throat.

"You've been talking to Nainaur." It wasn't a question. "You. Ren Eldanuer, who belongs to *me,* has gone behind my back, scheming to steal one of the most precious items in all the planes."

"No, I—"

"*Silence!*" he roared, slamming his hands on his desk, face taking on its iridescent and fiery appearance.

Hells.

Her body flushed.

"Have you been working with Xarek? Tell me now, and I might not lock you in the pits for the rest of your days," he snarled, showing the points of his sharp teeth.

She shivered, and it wasn't only due to terror. He was the epitome of power and dominance, exuding his spectacular wrath. The most terrifying beast of your nightmares and the king you got on your knees for. The lover you wanted to fight for you.

It was time to come clean. Ren opened her mouth, surprised that her voice didn't shake.

"I have never worked with Xarek, though I have been working with The Gilded Triangle. They brought me to The Hells to try to get the—"

"Vutar'ka Zhartun," he finished. "Do you realize what could have happened to Jester if you had involved him in this inadvertently? He is a Devil of The Hells. Becoming a sleeper would have been a *privilege* compared to what might happen if a soulless Devil entreated with the god of The Heavens."

Her eyes prickled.

Don't you dare cry.

She decided to trade her sadness for anger.

"I didn't know. I was only trying to help!" she fired back, clenching her fists. "No one is helping him, and he is *alone!* I know what that feels like. To be soulless and alone. If I can help him, I will."

"You are going to stand there and tell me that your motives aren't selfish?" he said, bolting to his feet. "What did *The Almighty* Nainaur promise you in exchange for your betrayal? What could have been so important that you would risk everything?"

"Everything? I have *nothing*, Azur! No memories, no family, no home! He offered me all of that *plus* redemption. If I recall, you told me that was impossible."

She was shaking now, her wrath taking its proper place and filling her with audacity.

"Is that what you want? To go back? Truly? For your memories to be restored?"

She considered. The truth was, she still didn't know.

"I know I don't want to live a life wondering if I was— am—good or bad. I don't want to keep living, trying to make up for all the things I might or might not have done without even knowing what I am working towards. Maybe if I know, if I go back, I can figure it out. Get on the road to redemption or...something like it."

Azur froze, staring at Ren as if puzzling something out. He finally sat, lacing his still-blooded hands together.

It struck her.

No. Jester!

"What did you do to Jester?!" she screamed, voice cracking with agony and rage. The tears came now, unobstructed.

He did not break eye contact with her.

"What if I hurt him, Ren? What would you do?"

She drew her obsidian dagger.

"I don't give a fuck if you're Immortal. I will stab you until you *wish* you were dead."

Her tone was venom. She would. She would die there, making this creature regret ever touching her friend.

Azur smiled wickedly.

That was *it*! She launched herself across the room, screaming and holding her dagger with both hands. She leapt into the air to swing down upon him as she vaulted the desk.

She froze—literally froze, hanging in mid-air.

Azur was holding a lazy hand up, still smiling. He sighed as if speaking to a lover.

"You are utterly remarkable. Though you would never allow yourself to admit it, we are similar. Beauty covering the heinous beast inside."

He let her drop, landing roughly on his desk, with papers and quills flying.

"You have surprised me, my dear, and I am so very rarely surprised. For this reason alone, I won't lock you up and torture you like that old fool in the dungeons. But to answer your question, no, it's not Jester's blood. I quite like my Jester, actually, and appreciate his unwavering loyalty."

Her breathing was shallow, and tears still streamed down her face, smearing the ink on the various documents on the desk.

"I didn't work with Xarek. I didn't *know* about the tome," she gritted through her teeth,

"Very well," he said firmly. "Then our next step is that we must destroy Xarek. You and I."

"Why should I help you?" she spat, anger still bubbling at the surface.

He raised an eyebrow.

"Did you forget that he plans to use you? Even if the prestigious Gilded Triangle *could* send you back, Xarek is a powerful High Devil who will stop at nothing to hunt you down. You want to take fate into your own hands? Help me kill him."

In her own hands. Freedom to make decisions for herself—to show The Planes, all the beings, Azur included, that *she* would decide her destiny. Killing a High Devil would definitely make her feel gloriously in control of her fate.

"What do I need to do?"

"That's my girl," he said, eyes gleaming. "I'm planning to host a party. All the High Devils, lords, and ladies of the plane will be invited. Xarek will not be able to resist this opportunity to challenge me. When he does, I will remove his head from his shoulders," he said casually.

"Why can't you just go do it now?"

"There are rules in my court. Xarek is Immortal, and as such, he is under my protection until he violates one of my edicts. Threatening his king publically would give me the freedom to act as I see fit in regard to his life."

"And where do I come in?"

Azur sat back, looking like the picture of comfort.

"Xarek wants to use you. I will take you as my consort to show that you are mine. Every Devil in the planes will know that you cannot be touched. I have a feeling, however, that Xarek, in his devilish arrogance, will try to see how far he can get with you, and try to collect information. Instead, I want *you* to discover his plans. Then I kill him."

"We," Ren stated definitively. "*We* kill him."

Azur tilted his head back and inhaled deeply as if treasuring a delicious scent in the air.

"Yesss, my darling," he purred, "*we* kill him. The event is tomorrow night—before we go, I need to brand you as mine," he said, almost as an afterthought.

"Absolutely *not*." She balked. "I'm not going to let you *brand* me. Are you insane?"

"Some people have said that, yes. Don't fret—it's temporary. But I cannot call you my consort if you have not been marked."

She narrowed her eyes.

"No one would believe it without my brand, it will also keep you safe. But I won't do it unless you give me permission."

"Will...it hurt?"

He tilted his head thoughtfully. "No. At least, they haven't told me it does."

"And...this is the only way?" she asked, hoping their contract extended to preventing him from lying.

"I am afraid so. Any more extreme action might place you at unnecessary risk."

"Fine," she said, huffing.

"Excellent. Now, if you'd please lay down."

Awkwardly, Ren realized that she was still splayed on Azur's desk.

"There is fine. Might as well," he grumbled, surveying the mess of papers.

He reached for her and lightly positioned her face towards his, hands still stained with dried blood. His eyes were hooded as they traced the curve of her neck.

"Yes, this will do nicely," he murmured to himself.

He then lowered his face inches away from her, and she knew he could see her pulse quicken.

"What are you doing?" she asked breathlessly.

"It must be where everyone will see it," he said, face still hovering at her nape.

The smell of roses on his breath made her heart skitter. With a start, she felt him trace the gentlest of lines down her neck with a sharp fang—the sensation already causing her muscles to spasm. She squinted her eyes, trying to concentrate on the necessity of the practice, not the caress. She knew that it would be all too easy to get lost in the experience.

"Oh, my darling, Ren. Just a pinch," he sighed at her soft nape.

He buried his fangs into her roughly.

Ren gasped as his teeth pierced skin. A momentary stab of pain and then a surge of pleasant prickling raced through her body. She began to pant, losing control of her desires, wanting nothing more than for him to devour her whole.

One hand shot up, grabbing the curve of his horn to pull him in closer—a beg for more.

Deeper.

He stopped with a jolt.

"If you do that, I won't be able to control what happens next," he grunted huskily.

She felt wicked as she deliberately unfurled her fingers one by one, then teasingly trailed each finger lightly down the horn's curve.

Azur sucked in air quickly, letting out a moan of excitement, his body shuddering. He trailed his tongue down her neck, licking up blood that was dripping there. A dark laugh escaped his lips as he kissed the small curve of her neck, stroking their mutual lust, moaning as he went. A low growl rumbled his throat as he jerked as if trying to contain his eagerness, drawing gentle lines of kisses to her chin. He paused, demanding her attention, a question lingering in his eyes.

Yes.

His lips met hers with a hunger—the ache in her core now a throb of desire. He pulled himself onto the desk and straddled her, breathing low groans into her mouth.

"You feel so perfect," he growled, lifting her hips up to meet his and clasping his hand around the back of her neck. She could feel his hardness as he pulled her leg up to wrap around his waist.

She was shattered, only able to breathe in gasps and whimpers.

He jerked, pulling her even closer as if wanting to crawl inside her. Another jerk—and his wings, large and menacing, ripped through the flesh of his back, shredding his shirt and vest.

Ren stifled a cry of surprise into his mouth but refused to break the embrace. It felt too perfect in his arms. She trailed her fingers down his chest, letting the tips of her fingers quiver in the pleasure of his perfect skin.

He slowed down, his kisses turning sultry and needy before he gently pulled away. He lifted her chin delicately and traced his gaze across her expectant lips—blinking slowly, as if seeing her for the first time. His breath ragged, his cheeks flushed. His glowing eyes, endlessly deep, surveying her as if she were the only person he wished to admire for the rest of his Immortal life. His eyebrows were tucked together, lips slightly parted.

"Ren?"

"Yes," she said, struggling to catch her breath.

"Please. Could you remove yourself from my desk?"

He straightened, vanishing his wings.

She let out a choked sound, and before she could stop herself—she reared her hand back and slapped him.

Both of their mouths fell open, hers in disbelief, his almost proud. She angrily hopped off his desk and left, slamming the door behind her.

CHAPTER 18

I am Greed. I will not allow him to take Vutar'ka Zhartun. Or Ren. I possess them fully.

She was done pouting like a child. Instead, she would put their encounters in the back of her mind and remain aloof towards Azur. This was all a game to him—he was chasing pleasure and envy. Fine. She would chase hers, too. If he was going to use her, then she would use him.

It was on her way to her rooms that she spotted Jester grumbling to himself and holding various ornate fabrics. He looked a bit frazzled, but other than that, unharmed.

"There you are!" he said, relief replacing his bothered expression. "I've been wandering around trying to deliver this to you." He strode over and pushed his load into her arms. "Dresses for you tonight—I raided Zelaia's closet. The garments in your wardrobe aren't appropriate as the *consort* of the King of Hells," he said with a knowing look.

"Could you not? I'm already dealing with enough right now."

"I can see that," he said, pointing at her neck. "The entire court is going to go *wild.*"

Her eyes widened. She had completely forgotten through her lustful encounter that Azur had *branded* her. She turned on her heel, dropping dresses to the floor, and ran to her room, skidding before halting in front of the vanity.

Starting behind her ear and following the curve of her shoulder was a red tattoo, iridescent and catching the light. It was unreadable to her but recognizable in its sharp, devilish writing.

"I've seen worse. At least yours glitters. Very thoughtful of him," Jester said, approaching and holding the dresses that had tumbled to the floor.

"What does it say?" she demanded.

"Property of Sexy King Lord Shiny Hair," he said, dumping the dresses.

"No, it does *not!*" she countered.

He giggled.

"No. It doesn't. There isn't a direct translation. It says Threxis elt Igdthen Mashrez. The closest it comes is *touch her and die*, or something. Maybe *touch her, and I'll stick my claws into your windpipe*?"

Ren tugged on the hair near her scalp in exasperation. "I suppose this is what I agreed to."

Jester tried and failed to hide his look of judgment as he stroked the fabric of a blue dress slung over the vanity.

"I'm trying to figure this out as I go, okay?" she barked.

He picked up an elegant and silky scarlet dress and held it up to her face.

"What goes with silver?" he murmured.

Ren relented to the conversation change. "What are *you* wearing?"

Not meeting her eyes, he continued to stroke different dresses with the sharp points of his fingers.

"I'm not going. Azur asked, but I'm...tired of being the butt of everyone's jokes."

"Aren't you the royal Jester?" she asked, trying to tease and then immediately realizing how insensitive she sounded.

He looked at her full-on with a strained smile.

"Yes! But even a Jester needs a night off, eh?

She shifted uncomfortably, a thought dawning on her.

"Is...Jester your real name?"

His smile disappeared, face becoming serious.

"I...don't know," he said quietly, cheeks changing color. "I've been Jester for so long. I've given up so much of who I was that I can't quite remember what I was before." He laughed ironically. "Not unlike you, I suppose—but I like Jester!" he said, his mood changing starkly. "It suuuuits me, don't you think?"

His grin stretched from pointed ear to pointed ear, dimples brightening his face.

She admired Jester for his ability to turn any conversation around, but it also made her sad. He was fighting to forget as she was fighting to remember.

"It does suit you, Jester," she said, giving him a warm smile and hesitantly reaching out to touch his arm.

He stiffened, and Ren was momentarily afraid she had crossed the line. His eyes told a different story, however, glittering at her in appreciation.

"Why are you always so seeeerious all the time?" he drawled, rolling his eyes.

He reached for her neckline and pulled out the vurmite necklace tucked behind her tunic.

"The red dress goes best with this. I know you were already thinking about it," he said affectionately. "Now, if you don't mind, it's late, and I need my beauty rest. Believe it or not, this fiery complexion doesn't maintain itself." He smiled once more and leaned in, kissing Ren on the forehead. "Sweet dreams, little Elfy."

And he was gone.

Ren turned and saw herself smiling contentedly in the mirror. Her smile grew as she realized she could finally call someone her friend. She would do just about anything to keep those dimples on Jester's face and liked to believe he would do the same for her. Not the dimples part. She didn't have those, but try to help her find herself in this hellscape.

Ren suddenly felt tremendously tired. The purple lightning was starting to appear in the sky. She'd forgotten that it was almost morning. Lazily and without undressing, she threw herself on the silky sheets and didn't awaken until midday—a cold meal already waiting for her at the edge of the bed. There wasn't wine this morning, to her great displeasure, but there was a note.

When you finally wake up from your beauty sleep, expect Zelaia. She will help you with your preparations for the party. Please pick out an appropriate dress from the ones Jester provided and meet me downstairs at a quarter past.

King Pelegros, Sir Maddeningly Muscular

Groaning, she shuffled over to the vanity and her pile of dresses. She pulled the red dress from the mix and held it in her hands. It was so silky that she felt that her rough skin would offend the delicate fabric. It was one solid color but could certainly not be called plain.

As she slipped it on, she observed that the low cut of the front cupped her breasts seductively, and the slinky material hugged her hips to accentuate her curves. Jester's selection made her vurmite look like the centerpiece of the whole facade. Like the dress was created to draw one's attention to her neckline. She loved how, even in something so soft, she could feel commanding.

After undressing so as to not wrinkle the delicate fabric, she jumped with a start as Zelaia let herself in without a knock. She had a large bag full of intimidating accouterment for styling, coifing, and contouring.

While Ren's first reaction was to snap at the Devil for walking in without notice, she knew she might need another Azur-sworn Devil on her side.

She plastered on a smile.

"Good afternoon, Zelaia, I appreciate you helping me with this."

The pink Devil pursed her lips and dropped the bag near the vanity.

"You know I belong to Azur, right? I didn't have much of a choice."

Ren struggled to keep her face from scowling.

"I see. Well, thank you anyway."

"Honestly, it's fine," the pink Devil replied, "I kind of live for this, helping clueless women find their sparkle."

Ren chose not to be offended as she sat at the vanity.

There was a tense silence before Zelaia interjected, "do you prefer that? Being called a woman? Or do you prefer female? You are Half-Elven, right?"

Ren opened her mouth to respond but paused. She hadn't thought about it before. True, she took more after her mother with her silver hair and was showing signs of longevity, but her eyes were undoubtedly from her father. Her ears were the size of a Human's, though they came to a point, giving away her mixed blood.

"Either is fine," she said quietly.

Zelaia met her eyes in the mirror.

"I just wanted to make sure."

As Zelaia ran brushes through her hair, applied powder, and did something or other with oils, Ren contemplated the question. The more she thought about it, the more her stomach twisted. It prompted her once more to linger on the knowledge that she didn't know who she was. Her identity was undefined and mysterious to her and so intrinsically tied to memories and learned behaviors. She didn't know enough about Elves or Humans to even begin to organize any sort of opinion on the matter. How was she supposed to *be* something without even knowing what it meant? What was the difference between an Elf and a Human? Or, for that matter, a Devil and a Human? Not physically, but something deeper. Leo warned her never to trust Devils, but besides Benji, Jester had been her only real friend. He'd shown her kindness, made her smile, and always tried to protect her. Even Zelaia, despite her bruskness, didn't seem evil or manipulative.

She felt frustrated with the concept of having to choose a box to put herself in. To be defined.

Just Ren.

Shouldn't that be enough?

After putting on the final touches, Ren had to admit Zelaia was a genius. She'd twisted her silver hair in an intricate knot, pulling it off her shoulders so as not to obscure her shining gem. She had applied coal to highlight the chocolatey hues in her eyes, and her lips were painted to match her dress.

I am beautiful as well *as commanding. But more importantly, I'm Ren.*

She reached up to brush the tips of her fingers on her vurmite.

"Good luck tonight. Many Devils would sell their souls to be where you are," Zelaia said before patting Ren's shoulder and letting herself out.

Ren's eyes followed Zelaia, and she wondered what had brought the Devil to Azur's doorstep—what desperate need this gorgeous creature had.

After adjusting her stone once more, she tore herself from the mirror and descended the wide staircase to the entrance hall, pride filling her chest for not snagging the perfect fabric on her heels. Azur was waiting, hands crossed behind his back, staring out the open door.

She'd seen several versions of Azur already, from the hellish negotiator to the unleashed terror, but tonight, Azur was all king. He did not wear a crown. He didn't need to. His horns were everything any king would need to display power and position. His wings were unfurled and tucked tightly against his back. The impossibly terrifying appendages looked every bit as noble as any mantle worn by royalty. His waistcoat was red, the perfect complement to Ren's dress, and his breeches were leather, as if he still wanted his subject to know that he was a warrior as well as a king.

He turned, hearing her approach, and grinned with approval.

"Jester told me you might pick that dress. I must say I am quite pleased."

She lifted her chin as she descended the rest of the stairs.

"You could just say I'm stunning and be done with it."

He raised an amused eyebrow.

"You look stunning, Ren Eldanuer," he said without a hint of irony.

Her breath caught.

Aloof, she reminded herself as she placed her hand in the king's and allowed herself to be led to the royal carriage.

While Ren wasn't familiar with all the creatures on the Mortal plane, she knew that those pulling her carriage were not one of them. Something so startling could only exist in The Hells. They were hooven, beasts of burden, but their manes were long, and their lower jaws were much larger than their uppers. They had no snout but rather breathed through small tentacles near where their ears should be.

Aloooof, her brain yelled as she tried not to rear back as one huffed in her direction, its breath warm and smelling like sulfur.

Azur guided her into the carriage and placed his hand on her waist to lift her into the seats.

She settled herself in the cushioned seat across from the male who owned her soul. He sat casually, wings spread out, relaxed.

"I feel I should warn you about tonight," he said as the beasts began to trot down the ashy street. "You will be entering the great hall with me as my consort. It will undoubtedly create quite the scandal since you are the first consort I have brought out in public."

He paused, letting the words sink in.

"You mean that in the thousands of years you've been alive, you've never brought a female—"

"Or male," he clarified.

"Or male—out?"

He shifted in his seat, wings flexing.

"No, my dear. I typically don't have many emotional attachments. Indeed, I strike a much more imposing presence alone. However, considering the circumstances, it seemed like the best move, and I'm sure my subjects will *devour* the gossip. One must indulge his followers on occasion, wouldn't you say?"

Ren didn't like the idea of being the subject of so many Devils' conversations. It felt like playing with fire.

Azur's face was suddenly very serious.

"I cannot be sure what plans Xarek has, but be on your guard. Do not wander far from me, darling."

Ren felt the knot in her throat tighten. The thought of seeing Xarek both terrified and excited her.

"What if he tries to control me?" she asked.

"He can't. To manifest a compulsion spell, the caster must touch their target. Your brand shows the court that you're mine and prevents anyone from touching you without your consent."

Ren wanted to shoot back that she wasn't *anyone's* but realized it was probably fruitless.

As the carriage came to a stop, an Elven footman offered his hand. Several attendants were awaiting their arrival, and the party had already commenced if the noise coming from inside was any indication.

Several attendants circled the king, ensuring every piece of his ensemble was in place. A short, Lesser Devil handed Azur a box and scuttled off, leaving the two alone.

"This is for you," he said, presenting the box. "It is a tradition in many of the courts. As I said, I've never had my own consort, so this tradition is quite new to me, but I thought it appropriate, nonetheless."

He lifted the lid of the box to reveal a thin circlet.

Ren could barely control her excitement, and her hands began to sweat. The circlet matched perfectly with her vurmite necklace. Reds and oranges sparkled around the band as it twisted artfully in what resembled two small devilish horns.

"I took some liberties with the design. I hope you don't mind," he said with a faint smile. "May I?"

"It's...perfect." She whispered and inclined her head, feeling a rush of excitement. This felt right—Elf, Human, Half-Elf, whatever. With this crown, she felt perfectly devilishly herself.

He offered his arm. "Shall we?"

Her heart was already thundering in her chest, but she felt it skip a beat when she wove her arm through his and felt his taut muscles.

He led her closer to the door and nodded at two porters. Obediently, they opened the door, and the music changed abruptly from a jovial dance tune to one that evoked power and dominance.

"His Highness Lord of the Planes of Hell, God of Devils and Ruler of The Underworlds, Azur Vincent Pelegros."

Ren felt like her legs were going to turn to liquid. Azur looked to his left and gave the smallest wink before tugging gently on her arm in encouragement. Ren kept her eyes forward, trying to concentrate on her slow stride. Her focus was short-lived—shattered when they entered the grand hall. The center aisle was lined with elegant carpets depicting fiendish creatures surrounded by smoke and hellfire. The room was dimly lit by immense pillar candles, casting shadows like beastly claws.

Azur grazed his thumb lightly over Ren's hand as they crossed under a massive chandelier. Ren could have wept with delight at the adornments of vurmite, which cascaded to the floor in delicate threads of crystal like dripping blood.

Yet, as impressive as the palace was, it was the music that she felt down to her bones. She knew it was for him, the king, but she felt then, on his arm, that the rumbling drums and deep notes were also praising *her* strength.

She kept her head high as she saw Devils all dressed in exquisite finery gasp, some clutching the partners tightly, as they watched their king escort a Mortal to his throne. Arriving, he let go of her arm and ascended the last steps. An attendant seemed to have been informed that Ren was inexperienced and subtly signaled for her to stand to the left.

Azur stood before his throne. It was imposing and monstrous, carved with screaming beings from Hellish, Mortal, and Fae planes. Yet the most monstrous creation on the pedestal was Azur. His red eyes scanned his subjects, stopping on a few who then bent their heads low to show subservience. His body began to pulse with power as black fumes emanated. His wings spread wide, making his form even more imposing. Ren was sure there could be nothing that matched this being's power with his magnificent presence reflected in the awe that he inspired in every face.

As the song ended, final notes echoed throughout the chamber, each and every knee bent to their king. He waited, greedily sucking up every second of the nobility supplicant before him. The last face he met was Ren's before he winked at her playfully and sat. The music immediately started again, and the Devils returned to their revelry.

Ren wasn't entirely sure what her role would be now, so she just stood next to Azur, hands crossed demurely in front of her, and watched the Devils dance around the ballroom. The trend seemed to be that the female High Devils kept their wings tucked away for greater freedom of movement while their male counterparts displayed theirs proudly. The dances accommodated these differences as the females didn't often circle the males but rather whirled in front of them. Yet, Ren preferred those who seemed to defy this conventional tradition and varied their steps to showcase both dancers' proud display of wings.

If it hadn't been for a swirl of smoke that began to blur her vision, she wouldn't have realized the change in

Azur. She saw his vice-like grip on his throne, and the tips of his fingers turned black as claws began to appear.

His glare was fixated on the revelry, and Xarek Wyvryn who was standing in front of his throne.

Ren held her breath, unsure if the two would attempt to rip each other's throats out right on the ballroom floor. Azur held up a clawed hand and instantly halted the music. Every creature stopped and turned their attention towards the throne.

The two males stared each other down.

A few tense moments passed before Xarek offered a revertant bow, his wings spread wide, touching the floor.

"My king. What an honor it is to be here tonight to celebrate the presentation of your consort. May I say how truly lovely she is."

He looked to Ren, offering a charming smile.

Ren clenched her jaw but kept her face passive.

"Lord Wyvryn," Azur's voice boomed, "just the male I wished to see. Lady Eldanuer is quite fond of music. She is quite a talented musician, in fact. She has shared with me that you are a decent violinist. Is it true?"

Ren watched as Xarek's entire body stiffened. It was a gross minimization of Xarek's talent to call his playing *decent.* It was certainly one of the most inspiring performances Ren had heard, and her heart recognized music above all else. But the game was being played, and Xarek had no choice but to comply.

"Perhaps you would play a song in her honor, Lord Wyvryn?"

Xarek's smile did not falter.

"I'd be honored, my king," he said, waving to a Human servant who passed him his stunning violin.

He positioned the instrument under his striking jaw and lifted the bow to hover over the delicate strings.

His eyes swung to Ren's.

"In fact, I wrote a song for you, Renata Eldanuer."

His pale eyes met Ren's, and she felt the world melt away as he stroked the bow down the strings, beginning.

The first notes were elegant and melodic, almost sad, with the long and slow pulls. Ren watched as his strong hands caressed the different rivets and glided down the neck of the violin. Azur had kissed her neck, but this male understood the ways to use his fingers on an instrument which was alluring in a wholly different way. To glide and brush across with care and subtlety created the most intimate experience of all. Music. She felt her throat tighten as his song moved from a slow pace to one that built—a crescendo that grew each note as the subtle plucking of strings caused the sounds to crash together in waves of harmonic resonance.

It made Ren want to fall to her knees.

Ren's heart stopped.

She tried to cry out but found that she couldn't breathe, couldn't move. Her eyes were locked on Xarek, and she noticed that he was smiling wickedly as the tempo of his song sped up.

Ren willed her body to act, her heart to begin ticking again, but it didn't. She was paralyzed and felt her mind begin to cloud over.

She could hear the distant voice of someone—*Renata?*—pleading with her to run. To cover her ears. But that was such a ridiculous idea, wasn't it? The music was so nice—so flawless in its presentation.

"Hello, Renata," she heard a voice say in her head. "I've been waiting so long to talk to you. How about we have some fun, yes?"

It was his voice. Xarek's voice. And she knew, as her body refused to respond, that her worst fear had come true. She was powerless and completely at his mercy because he had touched her—touched her in the way only music could.

CHAPTER 19

I wish I could tell her she doesn't have to bear the weight of her past alone. The way I do.

Xarek ended his song, a smile pulling at the sides of his perfect mouth.

Ren screamed, but no sound came out. Her face remained indifferent, if a little pleased.

Azur turned to look at her, and she shouted, entreated, and begged for help, but her body didn't move. He smiled at her expectantly, but Ren could not respond. She felt her lips move, and a voice belonging to her spoke.

"Lord Xarek, your playing delights me, as it did that first night. It is truly an inspiration to know that such a talented musician lives within The Hells. Perhaps you could teach me? Perhaps private lessons?"

She heard gasps from the throng and watched as Azur's claws scraped the metal on his throne.

Xarek smiled politely.

"Any moment alone with you would be a privilege that would give me great *pleasure*, my lady."

Xarek's voice in her head spoke. "Don't fight, little Mortal. If you're good, perhaps I can make you *my* consort."

Rage thundered through what remained of herself— not body or soul, but something still somehow alive.

Azur shot to his feet, fangs bared, and smoke wafted off of him, billowing large and filling the room.

Xarek took a step back and placed a hand over his chest.

"My king, I do not wish to offend. I am but your loyal servant."

He enunciated every word with disdain.

"I have had *enough* of your games, Xarek. It has been centuries of putting up with your pathetic plans to undermine my power." Azur flourished his hand, still black and clawed, dripping with inky fumes. "You have conspired to overthrow your king. By doing so, you have surrendered your Immortality and will be brought to justice."

"Oh my," Xarek responded, feigning boredom.

Ren wanted to tear the horns from his head.

"I have no idea what you are speaking of," he said with a performative bow. "This revelation wouldn't have anything to do with your little Mortal, would it? Perhaps she is trying to deceive you?"

Azur growled. "She is not involved in this."

Xarek clicked his tongue.

"I think she is Azur."

A few more unbelieving gasps at Xarek's lack of deference.

"I think she is very involved. But back to business. Seeing that I have nothing more to lose, I hope you would grant me a trial by contract."

Azur's eyes narrowed, and he bared his fangs.

"I'd rather rip your throat out and mount your head on a stake."

There was rustling in the crowd, the Devils started chittering, excited by the idea of seeing a violent confrontation.

"You think you can challenge a god?" his voice boomed, "that *any* of you could oppose me? I *made* you. I *allow* you to live. It is by my mercy that you are not enslaved and toiling in the mines with my sleepers. Your misery would only serve to fill my need for wrath and power. Xarek, you are but a pest beneath my boot—one that I will delight in stamping out. I *will* make an example of you."

Several Devils shrank back in fear. And despite Xarek's previous bravado, Ren noticed the quiver in his lips.

"My request stands. Trial by contract," he said, voice strained.

Ren tried moving her muscles, trying to cry out, writhing—anything! This was most certainly a trick, and Xarek was pulling at Azur's wrath and envy. If he had seen her, looked in her eyes, he might have noticed that she wasn't herself. But his eyes glowed menacingly, unyieldingly focused.

Xarek flicked his wrist, and a contract appeared and a blue Lesser Devil promptly grabbed it out of the air and began to read.

"Lord Xarek Wyvryn does henceforth challenge King Azur Pelegros to a trial by contract to determine the innocence or guilt of Lord Wyvryn for allegedly conspiring against King Pelegros and his unholy throne."

The Lesser looked up from the parchment, eyes as big as saucers.

"Lord Wyvryn, what are the terms of your contract?"

Xarek spread his wings wide.

"A duel in accordance with the king's laws. I do, after all, respect the precedent set by His Highness."

Ren watched as her hand involuntarily reached out to grab Azur's wrist.

"No, my Lord, it is not worth the risk to your life," her voice said.

That doesn't even sound *like me.*

This was the worst thing she could have said.

Xarek knew Azur—knew his pride. He knew how these words, from Ren's Mortal mouth, would cut at it.

The muscles in Azur's jaw flexed.

"I accept," he said, blinded—unable to notice the changes in Ren's face, her posture, the pitch of her voice. The two Devils cut their arms, sealing their terms.

Azur's smile grew, and all the candles flickered in warning.

"I will not be choosing a champion, Lord Wyvryn. I will be the one to defend my throne and my honor against whoever or whatever you decide to condemn to death in an attempt to challenge me. I swear by the contract."

Xarek did not blanch.

"Oh, how delicious. I was hoping you would say that. As you've probably guessed, I *will* be using a champion. I'm a musician, king, not a masochist."

Azur snorted. "Who would be foolish enough to agree to fight me?"

The rest of the room snickered at the ridiculous thought.

"Oh, I think you will be quite surprised," he said, his eyes finally flicking to Ren.

She understood now. This was worse than death—worse than forgetting. Worse than all the pain remembering could bring. She was powerless to stop what happened next.

"Renata, would you be my champion and fight for me against the god of the underworld?"

Internally, she fought with all her remaining energy—willed herself to throw her body in front of the two Devils, but none of her reached the surface.

"I, The Defender of The Planes, will fight for this innocent male!" her voice boomed. "I consent and swear by the contract."

The only sound in the room was Ren's own screams inside her mind. Every face was slack with disbelief.

Azur gazed at Ren, first treacherous and then in understanding.

"You fucking bastard!" Azur roared, throwing himself at Xarek, wrapping one hand around his neck, and lifting him off of his feet. "You've compelled her. She couldn't properly consent!"

Xarek's eyes were watering from pain, but he continued to smile, a strained laugh escaping from his throat.

"Compelled Mortals' consent counts towards contracts. You *wrote* those rules."

"It's not true consent," Azur ground out.

"So it matters to you now? That's sweet. You must really care for the—"

Azur tossed him aside, and he landed inelegantly, skidding across the floor.

The king hastened to Ren and grabbed her limp hands. "Come back to me, Ren," he whispered, looking into her eyes.

But she couldn't. She had to allow him to use his magic on her and Xarek had made sure that couldn't happen. She was buried too deep for even her thoughts to reach him.

Her body reacted on its own, recoiling from his touch.

"I have been waiting for this moment," her voice said clearly. "I will not allow you to victimize any more innocents, *King* Azur. Xarek is the rightful leader of The Hells, and even if I die, I will die knowing that my voice has been heard, the voice of the Mortals!"

"Oh, Ren," he said, almost inaudibly, his eyebrows tucked close together. "I'm so sorry."

"You have to fight, Azur," Xarek said, standing and flattening the wrinkles in his doublet in an attempt to salvage some dignity. "If you do not fight, you surrender your throne to me and admit to making false accusations against a Lord of Hells. A crime punishable by death, or in your case, imprisonment for eternity. I wonder how it feels to starve and not be able to die?"

Ren, or the body of Ren, kicked off her shoes and marched to the center of the chamber.

"No more delaying, Pelegros. Fight me or surrender."

Xarek approached and handed her a gilded dagger, almost identical to the one Azur had destroyed. Another symbol of how futile any combat would be against the god. Her avatar was unfazed by the metaphor, and she ripped the red dress's fabric up to above her thighs, revealing the piccolo strapped there. She made two practice swipes with the dagger before taking an attack position, knees bent.

Azur did not take his eyes off Ren. He strode carefully towards her, and as he did—she lunged, stabbing towards the god's torso. Azur didn't even need to react as her dagger glanced off a purple shield that flickered in front of him. Her body was breathing hard, and she could feel her facial muscles flex with anger.

Azur clenched his jaw, his breathing ragged as wrath welled within.

"You're weak, Azur." Her voice was low and gruff. "Only a real male can lead this plane to its true potential. God or no, you have failed. It's time to let go."

Azur's eyes darkened, infernal rage shining through.

Ren then bellowed furiously as her body darted, swinging around to try to stab at his ribcage. Azur did not move his body to face her, and her dagger veered off his impermeable shield. This time, her body froze as a current of energy from the shield blasted through her. Ren's true self could not feel the pain, but her body convulsed, and she saw as her hands lost grip on the dagger before she was thrown back, crashing to the floor.

Azur's face winced.

He took one step forward, but Ren's body scrambled towards the dagger, swiftly retrieved it, and sprang up to standing.

"Hmm," Xarek's voice came. "I didn't realize she was so feisty. This might be more entertaining than I thought."

Azur ignored Xarek and the uncomfortable laughter of his citizens, red eyes burrowing into Ren's as if his piercing gaze could break the spell.

Ren began to circle Azur. Her breathing was rapid, but her hands were steady. But the Ren within was whimpering with terror.

"Please stop," she pleaded with herself. "You'll kill us."

Azur reached out a hand, approaching her as if she were a rabid animal. Xarek allowed her to wait in an attack stance, curious to see Azur's next move.

He leaned close and seized the side of her face, holding her in place.

"Ren. I have to do this."

His strong grip tilted her head to the side, examining her.

"It would be so easy to end you now. But I need you to know that I did believe in you," Azur said, his lips only a whisper away. "I hoped that you would find redemption—find peace. I can't tell you why you did it. But that's why I agreed. I wanted you to carve your own path—to be free from guilt and the burden of grief. To live to be the person you always wanted to be and should have been. I still believe you can find it, Ren. You are worthy of redemption. Even if it's just in the eyes of the irredeemable."

Ren had no soul. The part of her that existed wailed in pain. Heartbroken and mind in pieces. She pushed against the Xarek's bind, lashing every ounce of strength in a desperate attempt to signal to Azur that she had heard. It was in this chaos of internal strife that she saw her arm shoot out as she buried her dagger, to the hilt, into Azur's stomach.

He gave a small start of surprise before looking down. Black blood seeped through the wound. Azur lowered his hands and wrapped them around hers, which were still clutching the dagger, and gently caressed the pad of his thumb across her fingers.

"I would let you kill me, Ren. If it would even matter, if it would make a difference. But it doesn't."

His hands moved up to her shoulders, and before Xarek could command her again, Azur lifted her and hurled her at the wall.

She knew the speed of the collision would break her body on impact. Her one hope, as she hurtled towards the stone, was that someone would remember her as Ren. That

Jester would tell people that one female, woman, Half-Elf, had existed for a time as herself. Free from the constraints and expectations of others and made her own choices, no matter how misguided they might have been.

The last thing Ren heard before a portal sucked her out of the palace was Azur's voice.

"I concede. I will not fight."

Ren careened off the carpet and tumbled towards her vanity, slamming into it with a *crack*! Fortunately, it was furniture, not bone, that had broken. She jumped up, having regained control of herself, and dashed to the hall.

"Jester! Jester, help!!"

Her mind spun as she tried to figure out a plan.

She ran to Azur's office and wrenched open the door. Nothing.

She crashed through every room screaming her friend's name, voice shaking.

"Where are you?!"

She saw Zelaia's form run up the stairs.

"What in hell's name?"

"Zelaia! Thank gods!" Ren grabbed the Devil by the shoulders. "You have to help me find Jester! Azur is in trouble!"

"What are you prattling about? Azur is a *god,* Ren. He is fine! If he's tussling with that dragon again, I promise that he will come out without as much as a scratch."

"No! He surrendered his throne to Xarek!"

"He—what!?" Zelaia's face vacillated between panicked and confused.

"I have to find Jester!" Ren, repeated near hysterics.

Ren moved to run down the stairs when Zelaia caught her arm roughly.

"Ren. He isn't here."

"Where is he? We need to get him. Can you portal because—"

"Don't you get it yet, you thick Mortal? Azur *is* Jester!"

CHAPTER 20

The contract cannot break. The tome cannot be found.

Ren scoffed.

"That's ridiculous. Jester is my friend. We've been—"

"Listen to me. Azur disguises himself as Jester. He's been doing it for longer than I've been indebted."

Ren's mouth moved as if trying to produce the words to reject her claims. It was impossible. Jester was nothing like Azur. She thought of Jester's quick wit, his playfulness, and how Azur was never—could never be like that.

"That's impossible," she stuttered.

"It's the truth."

"It was all a lie?" she whispered. "No. You're wrong."

She turned around and scanned the hall, desperately hoping that Jester would jump out from behind a curtain, playing and taunting her gullibility. Her mind refused to accept that her friend, her only real friend, wasn't real at all.

Zelaia stepped in front of a distraught Ren.

"Ren, listen to me," she said firmly, but not unkindly, "Azur *is* Jester."

Ren didn't want to listen. She wanted to cover her ears to stop the bells of realization beginning to ring in them.

"But why?"

Her voice was beginning to break.

"*Why* would he do this?"

"Azur has many reasons for doing what he does—It isn't for us to question."

"That's...absolute bullshit!" she shouted, leaning in closer to Zelaia, balling her hands into fists.

The Devil did not flinch.

Ren felt like such a fool. So embarrassed that she hadn't seen it.

"Does everyone know?"

"No," Zelaia said, looking at her sadly and crossing her arms. "Only the other soulless here in the safe house."

Ren felt the overwhelming urge to run—as if running from the news would make it less real. But there was nothing to run to. No *one* to run to. Her body moved, backing away until she hit a wall, allowing her exhausted legs to give way and slump to the floor. She felt like her friend had just died— ripped away from her life violently.

"I don't know what's real anymore," Ren whispered. "I'm so tired of feeling so powerless. Of being in the dark."

Zelaia didn't speak. She stood in silence for a beat, before walking to a nearby room. She returned with a tunic, pants, and some boots and bent down, leveling herself with Ren.

"If you want to know the truth. I can help. But please realize, sometimes the truth is a lot harder than the fantasy we paint for ourselves."

She set the clothes next to Ren.

Ren did want to know the truth. But she was so tired. She could just curl up here, on the soft carpet, and sleep.

"What's going to happen to Azur?"

Her voice cracked on the last word.

Zelaia's eyes became serious.

"I don't know. Your mark is still there, though," she said, pointing to her neck. "That means he is still king, has at least some of his power, but for how long, I can't say. Nothing like this has ever happened before."

Ren let her body work robotically as it pulled off the remnants of her once beautiful gown.

Zelaia helped her stand and steered her limp body to the bathing chamber. She insisted Ren wash her face with cold water and helped her pull the pins from her hair, remove her horned circlet, and redress.

Ren couldn't look at the shining gift from Azur; it was too painful. A visual that held too many conflicting emotions.

Zelaia also insisted that Ren drink at least a cup of tea and some stale biscuits. Ren complied numbly.

"We won't go until you're ready," Zelaia said with unexpected tenderness.

"You defend him," Ren swallowed, "but it's not fair what he does."

Zelaia exhaled sharply.

"He saved me, Ren." She looked up as if grabbing onto a distant thought. "If it weren't for him, I wouldn't be—I'd rather be a sleeper than what happened to me."

Her voice suddenly turned harsh. She closed her black eyes, squinting them tightly as though trying to ward away a bad memory.

Ren looked down. "I didn't realize—"

"No. You didn't. But...it's fine. I understand that it's easy to forget, seeing all the sleepers, that some of us willingly signed contracts and accepted the consequences. Others are more...naive."

"Maybe that was me," Ren whispered.

The Devil made a noncommittal sound. "Maybe...but I don't think so."

Ren nodded. "I...I'm ready to go."

Zelaia's expression continued to be sympathetic, but she said no more. She glided to the center of the washroom and flicked her wrist. Nothing happened.

"That's not a good sign." She said, examining her palms.

"What?"

Ren jerked her head towards Zelaia, bracing for more bad news.

"My magic is weaker. It still works, but...it's stifled."
She paused. "Luckily for you, I'm *very* talented. Even without
Azur," she said before another flick, opening a portal.

They emerged in Ogriazeth, still shadowed by
nightfall. But even with the glow of the street lanterns, Ren
didn't recognize the neighborhood.

Zelaia signaled for her to follow and the two females
walked, pace slow, eventually running into a small stream,
muddied with ash, that crisscrossed the middle of the city.
Ren did not try to engage with Zelaia, she was too numb, and
her brain didn't have enough energy for small talk. For her
part, Zelaia didn't seem to be a fan of empty words.

The stream began to wind down, feeding into a large
grey river that entered a new area of the Forest of Nahmir.
Zelaia ducked under several ashen trees and rounded a
corner to the river bank. There, mere feet away from the
ripples of the water, was a small patch of luscious green
grass, almost neon in the night light, next to all the ash and
gray. It was the first appearance of live vegetation that Ren
had seen since being in the hells. Sitting, legs crossed in the
middle of the patch, was an emaciated red Devil with stringy
black hair.

It took a second for Ren's sluggish brain to compute,
but when it did, she bolted and threw her arms around the
Devil's neck.

"Jester!"

Fat tears began to soak Jester's ragged shirt. He was
so excruciatingly thin that Ren could wrap her arms around
him fully.

Jester didn't respond or react.

She pulled back and looked at his face.

His eyes were open, but there was no life inside—
Jester was a sleeper.

She couldn't breathe.

She sank down on the small piece of grass and stared
at her friend. The feelings were too confusing and too

knotted to disentangle. Her grief for her friend was insurmountable, but this wasn't the Jester she knew.

"What happened to him?" she asked Zelaia, unable to see through her tears.

Zelaia joined her on the ground.

"I don't know for sure. It happened before I was with Azur, and he won't talk about it. I know that Jester was one of Azur's first souls, and somewhere along the way, he broke his contract and became Azur's first sleeper. I think Jester's real name was Ahdan."

Ren's ears started to ring.

"Ahdan? Jester—Azur—told me about an Ahdan. He sold his soul to save his mother from a disease."

Zelaia pinched her brows together in confusion.

"Devils don't typically share the contents of their contracts—usually we can't, but I remember my parents telling me that there'd been a blight on the Lesser Devils for several years. The stories of that time were terrible. I even had an uncle who succumbed. Then, one day, it just disappeared."

"He violated his contract. On purpose," Ren whispered. "Azur told me that something bad had happened to Ahdan. I had assumed he meant that he'd killed himself."

"So much worse than death," Zelaia said, frowning. "No one could be so naive as to willingly violate their contract."

Ren only partly listened as her eyes looked at Ahdan. He looked so much like Jester but simultaneously, a completely different male—no sparkle in his eyes or the threat of giggles. Whether Azur was a Jester or not, this creature couldn't be Ahdan either. Nothing remained of whatever he was before.

"Perhaps," Ren began, "Ahdan didn't know what it meant to become a sleeper, since he was the first. Didn't know what he was giving up."

She thought of herself then, how she couldn't imagine Renata knowing what she was sacrificing when she surrendered her memories, every speck of her identity.

Yet *he* knew. Azur knew what it meant, with every arm cut and every contract signed.

Zelaia's voice was hushed. "Azur comes here, you know—every week and talks to him. Sometimes, he brings food, coaxes him to eat. But most of the time, he just sits."

"But it's his fault!" Ren blurted. "It's Azur's fault he's like this, and Azur said he *loved* Ahdan! He didn't have to take his soul—he doesn't have to *keep* taking people's souls!"

"We also didn't have to come to him," Zelaia interjected sternly, "but we did. We asked him for something, and he gave it to us."

Ren couldn't accept that. She knew in some ways she was complicit, but she could never understand how Azur could willingly put others in a position to eventually become soulless sleepers, especially someone they claimed to love.

Reaching up, Ren touched Jester's—Ahdan's cold, unmoving hand.

"I'm not trying to defend Azur," Zelaia continued, "gods know he's made many mistakes and hurt countless creatures. But I also can't bring myself to hate him. I do think he is more complicated than just a monstrous devil god with no feelings. If what you're telling me is true, it was Azur who stopped the blight thanks to Ahdan's contracts. The contract must have—"

"But when is it too *much* Zelaia?" Ren snapped. "You said it yourself, he's hurt countless! When is ridding the planes of a blight merely negligible to his greater sins?"

Zelaia sidestepped the question.

"I've often thought Azur retreated into Jester to be free. Even if Jester was a soulless Devil. He is free in many ways that Azur is not. Azur stands with the weight of an entire plane on his shoulders. Right or wrong, that must be heavy."

Ren scrubbed her face. "He wouldn't fight me. He could have killed me and kept his throne. But he surrendered."

She told Zelaia about Xarek, the possession, the contract, and how Azur had saved her.

When she was finished, Zelaia let out a low whistle. "Why in hells would he do that for *you?*" she asked, with a genuine perplexity showing on her face.

"What will happen to our souls if Azur is locked away?"

"I'm not an expert in these things," Zelaia said, stiffening. "Azur's power is what keeps us and our souls safe. If he doesn't have those powers—we might all turn into sleepers."

"To hell with that!" Ren said, jumping up. "I've not come this far to lose myself again!"

Zelaia looked up at her, bewildered.

"I didn't give everything up for it to be for nothing," she continued, chest heaving, "I'm going to find Xarek, I'm going rip his ribs out of his chest, then I am going to find Azur."

Zelaia chuckled and stood.

"I didn't believe Azur when he said you had spunk. I thought you were just another privileged Mortal—honestly, I'm still not convinced you're not—but...you're something else, too," she said, placing one hand on her hip.

"Well, I thought you were just one of Azur's sex dolls, so I guess we were both wrong," Ren said, a smirk threatening.

Zelaia snorted.

"I *wish!* Do you know how long it's taken me to break down those walls?" She rolled her eyes. "That male is wound so tight!"

They met each other's eyes and Ren found understanding there—sympathy.

Zelaia's breath caught, her body going completely rigid. She opened her mouth, but before words could come, she vanished.

Ren's arms were reaching out to where Zelaia had been standing.

She spun around.

"Zelaia?"

She called into the forest, knowing there would be no response.

Hells hells hells helllsssss.

Reaching up she grabbed the ends of her hair.

This is really bad.

With a start, Ren jumped back, something having grazed her leg. She looked down and saw Ahdan's hand hovering in the air. His eyes were looking past her, but it still felt like the move was purposeful.

"I'll bring Azur back, Ahdan. I promise."

He did not respond—did not move.

His hand hung in the air motionless.

She wanted to stay with Ahdan, to try and comfort him somehow, but urgency was rising within her. She knew she must act fast.

She began to back away tentatively, afraid to take her eyes off the Devil lest he move again. Only when his features were too small to make out movement did she finally turn and make a break for the tavern.

The city was starting to wake up as the purple bolts of lightning appeared. She saw sleepers exit buildings and walk lethargically down the street in unorganized files.

Rounding the corner, she saw the female Half-Orc sitting in her usual spot at the entrance to the tavern.

Ren had no fixed plan, but the tavern always had answers, and maybe she could get them from The Gilded Triangle.

She bounded through the front entrance, startling Fred away with a jolt; he had apparently fallen asleep at his bar.

"Anything for me, Fred?" she burst out, more aggressively than she'd meant to.

The barkeep blinked several times.

"Jeez, ye scared me, Renata. It's barely light out." He rubbed the sleep from his eyes and gestured toward the glass filled with amber liquid. "Nothing yet. But I hear ye need to be movin' along soon."

Damnit to hell. The tome.

Ren laughed nervously. "It's all taken care of."

She tried to casually walk up the stairs.

The door to her room was oddly closed. Fred's custom had been to leave it open while she was away. She approached cautiously, warning bells ringing in her head.

When she touched the knob, she heard the slightest rustle behind her. Ren whirled around and lurched forward, hands finding purchase on plush white robes.

Leo's robes.

"What the hell, Leo?" she said, pushing him away and letting out an anxious breath.

He reeled back, "I'm...I'm sorry," he sputtered, hands held protectively in front of him.

He wasn't the same Leo she had come to know. Purple shadows lined his pale eyes, and his hair—usually neat and controlled—was now frizzy, unbound, and damp with sweat.

"Have you found it? Please tell me you've found it."

"Leo, are you okay?" she asked, trying to steady the shaking man.

He approached her fearfully, hands outstretched and shaking.

"I must help him, Renata. You cannot know how much I desire to help my lord! It is all that matters."

Ren felt her stomach drop. "I...I haven't found it yet, Leo."

A single tear dripped down Leo's face, and he hung his head, dejected.

It was then that Ren realized that this wasn't the incorporeal version of Leo. He was standing with her in The Hells.

"What are you doing here? I thought it was too dangerous for you."

"I...I had to come. I can't afford to fail this test, Renata. But the temptation." His voice cracked. "Is burdening my soul."

Her chest clenched. The pain in this adult man's face was so visceral.

A sharp breeze cut off Ren's words of comfort, so strong that she heard the bottles rattle from downstairs and a curse from Fred.

"No...I..." Leo sputtered, "I must go."

He spared one more look at Ren before he ambled swiftly down the stairs, robes billowing in the lessening breeze.

"Come in, Renata. We need to speak," the kindly voice said from inside her room.

Ren swallowed the discomfort in her throat and walked purposefully to her door, pushing it softly open.

Inside, the Lord of The Heavens was sitting on her bed.

"You've been gone," he said with a small smile, "I was hoping you would have brought Vutar'ka Zhartun."

Ren's throat bobbed. "My lord, there seems to be a problem with my contract and I—"

He raised a soft hand and stood.

"Renata. I was hoping that my insistence was enough to impart to you the enormity of what I've requested. It seems to me that you still do not grasp its importance and what you stand to lose."

Ren looked down at her booted feet, trying to look repentant but remembering Azur's insistence that this god should never find the tome.

"It is for this reason that I have come to you. I know you stray, my child. You have been taken in by my brother's manipulation. I cannot fully blame you for this. He is a powerful god in his own right, and his tactics, while vile, are brilliant in their mastery."

His blue eyes darkened.

"I have collected another memory. This one, though, will not remind you of the beauty you have lost but the pain you have wrought and the reason you must find the tome and find redemption."

Ren shivered.

"Lord, I do not wish to see these memories. I must believe that Renata surrendered them for a reason."

Nainaur tilted his head pityingly.

"Child, I was not asking for your consent," he said before raising his hand and flinging her from the room.

This transportation, unlike the others, was violent and sent her reeling through time and space. When she reached the other side into the memory, she felt like her insides had been jumbled around.

The image before her only compounded her shock. In her wake lay hundreds—thousands of Fae bodies. To her horror, the majority of them were unarmed civilians. She heaved and retched, the meager meals coming up as her body convulsed.

She stood in the middle of a destroyed town. Flames licked the sides of crumbling wooden structures and the agonizing cries of the injured saturated the air. They weren't just dead—they were butchered. The white sheen of Fae blood staining the roughened stone and coating every inhabitant as they feebly tried to save the dead and dying.

She ran to the closest figure who still looked alive, reaching for them to try to do something—anything to help.

But there was nothing to reach for. This was a memory. The past could not be changed.

Why is he showing me this?

She watched as desperate Fae ran from building to building, screaming the names of their loved ones and crying out in agony when they finally located their lifeless, dismembered bodies. Parents wailed, holding their children, while survivors screamed in pain over their broken bodies.

"Stop! Please, no! I can't watch!" she choked out, more on her emotional pain than the smell of burning flesh.

"But Renata, it was you. You did this to them," came Nainaur's voice, gentle but admonishing.

The breath from her lungs was sucked out.

It's impossible—Renata—no, I would never do this. I could never hurt the defenseless I—

She saw her. Renata. Standing in the throng, her back to Ren, gripping her piccolo.

"You don't *know* yourself, Renata. You *are* this person. By destroying this town and the people in it, you cut off the supply lines from the Unseelie court. You should be proud. You are a hero—The Defender of the Planes.

Air wouldn't enter her lungs. Her throat was closed, and her vision blurred.

It could be—she couldn't—

"You need me, Renata. Your soul, bound to hell, is where it deserves to be. You are drenched in sin."

The memory of her own words assaulted her. *"But when is it too much, Zelaia? He's hurt countless!"*

Nainaur continued.

"He helped you forget. Forget your deeds, the screaming faces of children that *you* murdered for your *greater good.*"

Ren fell to her knees, choking, hands clawing at her neck, desperate for air.

The god didn't intervene, did not help her. "The only way forward is through *me.* I can absolve you, Renata. One deed greater than all your sins. Find the tome or live your life knowing that you can never make up for the pain you have caused."

She lurched back to the present, still wheezing.

Nainaur stepped over her writhing body, leaving Ren alone.

Stop fighting.

She told her body.

Just die.

Her mind whispered.

Let go.

She tried, she wanted to, but something in her refused, kept hopelessly gasping for snatches of air. The piccolo at her side vibrated gently.

Ren wasn't sure how long she stayed there, twisting on the floor, but her lungs eventually caught enough oxygen to keep her conscious. She listened to the rhythms of her wheezing breath and watched her chest rise and fall. Everything hurt, but nothing more than her soul—or the place where her soul resided. She couldn't get up—couldn't will herself to move. She just stayed there, barely breathing, barely blinking, staring ahead at the dusty underside of the tavern bed and the discarded garbage underneath.

One piece was delicately folded, unlike the wrappings of other long-forgotten food.

At first, Ren could only look at it, body unwilling to cooperate. But after what seemed like an eternity, she moved a shaky hand, slid it to her, and unfolded it.

A note.

Do not trust *Nainaur. He* lies. Love, Jester.

CHAPTER 21

Would you have been proud of me, Ahdan? Would you have given me your blessing to move on? Would you have forgiven me?

Ren feared her throat would close again. She wanted to believe this note was real, a warning. If it were real, that meant that maybe that vision was just an illusion—a way for Nainaur to force her into action. Every piece of Ren wanted the vision to be false. She would forgive the god for this cruelty if it meant that she wasn't the cause of so much pain. Yet the images felt familiar despite the lock on her memory.

The note itself could be another devilish trick, a warning of a lie from a liar. She couldn't ignore Azur knew that she was seeking the tome and that this might just be another way for him to manipulate her. But did she not owe him the benefit of the doubt when he had sacrificed his throne for her? Did she owe the being that owned her soul anything?

She sat up and put her head in her hands, letting her silver hair fall to shadow her like a blanket.

What do I do, Renata?

One god was offering her redemption. Find the tome and be free. The other god was gone, likely locked away, and, in no uncertain terms, stated that Nainaur should never gain possession of Vutar'ka Zhartun.

Azur's abdication also meant the dissolution of his powers and potentially meant she and the other souls he possessed would turn into sleepers.

So pick a side, Renata whispered from her mind.

Nainaur, The Almighty, or, Azur, The Unholy.

Ren couldn't help snorting at the irony.

"I'm not picking a side, Renata," she gritted out, digging her nails into her scalp. "I want to pick me."

Such a simple desire and yet unimaginably difficult.

Nainaur had offered to save her, dissolve her contract, and give her redemption, restoring her memories in the process. A terrifying prospect. In her mind, restored memories meant waking up an entirely different person once again. A person in love with a male and had a whole life of experiences. A life where she lived in a small house and was safe and settled.

Ren, the woman she was today, didn't want that—couldn't imagine ever wanting that. Would Reneta, with her memories back, even remember what it was like to be Ren? Would these several months be lost to the tragedy of another deal made with another god? Forgotten?

Then there was the trauma—the overwhelming guilt of her actions. Guilt so heavy that her desperation forced her to seek out the most powerful Devil alive.

If she went after Azur, she would be rescuing someone who effectively ruined her life. The being that placed all these impossible questions in her lap in the first place. Yet, selfishly, she knew it was the safer option in some ways. Going up against Devils of nobility felt much less daunting than recovering her memories. It was too much to consider—she was too weak.

Do something good for once!

"How," she muttered, squeezing her scalp more tightly, nails digging in.

She didn't know anyone. What step could she possibly take towards good?

Zelaia.

Zelaia and the other soulless. If she couldn't fix this problem, a problem that was her fault, they would all become sleepers. She didn't know Zelaia very well, and she hadn't met the others, but she knew, without any doubt, that if Jester were at risk, she wouldn't even hesitate.

This was the answer.

She wanted to do good even if she was not, herself, good. She knew that without Nainaur's blessing, she wouldn't make up for her sins. But perhaps Renata's sins and her shame had to be secondary to the lives of others.

She wasn't naive that Nainaur would take it as a slight to his authority if she once again ignored his request. Additionally, once Azur knew the extent of his brother's ambitions, he would never allow her to continue her search. But those consequences would have to wait.

She pushed herself up on shaky legs.

"Time to rescue a fucking god."

She tied her hair back and made sure her piccolo was secured to her thigh before leaving her small bedroom.

One step at a time, Ren.

She rushed down the stairs and outside, ignoring Fred as he tried to speak to her. She was afraid that if she stopped, she would lose her nerve by allowing The Gilded Triangle another opportunity to convince her to look for the tome.

She had no real destination and didn't know where to find Azur's safe house. Her only plan was to find a Devil and get as much information as possible. Surely, word had spread about Azur's capture, and everyone would be talking about the next steps.

As she marched past the fountain, the female sleeper caught her eye. Today, she wasn't sitting but was standing straight up. Even more shocking was that she was looking directly at Ren with a quizzical expression.

"H—hello," Ren said with a small wave, allowing herself to be momentarily distracted.

The female Half-Orc did not return the gesture but rather reached into a deep pocket in her ripped dress and took out what appeared to be a brown rag. She did not break her eye contact with Ren.

"Is that for me?" Ren asked.

The female did not respond, only held out her hand.

Ren drew near the female and, testing hesitantly, extended her hand. No reaction. She laid her hand gently on the rag and picked it up. As soon as she did, the rag fell away, revealing a long dagger—the same that Azur had given her before her first trip to Dementiz. It was black and wickedly sharp, emitting small pulses of power. She felt the textured hilt under her fingers and sensed a small buzz of reassurance from her piccolo.

Dementiz—Castle Valdrock.

Ren had already walked there twice—through the forest of Nahmir—it was her best lead.

"Thank you," she said to the female, offering a small smile.

Sadly, the Orc was no longer alert. She gradually began to move again, plopping herself down on the fountain's pedestal.

This was the second time she wanted to thank her. Ren was at a loss. She couldn't even play her a song without alerting any patrolling Devils and didn't want the female to experience undue punishment. She raised her fingers to her chest and felt the large vurmite under her tunic.

"Azur," she whispered.

Predictably, nothing happened. She removed the chain and set the vurmite down next to the female. The only possession she had left to give.

Before she could change her mind, she turned and stalked away, trying not to think of how much the gem shone in the purple light.

As she marched towards the forest, she noticed how lightheaded she was, most likely from lack of food and sleep. She decided to relish it. The numbness was a welcome relief from her spinning thoughts and waves of guilt. It delayed her awareness that she didn't know the way to Dementiz directly from Ogriazeth.

Jester, or Azur, had portaled them closer both times they had traveled. She also couldn't recall if Azur had told her how long the trip would be without a portal.

Ren moaned in frustration and grabbed her head, shaking it from side to side.

"Just another fucking thing," she mumbled under her breath.

Ren started to search the ash for any signs of footprints or a path—some sign to give her any direction or clue of where to go. Then she saw it. The small ripple. The slight blurring of an opened portal.

Azur, as Jester had told her he could leave the portal open, like the one in her room, and come back to them later. This must be the portal they had taken to the forest on their first day together and the same portal that transported Gabriela back to the forest.

After Azur had opened the portal, it had led *to* the deeper forest and *from* the mines. She had no idea if this logic still stood, but her mind was foggy, and risk management non-existent.

She approached the airy fissure and apprehensively reached her hand out to brush the ripples. Flames immediately burst forth, circling in its now recognizable pattern. She wasn't afraid; she felt that she couldn't get lost more than she already was. She took in a gulp of air and held it before striding through the portal.

The air in her lungs was sucked out as she landed unsteadily on the ashy ground surrounded by more spiny trees but undoubtedly in the same part of the forest her Azur had taken her to. But she still couldn't completely be sure of her next direction as dead trees tended to look less than distinguishable. Ren began shuffling around, searching desperately for cracked tree limbs or...

Footprints!

Truthfully, it was even better than footprints—it was Jester's lively, shuffling gait as he kicked up the thick layers of ash. Her excitement at the clue quickly fizzled out at the memory. A memory that should have been pleasant.

Not Jester. Azur. She had to keep reminding herself.

Ren cleared her mind to keep any intrusive emotion at bay, barreling forward.

Making camp in the forest would be a necessity since it was already afternoon, and the walk took almost a day. She banished thoughts of the one-eyed creature from her mind and fondled the hilt of the dagger at her hip.

Her walk was only made bearable by her soft, mellow hums, being too afraid to play her piccolo again, and, probably for the first time, she wasn't in the mood.

She decided to write several songs to pass the time. She first attempted to capture the tragic love story between Azur and Adhan. Or at least, the way Ren saw it. When finally played, the notes would be slow and shallow. Each note overlapped to sound like they'd barely changed at all. Ideally, it would be a duet with two piccolos—both echoing their love to each other before a solemn farewell.

She felt an uncomfortable sensation in her chest. She wondered what an in-love Azur was like. Ren had only known him to be fierce and possessive. Demanding in his needs and desires. Perhaps a younger Azur was tender—his caresses filled with care and sensitivity.

She couldn't stop imagining how different their experiences would have been. Azur might have traced the seam of her lips with his hands, and his eyes would have looked almost tormented with longing before he lowered his head, lips barely brushing hers before he finally kissed her. How the kiss would start gradually, agonizing in its slow intensity, almost reverent. She imagined how his breath would catch as they deepened their kiss and how his hands would cradle her head, brushing his thumb across her cheek. Perhaps he would even tremble with anticipation as their bodies touched and hands began to explore. Had she ever been kissed like that?

Ren's mind shifted unexpectedly to Nephele, as it so rarely did, and guilt squeezed in her gut. She was out on another plane chasing her identity. She was fantasizing about kissing Devils as Nephele waited, alone, in Vergessen. Nephele had joined a war for her, agreeing to risk his life. He stood by her, even when he knew her to be a monster. How much loyalty did she owe Nephele?

She had decided, alone on the floor of that tavern, to choose herself—to be Ren, but it was becoming increasingly clear that this choice had its own set of painful consequences. She had shut the door on people that loved her. Despite her best efforts, she would still be the villain in someone's story.

Ren blinked several times, realizing that the purple lightning was decreasing with intensity, and she was having a hard time distinguishing which trees she had already passed. Following her instincts, she searched for a large tree to sleep in for the night. Balance had yet to be a problem for her, and she noticed that once she had scaled a gargantuan one, she felt quite comfortable being held by its branched arms.

Ren was already asleep by the time the final streaks of lightning vanished from the sky.

But her sleep—so desperately needed—did not give her the reprieve she sought.

Her mind saw layers of white clouds, each pulling away lazily like curtains to reveal an aerial view of Vergessen. It was night, and the small town was quiet, with twinkling lanterns in old lamp posts lining the main street. She watched as she floated through the air, making her way through town. Ren was surprised that she was glad to see the familiar streets. The potted plants on sills, so green and lush, and the twinkling of stars reminded her that life existed outside The Hells.

Her incorporeal body drifted until she approached her parent's home. A male was standing outside wearing a white robe with touches of gold. Ren immediately recognized his white hair, which was tied in a low tail.

Leo.

She watched as her father, bleary-eyed, answered the door.

"Good evening. Is this the residence of Clara and Atlas Eldanuer?" Leo asked.

"Yes, I'm Atlas. Is everything okay?" he asked, panic evident in his voice.

Over Leo's shoulder, she could see her mother turn the corner.

"Who's at the door, my love?"

Leo raised his hands and motioned to someone standing a few feet away. He was dragging an Elf who was gagged and blindfolded. Ren watched in horror as the other two acolytes, who she recognized as Brennan and Claudia, shoved a thrashing Nephele through the door before they pushed their way inside.

Atlas hit the floor harshly, and Claudia slapped a hand roughly around Clara's mouth to stifle her screams. Brennan shut the door behind him, Ren's form following close behind. She had no body, no voice, and was once again powerless to help.

"Don't fight," Claudia hissed, white puffs of air flowing from her fingers like steam.

Brennan and Leo clapped hands over their own mouths as the fluffy air floated down and entered their victims' nostrils.

Atlas, Clara, and Nephele promptly stopped struggling and settled themselves passively on the floor as Brennan scrambled to tie them up.

"Is she here?" Brennan asked Leo, eyes wide.

Leo turned and looked about the room.

"She is. Renata. I know you can hear me. Please do not make me hurt your family."

His words were biting, but there was fear behind his eyes.

"Find the tome. I will not take responsibility for your inaction. Nainaur will forgive my sins," he said, voice cracking. "He will absolve me as he will absolve you, but only if you find the tome."

Ren woke with a start, lurching forward, almost pitching herself off the tree.

Her breath shook.

"What the fuck do you expect me to do?" she screamed at the heavens.

It was already morning, and several startled bird-like creatures launched themselves into the sky.

"I don't know where to look! You haven't helped me!"

She was vibrating with anger and whirled on the tree, slamming her fist hard into its rough bark, splitting skin. She inhaled sharply as the pain surged through her fist. Angry tears welled in her eyes, and her whole body shook. She put both fists to her eyes and tried to steady her breathing. She knew enough to realize it wasn't a mere dream. It was either real or a threat. Either way, she had to act.

Don't lose control, Ren.

She couldn't afford to panic.

Ren growled in outrage, producing a sound she didn't even know she was capable of. She had no leads on the tome and nowhere to start looking even if she wanted to. She needed to get back. Return to Vergessen and help her family. But she was on her own with no magic to portal and barely understood her bearings as it was.

She looked at her bloodied hand, wishing she could smash it through Leo's head.

Her only option was Azur. If nothing else, he could portal her to Vergessen, and she could carve the faces off of the three acolytes.

Ren slid down the tree and quickened her pace. Her wrath drew her forward, spurring her on with every movement. She did not allow herself to falter in momentum. It took her only three hours to approach a familiar hill overlooking Xarek's castle.

"You're first, Xarek," she seethed.

Unlike the previous time she had snuck in, it was daytime, and the grounds had twice as many guards patrolling the lawns.

A good sign.

Patrols meant Xarek was worried, which could mean that Azur was somewhere inside.

Ren hunkered down and waited. She watched as each patrol passed and timed how long each pass took before the next guard circled around. She then formulated her strategy. Lulling the Devils to sleep didn't seem logical here. Her piccolo were not loud intruments, and if the notes reached the ears of one set, the others would immediately be alerted when their comrades were asleep on the lawn.

She watched as a large yellow Devil curved around the corner, showing Ren his back. She had less than a minute to slide down the hill without attracting attention. She'd coated the bottom of her leather pants in ash to aid her momentum and pushed herself down on her bottom. She kept her eyes locked on the Devil to make sure he wouldn't glance back.

Once there, she dashed for cover behind a small pedestal. Her heart hammered, but she held her breath. The second guard passed.

Ren knew that the next part would be the hardest.

Once the second Devil had turned his back, she crept to another pedestal, which gave her the perfect view of a fountain the size of a small pond. This Devil, standing alert, would not be making the rounds. He would stay, eyeing the back entrance.

Patience.

A third Devil turned the corner. Once the third was out of sight, Ren pulled her dagger from its sheath and flipped the blade in her hand.

You've done this before.

She reared back and threw the dagger at the fountain guard's neck. The dagger buried itself to the hilt, and the guard collapsed, unable to move from the paralyzing magic of the dagger. Ren charged at him and pushed his body into the deep water, removing her weapon as she did. She then ducked herself in the water, pulling her victim deeper. She hoped that the splashing from the fountain's spouts would cover any noise they'd made.

She counted, watching as the bubbles stopped emanating from her victim's lips. With little time to waste, she raised her head cautiously from the surface of the water right as another patrol passed. She lifted herself up from the fountain and sprinted towards the grate. She had to beat the next pass, and her timing had to be perfect. She could see the familiar wall she needed to scale before finally dropping into a hidden alcove.

When she finally reached the wall, she threw her body and scrambled to pull herself up. She laid flat just in time to hear the grumbling guard pass by. Ren allowed herself to lie there, letting her heart rate settle while listening for a few more guards before she dropped down in front of the grate. Ren held her breath as she tried the lock. She no longer had her lock kit, so her only hope was that they'd forgotten to secure it. The grate moved soundlessly.

Unlocked.

Ren almost smiled before she felt her body seize up. Her hand, clasped around a bar, felt like millions of needles were penetrating her skin as her body convulsed, collapsing to the ground. She could taste metal, and she wanted to vomit before the jolts finally halted.

In her haste, she had completely forgotten about the trap.

Jester would never let you live this down.

She examined the damage to her hands. They both were charred black, skin rough and peeling, small pustules beginning to form. On the bright side, the shock hadn't produced much noise, and she could stumble in unnoticed.

The small tunnel was still abandoned, and she had to feel along the wall until she found the opening. From there, it was easy to follow the smell to the circular grates below the torture chamber. Today, the area was sticky with fresh blood. She could see the black matter dripping from the hole, slow and viscous.

Someone's in there.

"I must admit that getting the chance to see you this way, unarmed and…well, *dressed down*, has given me quite the thrill," came Xarek's voice from above. "Your power is waning, Azur. You know that you are delaying the inevitable.

She could also hear him, Azur. But he wasn't moaning in pain. She heard him laugh darkly and spit, "Your torture tactics are almost as bad as your violin playing."

Something made a loud *crack*! Followed by a muffled grunt of pain.

Xarek scoffed.

"Oh, you *are* funny. You really should just tell me, Azur."

Another *crack*—then a stifled noise.

This time, Ren heard thick liquid hitting the floor and felt its warmth as blood trickled down the back of her neck before it continued its journey down the drain sending unexpected chills through her body. She screwed up her face in disgust.

"If you tell me," Xarek continued, "then perhaps I'll let some of those little souls of yours live." A pause. "No? Very well. You know, I think your Renata quite likes me. If I'm as poor a violinist as you say, perhaps I should let Renata help me with my *technique.* I'd like to see what she thinks of my fingering."

A jarring growl reverberated through the room.

"If you touch her, I will rip your wings off and make you *eat* them."

Xarek sighed. "I will get what I want. I always do," he said wearily. "Next time I'm here, we will practice your bow. I've always wanted to see what it's like, you on your knees before me. After all, you have to practice for my coronation."

Ren listened to boots hit stone and the distinctive scraping of the metal door. After a few moments, she heard nothing but Azur's strained breathing. He had been hiding behind a mask of audacity and pride, but the crackling in his lungs revealed the true extent of his injuries.

She wrapped her hands around the bars above her, biting her lips against the pain of her charred palms, and pushed, feeling several blisters burst from the force.

She heard Azur suck in air, having seen the movement. It took her several thrusts to dislodge the grate on her own, but she finally pulled herself into the chamber.

There he was—dripping black blood from hundreds of long, jagged cuts. His arms were chained to the ceiling, shoulders straining under the weight of his body, muscles bulging. His hair was stuck to his forehead, wet with sweat and blood. He looked at Ren, chest heaving, blood dripping from his mouth, fangs bared. He was completely nude. Even at this moment, at his most vulnerable, she could not imagine a more stunning and terrifying picture.

The Angel of Death.

Azur hitched his mouth into a crooked smile.

"Hello there, my Elfy girl."

CHAPTER 22

She came to me, soul in tatters. She hardly had anything to offer. But I listened.

She wanted to strike him. Wanted to add another wound to his stupid abs for using Jester's words against her.

"You *lied* to me."

Drops of blood splattered to the ground as he chuckled.

"Call it a personality flaw of the god of lies," he breathed in shakily, "did you come here to admonish me, or are we going to get out of here?"

Ren stomped towards him, getting within an inch of his face.

"Listen! I am here to help *you* because I owe it to you *and* to me. But my parents are in trouble so after we are out of here you're going to answer *all* my questions! Got it?"

She would have felt proud of her tenacity if she hadn't been trying to avoid looking at his huge cock.

The color drained from his face.

"Your family?"

"Yeah, so if you could stop with the theatrics, I'd appreciate it."

"Yes, ma'am," he purred, red eyes annoyingly sparkly.

She grunted and sauntered over to the wall of torture instruments and examined each closely.

"Ren? I promise I will help you with your family. No need to get violent. Though I can't say I'm not curious about how that seductive little brain works," he said, coughing.

Ren flashed him a warning glare and plucked two sharp scalpels off the wall.

"They really should have gagged you," she grumbled.

She had to push the table closer to Azur to reach his dangling wrists. Leaning in, she inserted the scalpels into the pin chamber. This might have been her hardest lock so far, mostly because she was inches away from Azur's bare chest, and he still infuriatingly smelled like burnt roses—skin glistening from moisture and his eyes gazing up at her face.

"Has anyone told you that you're very good with your fingers?" he teased, trying to hide the rattle of pain in his chest.

She heard the final click, and the manacles popped open.

"Don't do that, Azur," she hissed, making her way to his second arm.

"Do what? Be exceptionally charming?" he said, trying to flash a smile through his split lip.

"No! Act like Jester. It isn't fair," she whispered, the final manacle clicking open.

He massaged his wrist delicately. They were bloodied, skin scraped away almost to the bone.

"I suppose it would be useless to remind you that I *am* Jester?"

She ignored him and looked through the small window in the metal door. There were two guards standing at the entrance of the distant spiral staircase.

As she unstrapped her piccolo, she could feel Azur hovering nearby, his scent overwhelmingly decadent.

"What's the plan, captain?" he asked.

"First," she said, all business, "I'm going to deal with these fuckers, then we are going to rip out Xarek's spine."

Azur sighed contentedly.

"Are you trying to make me fall in love with you?"

She shot him another glare before lifting the piccolo to her lips. She felt her instrument vibrate with excitement, telling her the notes she needed.

She played the slow piece, allowing it to reverberate off the stone walls, enjoying their melodic echo.

The two guards immediately snapped to attention, hesitating only briefly to locate the sound of the music. With a confused look, they charged the door, spears in hand.

Both collapsed on the ground before they could reach the chamber.

"Damnit," she cursed, "I was hoping they'd unlock the door before they passed out."

She knelt down and inserted her makeshift pics in the door, but before she could finish her task, Azur grabbed her hands, examining the injuries there.

"What. Happened?" he demanded, voice low and menacing, bloodied fangs bared.

·She blushed despite herself, both injuries to her hands and knuckles having been entirely preventable.

"Nothing. Just clumsiness, that's all."

His face reddened even through the crusted blood.

"If someone hurt you, Ren." He cleared his throat and moved his jaw. "I am contractually obligated to eviscerate them and—rip their *fucking* face off. Who was it? Which guard?"

His voice rumbled, losing all self-restraint, small fumes of smoke appearing by his head.

"Don't bother," she said, pushing him away to continue with her work, attempting to ignore the flutter in her stomach.

He grabbed her hands, halting her progress.

"Consent *now,*" he demanded roughly.

"What?!" she hissed, trying to keep her voice level. "You can't just *demand* I consent to you."

"I'm trying to help!" he snapped.

"Help yourself! You're a mess!"

His jaw worked.

"I...don't have enough power to heal myself," he forced out.

Ren's eyes widened. She knew that it was a feat for Azur to admit weakness.

She met his red eyes and nodded slightly, "I consent."

Azur breathed out a shaky sigh as the black tentacles swirled around her palms. The injuries warmed and sewed themselves together. When his fumes disappeared, her hands were still red—not fully healed—but significantly better.

He was glaring at her hands, noticeably frustrated at his dampened magic, and dropped her hand.

Ren couldn't handle the awkwardness and quickly turned around to continue her work on the lock. Finally, after one of the most uncomfortable minutes of her current life, the familiar sound of release from the cylinder.

"Grab their pants," Ren huffed, opening the door and pushing one of the guards with her foot.

"You don't like me this way? Ren, I must say I'm quite hurt," he said, his humor returning.

She ignored and began undressing the larger of the two guards.

"I don't think those quite will fit," he said smugly.

Indeed, even the larger of the two was still a head shorter than Azur. Additionally, Azur's thighs were monstrously muscular, not that Ren had taken any particular notice.

"They'll have to do!" she barked as quietly as possible. "I'm not running around with your cock swinging in my face!"

"Oh, we couldn't have that," he said coyly. "Cocks should be saved for more *pleasurable* activities. Though, I wouldn't take cold-blooded murder off that list, personally."

"Could you stop being flirtatious for one godsdamn minute!"

"Absolutely not. It's like asking me not to breathe, darling."

"Well, you're Immortal, so stop breathing and stop speaking!" she shot back.

He smirked, dressing before they ascended the spiral stairs to the main floor.

Peeking out, they noticed another patrol of guards.

"Why is he so paranoid?" Azur whispered. "It's not like he has a god shackled in his dungeons or anything."

Ren tried not to snort, failing at keeping her wrath at the forefront of her mind. There was a part of her, a small part, that enjoyed having her friend on adventures again. Even if it wasn't in the form she had expected.

"Okay, *god*, strike them down with your almighty powers or whatever. The sound of my piccolo won't carry to them all."

Azur looked sheepish.

"The thing is, my powers are a little dampened at the moment, having surrendered my throne for *you*." He looked away, trying to hide his embarrassment. "I need to conserve my energy."

"I see—performance anxiety. Don't worry, Azur. I hear it happens to many males."

She grinned enthusiastically.

It was his turn to glare.

"A real male knows how to improvise."

Azur teleported, appearing in front of the first guard, a female Lesser with blue skin. Before the female could react, Azur spun her around and snapped her neck while half a dozen others rushed him.

Ren took this as her cue to unsheathe her dagger and pounce. She landed on the back of the guard closest to her and pulled it quickly across his neck. She tried not to flinch as the blood spurted over the gorgeous painting on the wall.

Before Ren could tackle her next target, Azur had already made his way through three more, several having been dismembered.

No finesse, this male.

Despite her mental grumbles, Ren couldn't deny that she'd enjoyed seeing Azur in his element. Muscles flexing, showing the perfect image of the god of wrath.

Having taken out all the guards in the hall, they heard running boots from the next.

The two sprinted toward Xarek's study and encountered four more guards. One, a High Devil with tanned skin and massive horns.

"Ladies first," Azur said with an ironic bow.

Ren dashed towards the largest, spinning out of the way of his longsword and jamming her dagger into his side. He screamed in agony, falling to one knee, the dagger having less of a paralyzing effect on this High Devil. Ren pulled the blade out, watching the wound bubble before stabbing once more into the side of his neck.

"Good, girl," Azur said, walking cooly past her, already having dispatched his own targets.

The pair narrowed in on the doorway, having encountered no other guards. Ren supposed that after seeing the wake of bodies, the rest had decided to keep their distance.

Cowards.

Ren's bloodlust had yet to be sated.

"May I?" he asked politely before the double doors.

Ren gave a formal and perhaps slightly playful head tilt of approval before Azur kicked the door open, blasting it from its hinges.

Inside were ten guards, all standing to defend Xarek, who was cowering with his violin behind the large stone desk. The guards didn't have a chance to charge before Azur lifted two hands, wings springing from his back. Each guard seized up, black blood spurting from each orifice before falling limp to the ground.

"What happened to conserve your power?" Ren murmured.

"Sacrifices have to be made for showmanship," he said with a flourish.

Xarek's hands were shaking. It seemed like he was trying to squeak out notes on his instrument but was unable to settle himself.

Azur teleported in front of the Devil and ripped his violin from his hands, tossing it to Ren.

"Y-you can't-can't hurt me without c-cause! I'm Im– Immortal" Xarek sputtered.

Azur's hand darted out, lifting Xarek off his feet by his throat. The Devil made a choking sound, struggling for air. Azur lowered his face within a whisper of Xarek's.

"Oh, but I *can* Xarek. You touched Ren. You touched what's *mine.*"

His voice had lowered several octaves and sounded more monster than Devil.

"I would crush your windpipe right now, but I promised a *very* special little Elf that we would do this together. So please relax, Xarek. It will all be over soon."

He threw Xarek across the room, his body landing with a crunch beside Ren's feet.

He wailed in pain, one arm bent at an unnatural angle. Ren then slammed her booted foot across his other arm, relishing the loud *snap*!

"I've always wanted my own set of Devil horns. They'd suit me, wouldn't you say, Azur?"

A momentary startled look crossed Azur's face before he smiled wolfishly.

"Darling, and you call *me* the tease. I wouldn't be able to keep my hands off of you."

Azur approached Xarek and bent down.

"Are you going to tell us who you made that deal with, Xandy?" he said with fake sympathy. "It won't save you, but perhaps I'll make your death a little quicker."

Xarek was trembling with fear, his eyes wide, blood beginning to drip from his nose.

"Just do it. I'm as good as dead, anyway. When he finds out you escaped—"

Azur kicked him in the side.

"*Who!*?" Azur roared.

The pale Devil was crying now, tears streaking down his face and mixing with the black blood.

"I can't...I can't say! The contract!" his voice bordered on hysteria. "But I think," he swallowed, "you already know."

Azur stiffened, barely breathing.

"Do it," he said without looking up at her.

Ren didn't hesitate. She knelt down, bringing the blade to his throat.

"Xarek?" She paused. "Fuck you."

She sliced his neck open.

Xarek gurgled the sweet sounds of approaching death.

Azur bent and whispered into Xarek Wyvryn's ear.

"If it is him you made a deal with, then I'd be giving you a precious gift by ending you now. Unfortunately for you, I am not a merciful god."

He kicked Xarek once more and crossed the room with Ren, leaving the Devil to torturously choke on his own blood.

When the two entered the hallway, Azur stretched his limbs.

"That was fun. Why don't we stop by the kitchen on our way out? I'm starving," he said, heading towards a large staircase.

"You want to *eat* at a time like this?" she yelled. "They're still after us—and—what about my family?"

Azur didn't stop his pace.

"Ren. How long has it been since you've eaten? If we are to recover your family, you will need your strength. There isn't much in the way of food along the way to where we are going. Dining accommodation in the forest of Nahmir has gotten pretty subpar as of late."

There it was again, the urge to strike him.

I could push him down the stairs.

Relenting, Ren followed Azur to the kitchens and noted that the palace looked abandoned.

"Not the most loyal of guards, are they?" Ren observed.

Azur shrugged. "Loyalty rarely comes into play for Devils. Fear always conquers loyalty, and little is more terrifying than their King."

Arriving at the kitchens, Azur began pulling out cheese, fruits, and vegetables, throwing some on the table, and shoving others in a rucksack.

"Eat," he demanded, pointing at her.

She would have protested, but her hunger won out against her pride and she began to break off pieces of cheese.

"Catch!" Azur hollered, tossing her a bottle of wine.

She caught it easily, trusting her natural dexterity, and pulled the cork off with her teeth. She took a large pull, relishing the bitter taste and anticipating the wonderful fog that would soon dampen her thoughts.

With her lips around the neck of the bottle, she passed Azur the violin, which she had kept close, to also store in the sack.

Azur walked out of the storage area, holding two large crates of liquor.

"You better not be suggesting we get drunk when my parents are in Mortal peril," she said through a mouthful of cheese.

"Don't be *ridiculous*, darling. I would never serve you such inferior spirits. If we are going to lose our inhibitions together, it will be with the best wine in all The Planes."

He flashed her a large smile. Ren's stomach clenched when she realized that it looked exactly like Jester's, minus the dimples.

He bounded up the stairs, and Ren heard a large *crash* from above.

What the hells?

The crashes continued at random intervals, but Ren heard no shouts of fear or running feet. After several minutes, Azur descended the stairs to the kitchens, apparently having raided Xarek's closest.

He was wearing a starched white shirt and leather pants. The shirt, still too small, had several buttons missing from the top, showcasing the alluring lines of his chest.

"Time to go, Elfy!" he said, scooping her up with more urgency than she was comfortable with.

"Wait! I didn't finish my wine!" she shouted, leaning over.

"Are...you serious?" he asked as she wiggled her way out of his arms to drain her glass.

"Look, It's been a long few days!" she said, licking her lips. "Okay, I'm ready to escape now."

She grinned, her teeth stained purple.

"You're devastatingly beautiful, you know that?" he said, raising a brow.

She swatted at him, and he took the opportunity to catch her hand, pulling her quickly to the kitchen exit. Once outside, he spread his wings wide.

"We have to fly. I don't have enough power to portal."

"You can't portal? Then how am I going to save my parents!" she said, pulling away.

"Ren, I promised I would help you. Do you want to sign a contract? Because we can. Or you can just *trust* me."

He looked at her, eyes serious.

She swallowed and nodded, allowing him to pick her up and tuck her close to his chest.

He shot to the sky, and as they began to fly among the fading streaks of light, Ren saw the smoke billowing from the palace.

"You're burning it down?"

He grunted, wind blowing his curly hair from his face.

Ren tried to crane her neck for a better look.

"What about the rest of the people inside? I'm sure there were guards, workers?"

He kept his red eyes on the horizon.

"They knew what they risked when they sided with Xarek Wyvryn. They still have time to escape. But they'll all be sentenced to death either way."

Ren opened her mouth to object, to defend the beings inside, but that was hypocritical. She had killed several guards for only doing their jobs.

After all the purple had winked out, Azur landed hard in the middle of the Nahmir forest and set Ren down.

She immediately turned on him.

"Okay, Lord Pelegros. It's time for some answers."

Azur stretched his wings and sat down, leaning against a nearby tree.

"As you wish. But remember, I can't answer anything about your past."

She was slightly thrown at his serious tone and half expected him to make a lude joke. But he was all Azur now, Jester nowhere to be seen.

She joined him near the tree.

"First, my parents. Leo, The Gilded Triangle man who sent me here, is holding my parents hostage. Why would he do that? Why are they so desperate to find this tome?"

He sucked air through his teeth.

"I hope you can understand that some information cannot be shared. I have contracts."

Her face turned skeptical.

His jaw moved as he looked up, thoughtful.

"I can only venture a guess as to why Leo would take your family. If he is working with my brother, then he is afraid of disappointing him. Of failing his holy mission."

She blanched.

"He would go as far as kidnapping innocents?"

"As we've discussed, Ren, people do a lot of things when they are desperate."

She clenched her jaw. "And why is this stupid book so important?"

"It isn't just a book. It's a holy relic written by my younger brother Faydir. It was…the reason he died."

Ren struggled against her urge to interrupt with a litany of more questions.

"Vutar'ka Zhartun, in the old tongue of the gods, means The Ultimate Truth, and that is simply what it is. A truth so powerful that gods quake in fear of it. Sometimes, truths, like your memories, are hidden to protect. The Ultimate Truth was never supposed to be written. It was thought to be impossible. Faydir gave every ounce of magic he had—all his godly life force, to write it. Before he died, he gave it to me to read and keep secret lest it fall into the wrong hands and The Ultimate Truth be forever destroyed."

"If the truth is so important, why don't you just…tell it?" she asked, forehead creasing.

He breathed out.

"Who would believe me? I am the King of The Hells. The god of lies. My word means nothing, and The Ultimate Truth…" He shook his head sadly. "It doesn't matter anymore."

Ren's mouth fell open.

"Of *course* it matters—"

"But would it change anything? Would knowing about your past, *your* truth, help you? If you can't change the past, why would the reasons why you got there make a difference!"

His voice was raised now and his eyes were on Ren's, intense.

"I'd believe you," she said gently, laying a hand on his scratched arm. "If you told me. I would believe your truth."

He swallowed.

"As I said, I can't tell everything because of the contract."

"What does our contract have to do with the truth?" she asked, exasperated.

"Nothing Ren. I mean *my* contract. The one I signed with my brother Nainaur—when he enslaved me to The Hells."

INTERLUDE

1,203 years ago

The air was sticky with moisture—soil soft underfoot, as two gods strolled.

"Peace, brother. You must control yourself lest he destroy you," Ziemia hummed, words making the plants around her twitch.

She was unquestioningly the most beautiful creature in existence.

Her caramel skin was glistening from the sun, her most favorite creation, and her hair curled and flowed wildly in the morning breeze—strands collecting stray twigs that nestled themselves there. Her eyes had a neon green glow, and sparkling green motes hovered over every inch of her skin.

Azur ground his jaw.

"I can't *do* this anymore, Zem. I...no longer care what he does to me. I am irredeemable. Destroyed, already."

The goddess stopped.

"We all have our part to play. This one is yours. If you want to protect them, you have to fulfill your role."

His anger was rising, he wanted to scream at his sister, but he knew his anger was misplaced.

Her voice was soft, almost a whisper.

"Nature is cruel. I watch as it grows, thrives, and blossoms, but I must also watch as it destroys my people. The innumerable lives lost to the fierceness of nature weigh heavy on my heart each day, but without nature, there would be no beauty. And this is the cost."

"It's not the same," he snapped, "you know it's not the same."

She gave him a slow nod of acknowledgement.

"I know," she said, placing a thin hand on his robed arm.

"But the planes cannot survive without you—wouldn't survive the chaos he would unleash. *Nature* could not survive without your balance. This is your charge. They will never know what you do for them. But that isn't why you do it."

CHAPTER 23

The truth feels like a pathetic excuse. I am responsible. My Wrath, Lust, and Gluttony are all real. They feed my power, and I revel in them.

"You're enslaved here? Then...all of this isn't your fault?"

"It is my fault. I signed a contract, and I take full responsibility for that."

"But how?" she pleaded.

Azur ran a hand through his disheveled hair.

"My family has always existed. We were happy once—together in the heavens. But we were lonely. One day, my sister Ziemia suggested that we all impart our essence in the cosmos and create living beings. We knew it would drain the majority of our power, but we all agreed. We wanted to do something important—fulfilling. We wanted to share our lives. Wanted children. We hadn't realized at the time how selfish our decision was.

"We created them in our likeness. My brother Faydir created The Planes of Fae, creatures blessed with mischief and whimsy. I created The Hells, a plane glittering with riches to delight. The Devils with their vibrant skin the colors of my beautiful vurmite. Ziemia created yours—The Mortal Plane and the luscious nature within." He smiled. "My other siblings could never compete with her imagination and ingenuity—the reason your plane has the most variety of life. Finally our eldest brother, Nainaur, crafted The Plane of Heavens, only imbibing it with a small number of ethereal creatures.

"One of the few traits we all agreed on was that we wanted to give our children the ability to reproduce, a capacity that had become one of our greatest joys. But these gifts had unforeseeable consequences. It was becoming evident that our creations were populating at an alarming rate. We could not expand our created planes, for we had expended the majority of our Immortal power in their creation. Nainaur, the wisest of us all, suggested limiting their lifespans. He promised that after their deaths, he would take them into The Heavens, blessing them on his plane and allowing them to live with the ethereal beings.

"Ziemia, as is her way, was creative. Humans and Orcs always lusted for each other, reproducing the fastest, so they were given the shortest lifespans. While Elves and Gnomes tend to mate less, and thus, she gave them more years. Faydir followed her lead, allowing his passive children to age slowly but ultimately pass on.

"But in my greed, I couldn't let go. I couldn't stand the idea of my children dying and something taking them from me. Death meant pain and abandonment, and the thought of their lives living elsewhere made me envious. Therefore, I allowed my creatures to remain Immortal, living long lives full of adventures and experiences."

He paused, eyes darkening.

"This gluttony to see them thrive pushed me to start offering them small doses of my power. Signing contracts that I naively believed would help them. I allowed them to surrender their Immortality in exchange for magical prowess. After all, not everyone wanted to live forever, and it felt like a fair compromise. But understand, I also received power from these exchanges. More power to create and control—I loved it.

"But something went wrong. For millennia there were no sleepers, only Devils with their small gifts. Then, one day, when Adhan tried to pass over to The Heavens...he didn't. He stayed and turned into what we now know as a sleeper.

"I was devastated. The only creature I had ever given myself to fully was gone. A shell. I tried all the magic at my disposal to help him, to bring him back, but it was no use.

"I couldn't fathom why this had happened. The only consequences for Devils in the past were their lifespans. It was the only way for me to give power and, while harsh, only meant they would eventually go live with my brother. I hadn't realized my brother Nainaur's growing ambition for power.

"It started small. He began visiting the Mortals on my sister's plane, evangelizing. Ziemia was the shyest of our siblings and preferred to show her love through plants and nature. Blessing her children with the light from her sun and the blooms of her flowers. She didn't mind Nainaur receiving the worship and the power that came along with it.

"Then our planes began to change. Ziemia's nature began to betray her as natural disasters destroyed her beautiful creations. Faydir's plane was blighted. The fragile ecosystem he'd created began to die, and so did its occupants. On my plane, the people started to change. More sleepers appeared each day, many of whom I had signed contracts with. Others from my High Devils, a creation I also gifted with the ability to offer contracts. Then suddenly, there were too many sleepers to count.

"All the gods gathered together to find a solution to the suffering of our people. Nainaur blamed us for refusing to create the proper balance. He said balance was the only way to true happiness and for our children to reach their full potential. Nainaur swore to us that day that he would help us maintain that balance, gifting us some of the power he'd collected from the Mortals to aid us protect our planes. He pointed out that the transfer of power could only occur via contract. I, having invented the process, believed him and was the first to sign. I trusted my brother, the self-proclaimed god of truth, to keep to his word.

"One of the exchanges was that he would intervene on behalf of the sleepers if I remained their constant custodian in The Hells. The contract, worded strategically, trapped me here, in The Hells, in exchange for his help. I had no desire to leave, so the sacrifice felt minimal at first. But to my horror, his intervention amounted to forcing the sleepers to work in the mines, extracting my precious vurmite. It took me several centuries to realize why he was doing this. These stones, magic in their own way, have been fueling my brother's power. It was the vurmite, along with the mass worship from followers of The Mortal Plane, that allowed him to lord over us, all the creatures and my siblings included. Since this realization, I have tried to stop it, but..."

He stopped, eyes distant.

"He punished me. Captured me and unleashed an Immortal god's level of agony and torture upon my person. He didn't scar my body, but—but my people. Diseases and destruction erupted across the lands. Devils were dying by the millions. One for each piece of vurmite I had stolen from him before finally releasing me.

"It went on like this, the suffering, the death until Faydir suggested we write Vutar'ka Zhartun. He wanted our children to know the truth. He believed they were intelligent enough, wise enough, to see past Nainaur machinations. They would turn from him if they realized his depravity, weakening his power enough for us to intervene. But Faydir had also signed a contract, and he knew the consequences of sharing his knowledge. He was a god, so he could not become a sleeper. He simply died—vanished rather. He and the power he provided to The Fae Plane. It is because of The Ultimate Truth that I can speak to you now without vanishing myself. It protects us from certain consequences of our contracts.

Since our brother's death we've kept the tome secret, my sister and I, believing that one day we would find a way to stop Nainaur and bring peace to the planes. But somehow, my brother discovered its existence and will stop at nothing to destroy it and silence us again—prevent us from sharing The Ultimate Truth.

"It wasn't long before Nainaur began the rumors of my malevolence. I didn't deny them because they were true. I had created the sleepers. I had already signed innumerable contracts before I realized what I had done, and I couldn't stop. At first, I felt like I was helping, allowing my children to choose. Then it just...spiraled. I forgot why I was doing it, and, in my grief, it didn't seem to matter. Once you've caused so much pain, you become numb. I was numb, have been numb for a long time. I have become what my brother always said I was. The embodiment of evil.

"I know now that no matter what I do, there is no going back for me. I am too far gone. My sins, the souls I have taken, and the agony I have caused outweigh any good I can do. I am lost to evil. It is my only companion. My lust, greed, envy, sloth, gluttony—it feeds my broken soul. It is the only way I *feel* anything besides the overwhelming numbness."

He paused, pain carving deep lines in his face. Azur closed his eyes and leaned his head back against the tree. Ren noticed his pulse throbbing in his long neck.

Ren didn't say anything at first. She simply reached out and touched his leg. His head jerked as if he'd forgotten she was there.

"I'm so sorry, Azur," she whispered.

"Don't be," he said, perhaps harsher than he'd intended. "I am what I am. I could have let him take me the way he took Faydir, but I didn't—I continued."

His eyes looked shiny, glistening with emotion.

"I could have found a way to use The Ultimate Truth before now—but I didn't—I haven't."

Ren hugged her knees to her chest. This revelation would indeed turn The Mortal Plane on its head. Societies were built on their belief in Nainaur. Even with the tome, with The Ultimate Truth, it seemed impossible that people would turn their back on their god. The one they credited for creating and maintaining their life by blessing their crops and keeping them safe.

But Nainaur was not the benevolent almighty that they believed him to be. He was using their worship to fuel his power by manipulating their love. Faydir had believed Mortals wise enough to make the right decision, but Ren wasn't so sure. After all, ideological differences were the catalyst for starting the Fae wars. There was a price to this truth.

She understood why Azur and his sister hadn't yet moved against their brother.

She ventured one more question.

"But why me? Why did Nainaur send *me* to get the tome?"

He smiled sadly to himself.

"He knew what you meant to me—what your *request* meant to me—your contract. I can't reveal much else, but I can say that you were the first being to come to my doorstep that reminded me of myself. You desired the same things I did, and I craved to give them to you. You stood before me, the embodiment of wrath, envy, gluttony, lust, pride, and yes, even sloth in some ways. I wanted to see you—and selfishly, as I am selfish—see if you succeeded.

"You did it because you saw the sinner in me. I've done evil on a grand scale, and I wanted to forget," she spoke softly.

He did not answer.

"He sent you back here as another torturous reminder that he has control. He wanted me to know that any good I tried to do would always fail—to remember that sharing the secrets of The Ultimate Truth would only bring more pain and despair to my people.

"Yet at that moment, in the palace, I couldn't let him win. I was so exhausted from fighting his way. He never would have truly let me abdicate. He could never control Xarek as he controls me with the bond we share. He likely thought I would kill you, destroy you, my project of hope. In the unlikely scenario that I didn't kill you, he knew what stripping my powers would do to me. How it would wound my pride. Indeed, I am more vulnerable than I have ever been," he said, his face twisting in contempt.

"How do we get your powers back?"

"They will return on their own, but likely not in enough time to rescue your parents." He massaged his temples. "The only choice we have is to retrieve the tome. It still contains my brother's magic. We should be able to siphon just enough to send you home without breaking any important enchantments."

She inhaled, giving him a determined look. "Then I guess we are getting that tome after all."

"I guess so, Elfy," he said, finally smiling.

Suddenly, they heard a low rumble.

"Fuuuuck, really?" Azur grumbled.

Ren leaped to her feet, drawing her dagger.

"Relax, Ren, it just means it's going to rain," Azur said, crossing his arms.

As soon as he said it, a small blue droplet hit her nose, causing her to blink rapidly. The drops weren't like The Mortal Planes.

They glowed neon in the blackness and shimmered as if they were filled with diamonds. She watched in awe as her clothes began to glow, collecting the shining beads. She lifted her hands to the sky and caught several droplets. They splashed off her hand, sprinkling neon sparkles into the ash.

"You...made this?"

Azur blushed, actually *blushed,* and cleared his throat.

"Yes. I don't know if you've noticed, but we share an affinity for the beauty of all that glitters."

She smiled and watched the droplets soak his hair and drip down his cheeks. The shimmers eventually dissolved like snow, but the rain kept falling, and the black ash began to glimmer. It looked like she was standing in starlight.

The snow and starlight, unfortunately, also *felt* like snow. She bit down on her teeth, trying to control their chattering. She was proud, had to admit it now and didn't want to show frailty. Hoping he wouldn't notice, Ren casually walked next to Azur and sat down. His body was radiating warmth.

"You're like an oven!" she sputtered, pushing wet hair out of her face.

He rolled his eyes and put one large wing around her.
Burnt roses.

She couldn't stop herself from closing her eyes and breathing deeply. She listened to the pitter-patter of rain hit the leafless trees.

"I believe you," she said, looking up at him.

His eyes were the only other color besides the glowing blue and she shivered from the effect of the contrast. His face looked confused. As if he couldn't understand the language she was speaking.

"It's just that," she babbled, suddenly feeling awkward, "you said no one believed you, god of lies and all that, and I just wanted you—"

He kissed her.

Cupping her head with his hands. It was soft but passionate, sending words he couldn't say. He suddenly pulled away. His eyes looked tormented, the glow like fire reflecting from within.

Ren's mouth was parted with shock.
Pick yourself.

She leaned in, kissing him back—an acceptance of him and herself.

It might have been their vulnerable state, it might have been the culmination of longing, but as she pulled him down to the ground, deepening the kiss, there was no doubt about what she wanted. Azur allowed himself to be led to the ashy forest floor, circling her with two muscular arms.

She wrapped both legs around his waist, pulling closer by grabbing onto his horns, knowing it would drive him wild.

In response, Azur groaned with delight, his lust awakening.

Kisses became harder, needy, tongues and teeth colliding in desperation. He gripped the back of her head, his other hand tracing down her neck possessively.

Don't stop. I need to feel you.

A low noise emanated from the back of his throat. Ren could feel his hardness through his trousers, straining.

She was done waiting.

She lifted herself up, momentarily breaking the kiss, and pulled her tunic over her head.

Her skin shimmered and glowed, slick with water. Her breasts pebbled from the exposure and the tickles of rainfall. Azur stared at her body, first with what looked like awe, followed quickly by uncontrollable want.

"Show me what a god can do," she demanded, voice husky.

He cocked his eyebrow.

"Oh, I certainly will, but I'm thousands of years old, darling. I like to take my time."

He lingered there for a moment, warm breath tenderly brushing her skin, causing each hair to stand on end.

He lowered his head gently to her breast, taking her hard pink nipple into his mouth. Ren inhaled sharply as he teasingly grazed her sensitivity with his fang while looking up to her with hooded, almost menacing eyes. A threat that he would devour her. She panted in pleasure as the sensation made its way through her and settled between her legs.

She was hungry, impatient. She pushed her hips up to his hardness and ground there, taking what she wanted.

"Naughty girl." He sniggered, continuing to work her breast, placing the other nipple between two fingers and kneading the tender skin. She mewled with delight as the same hand then drew lightly down her breast and to her stomach, stopping to caress the skin above her trousers. He let his hand linger there, teasing as he dragged a slow finger slightly under the line of her waistband.

The implication was enough to drive her to madness.

"May I?" he said, face still partially buried in her chest, cheeks rough against her soft Elven skin.

Ren gave a breathless nod, and he trailed his tongue down to her waist and undid the ties with his sharp teeth.

"Show off," she murmured, suppressing a gasp.

He winked before jerking off her trousers, exposing her to the crisp night air, goose skin appearing. Her gasp broke free as the chilly wind brushed against her exposed wetness.

"Oh, you poor thing," he said, looking at her devilishly. "I'll just have to warm you up, won't I?"

Ren could not respond. She could only sigh contentedly as waves of pleasure continued to build.

Azur lowered his hand and traced a slow finger down her opening, testing the wetness before sucking it off his finger.

Her entire body convulsed.

"What a good girl," he purred.

He returned a gentle finger to her, tracing the seam of her wetness.

"Such a pretty little pussy."

He kissed her opening reverently before, without warning, he took her fully in his mouth. Ren lost control of herself and grabbed Azur's thick horns to push him deeper between her legs. Azur breathed a pleased sound into her and grabbed her hips roughly, lifting her up for easier access. He flicked his tongue over the small bundle of nerves at her apex before sucking tenderly.

"Gorgeous girl, you were positively alluring the other night, but let me show you what it feels like when the god of lust makes you come."

The tightness in her center was unbearable. She shifted her hips expectantly, begging for release. He sneered and placed two long fingers at her entrance.

"Ren. I want you to listen," he said commandingly.

Her bleary eyes opened, searching his face.

"You will *not* come before I tell you to."

Then he slid his fingers in with excruciating slowness.

She flung her head back in ecstasy and moaned loudly, every inch of her body quaking with rapture. It was perfect. He was perfect. He pressed his free hand lightly on her abdomen while he curved his fingers, stroking and beckoning her, daring her to break his rule.

Ren was actively writhing, hips bucking and moans echoing through the rain. She was ruined. There was no one or nothing that could ever compete with this mind-shattering bliss. She felt the build, grabbing her own breasts and fondling them.

"Oh no, my darling. Not yet," he teased before taking her clit into his mouth once more and sucking.

He released a heavy growl as he devoured her.

She'd lost all sense of time and space, not knowing where he started, and she ended. He raised his head, leaning forward to grab hers forcefully, and turned her to look at him. He had momentarily paused the strokes of his fingers within her.

"You may come now," he said with one long pump of his hand in and out.

She exploded. Arching her back in release. Everything in her life felt like it made sense at that moment. Everything seemed to be leading up to this single release of ecstasy. Of pure pleasure.

Surely, this was why she was still alive—to experience this feeling.

Her head felt light, and she could feel her insides contract with reverberations from her climax. She blinked several times, trying to ensure that she hadn't lost consciousness.

Azur met her eyes and stuck his two fingers in his mouth, sucking off her wetness. Ren closed her eyes and reveled in the moment, knowing the next day would bring more challenges. But right now—right now, she'd chosen her pleasure, and she was content and spent.

She felt Azur shift to lay beside her prone body, wrapping his two wings around her tightly.

"Don't get any ideas, efly. This is not cuddling."

The side of Ren's mouth cocked up.

"This is purely practical. As pretty as this rain is, you'll freeze if you stay soaked, though I have a feeling that soaked is exactly how you want to stay."

She would have guffawed at him, but she was too drained and simultaneously too relaxed. She didn't remember the last thing Azur said before she lost consciousness, sleeping dreamlessly.

CHAPTER 24

I don't remember a time before existence. I have always been, but sometimes even the infinite learn. This was what I wanted from my children. To learn. But I wish that learning did not come with such regret and shame.

Ren woke up the next morning to the smell of grilled meat. Azur was sitting by a small fire, holding the sizzling food with his bare hands.

"You don't burn?" she asked, wiping the sleepiness from her eyes.

"I'm immune to fire. Hell-god and all that."

He spun the meat a few times before offering it to her.

Ren had no desire to talk about the night before. She wanted to keep the memory safe and untarnished by awkward conversation, and Azur didn't seem the type to put any great value on a sexual encounter with a Mortal. She wouldn't give him the satisfaction of reminding him that it was her—Ren's, first time.

"So where are we going?" Ren asked, tearing off a piece of meat, forcing her mind to other matters.

Finished with his cooking, Azur stood up and dusted off his breeches.

"The inside of a volcano. Specifically, Mount Maleth. A wonderful tourist destination—if you like lakes of lava and not seeing the sky."

"*Inside* a volcano? Azur, you might be immune to fire, but I certainly am *not.*"

He leaned down and touched her nose.

"Yes. You. Are. My. Dear."

He emphasized each word with a tap before taking her hand and kissing the ring Jester had given her.

After everything that had happened, Ren had completely forgotten about her little jewel.

"The hard part will be arriving. I still can't portal, but there should be a shortcut after we reach The Lacerated Valley."

"The *Lacerated* Valley? You thought naming something The Lacerated Valley wouldn't encourage people's negative opinion of this plane?"

He glowered at her.

"It's called that because it is a cavernous valley. Additionally, I never said I didn't like instilling a modicum of fear." He flashed a wide smile. "You should try it sometimes. You're about as terrifying as a daisy."

She gaped at him.

"I am very terrifying! You should have seen the look on those guards' faces! They were basically pissing their pants!"

Azur looked at her pityingly.

"Yes, yes, my dear. I'm sure you were quite monstrous."

Ren stuck her tongue out at him.

"Very mature," he said, raising an eyebrow and slinging the rucksack over one shoulder.

He leaned down and opened his arms.

"Okay, Elfy, time to go!"

She stomped over to him, and he scooped her up before launching into the sky.

They flew for several minutes until Ren's mind began to wander.

"Azur, why did you save Gabriela?"

Azur looked taken aback by the question.

"Because she was being held against her will. She was being mistreated and abused. Why wouldn't I help her?"

"I just mean—you said you'd given up—on being anything other than evil. Saving an innocent female doesn't sound like you've given up."

Ren could feel Azur's muscles tighten, but he didn't reply.

Their flight continued in the uncomfortable silence for another hour before the smog started to thicken, and Ren had to shut her eyes to keep out the ashy particles. Azur began to glide under the gray clouds, and the land below became visible. Streaked with caverns, some of which glowed red from the fire in the pits below. Azur was right. It did evoke the image of a giant beast that had raked its claws down the valley.

Azur slowed his descent before landing gently on a large bank divided by two massive craters. The air was stifling hot and Ren knew, from the way her body perspired uncomfortably, that the ring was the only reason why she was able to withstand the heat.

The terrain was all craggy rock and mountainous planes. Several, far off, were spewing black ashy smoke. Despite the distance from the smog, the air still felt gritty. This hell, with the threat of fire and brimstone, genuinely looked nightmarish.

"It's...horrible."

"Why would you say that?" Azur asked, stepping up beside her.

"This plane is so...dead. Nothing can survive here."

Azur scoffed.

"I know it isn't like Ziemia's plane, but it still has its beauty."

"Beauty? What makes this beautiful?" she asked skeptically. "Or are you just envious of your sister?"

Azur muttered something audible under his breath before responding.

"Ziemia created her land with delicate creations on the surface. The beauty of my creations exists *below* the surface. The glitters of vurmite, that you so love, the fires from the mountain. Fire is not just destruction, my darling. It can be used to forge, rebuild, and strengthen. My plane isn't what it used to be before my brother, but it is still beautiful in the ways that matter."

Ren considered, returning to observe the billowing smog.

"I suppose you're right. I can't say I'm very comfortable here. It's dreadfully hot."

She wiped the beads of sweat that were beginning to trickle down her temples.

"But I agree, vurmite is truly something spectacular to behold."

Ren turned, having heard a dull popping sound from the direction of her companion, but it wasn't Azur before her any longer—it was Jester.

"No. Absolutely not!" Ren barked.

"There might be creatures down here, and I can't be The King of The Hells walking around a random layer of The Underworld. It would be too suspicious. I'm trying to keep the most powerful relic in the universe hidden, after all."

Ren ground her teeth.

"It's just—I don't like it," she said, crossing her arms.

Azur, as Jester furrowed his brow.

"Please explain."

"Jester was my friend!" she blurted.

Azur cocked his head, a strand of Jester's straight hair falling into his eyes.

"He was…the first real friend I've ever had, and now it feels—it was like a lie! Like our friendship was all a manipulation." She swallowed a lump in her throat. "And I feel like my friend died, and now he's here again, but not and—"

She choked back her angry tears.

Azur reached for her, grabbing her hand.

"I won't say that manipulation wasn't part of why I chose to be Jester around you. But the times we had together, the laughs we shared, that was all real, Ren. At least, it was for me."

She wanted to interrupt, to vent all her unexpressed outage at him, but she let him continue.

"Sometimes, all the time, I can't be who I want to be. I am a god. I am the villainous King of The Hells. I can't be seen jumping from walls and telling jokes in halls. It would be— disrespectful to all the beings who are hurting. And it—" He cleared his throat. "It's also a way for me to see Ahdan again."

It felt almost unfair that he could use Adhan to defend his actions. Yet Ren knew he was being genuine. If she thought about it, it made sense why he'd want to keep his identity hidden from her. But this reasoning didn't stop the hurt that bubbled in her stomach.

"Let's just go. I don't want to talk about it anymore." She dropped his hand. She was beginning to realize that most decisions were double-edged despite their intentions.

Azur looked over her head.

"It's that way."

Ren turned, noticing for the first time how the two large craters dipped down and formed a hollow. It would have been almost invisible from the sky, and she imagined it would be easily overlooked if one didn't know its exact location. From this vantage, she couldn't see any towns or cities close by. The area looked positively barren.

Except for under the ground, she reminded herself.

At the entrance, the hollow sloped down sharply. If Ren wasn't so adept at balance, she would likely have slipped, crashing to the ground below. Even going slow, she lost her balance, boots beginning to slide. Azur reached to steady her, but she stubbornly batted his hand away.

The bottom opened up into a small room scarcely large enough for the two standing side by side. Perhaps it would have been if Jester hadn't been so tall.

The only distinguishing feature was the adjacent wall, which was carved with the devilish script of The Hells. Azur leaned in and brushed off layers of ash. He read them aloud, the words sounding harsh and guttural to Ren's ears.

"Did you gods create your own languages?" she asked.

He smiled proudly. "Isn't it lovely?"

"No, actually. It sounds like you're gargling with gravel."

She refused to temper her grumpiness.

It was Azur's turn to scowl at Ren.

"It's a riddle, little Elf," he said, pointing a long red nail at the wall.

She snorted. "A riddle? A bit cliche, don't you think?"

"It was a thousand years ago. They were very popular when I wrote it!" he said, indignant.

"Just give the answer, then," she groaned, rolling her eyes.

"There is just one problem," he paused. "I don't remember the answer."

"You're kidding. Please tell me that Jester's face is just screwing with me?"

He turned to her sheepishly. "As I said, it was a thousand years ago, darling."

She pursed her lips.

"Right. Let's just figure it out, shall we? I'm sure the answer will come to me," he said, trying to break the tense standoff.

Ren sighed loudly.

"Okay, let's have it."

"It says, I prefer the dark, yet in the skies I soar, the glitters of the world are what I adore. I can change my face but not my mind. It isn't just fire that is my kind." He finished and bit his lip. "Any guesses, Elfy?"

She thought for a moment, stumped.

"I...don't think riddles were one of the things that Renata was good at."

"You mean that *you're* good at?" He rolled his eyes. "Memories aren't related to deciphering riddles."

She pursed her lips.

At some point, you have to stop blaming her for everything.

"Hmm. I think it's stars," he said, scratching the back of his head.

"Stars? That makes sense. Dark and in the skies—glittering—we know you like lights."

Azur, with Jester's face, grinned until his dimples appeared.

"You're right." He cleared his throat. "Magic wall! The answer is stars!"

They both flinched as a loud *crack* echoed through the small chamber as the wall split into two hulking pieces and fell forward. The impact threw ash into the air, momentarily cutting off their light source. As their vision cleared, they could see that the wall was actually an entrance to a massive underground grotto. Pools dotted the room, but instead of being filled with water, they were filled with molten rock.

"This tunnel should lead us to the volcano. Overland would have taken us days to cross the mountains," he said.

"It looks pretty volcanic already," Ren murmured, wiping the sweat from her forehead.

Azur strolled into the grotto, looking around.

"Wait," he said, holding a hand to stop Ren, tail lashing nervously.

"I remember the answer. And it wasn't stars."

They heard a low rumble as the heat intensified.

"Ren—"

A tremor rocked the cavern, and both lost their balance and stumbled to their knees. More ash wafted into the air, and rocks began to fall from the ceiling.

Ren rolled aside just in time for a large boulder to miss her.

"What's the answer!" she yelled, staggering to her feet.

As more rocks fell, crashing to the ground, Azur teleported to hover over her, blocking the onslaught. He had changed again, no longer Jester, he was The King of Hells—wings spread and face shimmering like coals.

Another low rumble vibrated the room before—

Stillness.

Then, through the brown and gray ash, she saw two giant yellow eyes.

"Dragon," she whispered before the air left her lungs.

Azur grabbed her around the waist and shot into the air, the dragon's eyes following closely, tracking them.

It was the size of several buildings, scales inky black, and shimmered in the light of the magma.

"You kept a dragon down here?!" she shouted. "How could you forget about a *dragon?!*"

Azur was flying in circles around the room.

"I didn't *forget* the dragon!" Another tremor tossed rocks around the room as the dragon beat its massive wings. "He's only meant to appear if you get the riddle wrong!"

"Which we did because you forgot that the answer was *dragon!*"

The creatures breathed in the air, pulling like a whirlwind. Its throat began to expand, and green veins appeared under its enormous maw.

"But we can't be hurt by fire, right?" Ren hollered, predicting what came next.

"This dragon doesn't breathe fire!" he shouted over the sound of crashing rubble.

The dragon's throat began to pulse, threatening to explode, before it released a spew of liquified mucus towards the two. Azur dove—barely avoiding the eruption.

The green liquid splattered against the far wall and began to sear into the rocky exterior.

"Fire isn't the only thing that burns, Elfy!"

The dragon bellowed in agitation and lashed its tail wildly.

Azur dashed to the left side of the grotto, where there was a narrow indentation on the rock.

"Stay here." he said, releasing Ren and taking off again.

Ren, exasperated at being left behind, bent down, hiding behind the protruding barrier.

Azur's talons burst from his fingers, and his eyes beamed red light, grabbing the dragon's full attention.

The enormous creature screeched as it swung its barbed tail in Azur's direction. He pivoted in the air just in time for the dragon to miss—tail colliding with another wall. The collision shook the grotto, and more rocks fell from above, landing in the magma pools and spraying sparks of red fire.

Ren's mind swirled, trying to think of how she could help. She wasn't sure how much power Azur would have over the beast in his weakened state. She watched as he glided down, slashing his large talons across the dragon's face. The creature slung its head to the side in pain and collided with Azur's body, sending him flying. Azur spun twice before redirecting himself and darting back for another attack.

Ren fumbled for her piccolo and raised it to her lips. She squinted her eyes, willing the music to come. But as much as she concentrated, her piccolo remained obstinately silent.

She tapped the piccolo on her hand.

"Come on, girl! What's wrong?"

She heard another screech from the beast as it gnashed its teeth at Azur, who was still darting around its head. Realizing with a start what he was doing, Ren unsheathed her dagger. She hesitated. If she did this, successfully or not, she would be losing her only defense.

Ren observed closely as the dragon whipped its head back and forth—green acid seeping from its open mouth, sizzling and melting any object it came in contact with.

Azur avoided the barrage deftly, flying high above its head, preparing another charge.

It was her moment. Ren steadied herself before rearing her arm back and hurling the dagger at the dragon.

Her aim was true.

The dagger flew through the air before lodging itself with a spurt in the dragon's large yellow eye. The creature wailed with pain and spewed acid in every direction, and Ren was exposed, no longer shielded from the barrage.

Acid rained down, burning through her clothes and searing into her skin.

The pain was immediate and excruciating. The skin on her torso and legs bubbled and dissolved as the green liquid melted through layers. Ren shoved her fist in her mouth, biting down a scream.

The monstrous dragon continued to roar—spitting, lashing, and thrashing.

Azur circled again, hands dripping with gore, having successfully blinded the beast's other eye and now able to fly unhindered. He made two rapid passes around the grotto, picking up speed. He was moving so fast that his fiery face blurred. He then bulleted himself towards the beast's chest, slamming his entire body in and through the monster, emerging from near its spine.

The dragon, heart pierced, and bones shattered, began to sway on its clawed feet, futility swiping once more before it crashed its long neck into the wall—the sickening sound of bone splitting apart echoed as the infernal beast's neck snapped in two.

Ren barely noticed. She was yelling and squirming on the ground, her whole body in tremors from the pain as the acid continued to eat away at her skin. She had no way to stop its spread. Her hands began to split apart as she tried desperately to wipe off the fluid. Blood was starting to pool and mix with green ichor as her skin continued to bubble and dissolve. She wasn't sure at what point Azur landed in front of her.

"No, no, no. Stay with me, Elfy," he said, grabbing her and pulling her onto his lap.

She hardly felt him lift her head and try to move her arms, but all she could hear and discern was pain. She wasn't sure if she was still screaming or if the cavern continued to echo forever. Her body started to convulse, and she tasted blood.

"Play Ren," his voice sounded desperate. "Please play."

She felt a familiar shape glide across her ruined hands, scraping against the new wounds.

My piccolo.

It was impossible. She couldn't play—couldn't move. She could only lay there and exist in agony.

"Ren, my darling, please listen," his voice was gentle and desperate. "You have to let me have control. Just for a moment." She heard another scream echo off the walls. "I can save you if you let me in."

What was he saying? She couldn't comprehend the words, nothing made sense, and thinking was unbearable. All she wanted was for the pain to end.

He could end it. Yes, I think he could end me. End all of this. Yes, end the suffering, Azur.

Through the waves of anguish, she felt her heart stop, and the pain disappear. She came to consciousness inside her body, existing in the space that was her and also not her.

She watched as her body—bloody and destroyed, lifted her piccolo to her lips, smudges of blood painting the instrument. She felt the flutter of the openings begging for her to play, longing for the next notes. The piccolo took over, forming a quick cascade of lilting harmonies twinning with a tune Ren could swear she'd heard before. Ren saw her fingers caressing the wood and watched as the skin, burned almost to the bone, began to stitch itself together. Ren finally noticed Azur's face, creased with distress and desperation.

Azur gasped, and the song ended. Ren could feel the tightening in her chest as small thumps returned to her heart space.

She began to come back to herself and surveyed her body, starting with her hands. Her left hand looked completely normal, but her right, having taken the brunt of the acid, was maimed with raised scars. She moved them, testing. The skin felt tight, straining to stretch, and felt a similar tightness in her abdomen. Looking down, the lower half of her shirt had burned away, and she was deeply scarred.

Azur's whole body slackened in relief.

"Fuck, Ren! I can't even remember the last time someone scared me like that."

Her head was swimming from the shock.

"Medical magic should be able to heal the scars," he spoke clearly, "if that's...something you'd want. Personally, I think you're looking less like a daisy every minute, and I mean that as a compliment."

"How did you know that my piccolo could heal me?" she asked, mind still fuzzy from the shock.

He shook his head.

Something else he couldn't tell her.

"You saved me," she said, groggily.

Azur thought it was a question. "No, your piccolo saved you. I just made it to where you were strong enough to play. Plus, I owe you. This dragon business was my fault."

Ren reached for him, needing aid to sit up.

"Are there any other giant beasts I should know about?" she said, trying to inject a bit of humor despite her lingering soreness.

"No. I was pretty confident no one would survive Tevlov."

Ren tried to stand, but her legs wobbled, and she had to sit again.

"Rest for a moment. We are close," he said, steadying her. "We can't help your parents if you can't reach them."

"And Nephele." she said between shaky breaths.

"Nephele?"

"Yes, my partner—"

"I know who Nephele is," he interjected.

Feeling a bit less woozy, she grinned.

"Don't tell me you're jealous, Mister Envy?"

"In the first place, I am within my rights as The King of Sinners to be envious. Secondly, I am not jealous of *Nephele*. I just didn't realize I was on a mission to save your boyfriend."

"And my parents!"

"Which is why I'm still here," he said, helping Ren to her feet.

Her brain had mostly cleared, and her vision was no longer blurry, thanks to her piccolo's apparent healing properties. Besides the scars, the only evidence that she had been close to death was the large burnt patches on her clothes.

"Why didn't my piccolo work on the dragon?" she asked, remembering her desperate attempt to pacify the creature.

"Tevlov was a magical being. He would have been able to resist your song, or your piccolo was trying to protect you. Didn't want you to give your position away—again—only for it to fail."

"My piccolo has full sentients, then?"

His lips thinned, carefully considering his next words. "Honestly, I'm not entirely sure. Contracts siphon some of my godly powers. That's what allows me to grant the desires of the recipients. Your contract, your piccolo, could have siphoned off more power than most. But it *could* be that your piccolo was already imbued with some power before our...negotiation." His words were delicate, dancing around as to not give away too much of her past.

Ren fingered the rough surface of her instrument.

"So...just another thing connected to my past."

She huffed.

"Perhaps this is a question you can ask *Nephele* once you return home." He grunted.

There was something new in his tone. Something outside of envy.

He offered his hand to Ren's and gently guided her to standing. He flew them down to the dragon carcass. Ren retrieved her dagger, still buried in the dragon's eyes, as Azur surveyed the path ahead.

"This way," he said, once again taking Ren's hand, and her head began to swim for a wholly different reason. His stride was more confident as he led her through the magma maze. Apparently, his memories of the volcano had returned.

They walked hand-in-hand in silence, and Ren didn't feel the need to break it. It was peaceful despite their surroundings. She knew his hold on her was more utilitarian than affectionate, but she let her mind wander and enjoy the contact.

Eventually, Azur stopped in front of a large magma river. Her brain warned her to run as waves of heat wafted off its slow ripples.

But unlike Ren, Azur was not looking at the river. His piercing eyes were burrowing into her. Once she met his penetrating gaze, he lifted her hand and kissed her ring tenderly.

"Ren." He swallowed, looking down at her. "Take off your clothes."

CHAPTER 25

At first, I hated her. She forced me to see the parts of myself that I had locked away and buried deep. She stabbed at the sensitive parts in my own soul. In due course, I was taken in by her after so many years of refusing to lend my power. Her request was simple: forget. Forget long enough to redeem herself. Live without the torturous memories haunting every waking moment. I had to help her the way I could never help myself. I thought about her and her journey on The Mortal Plane constantly, and yet I knew, deep down, that she would return to me. We are too connected, and neither can be forgiven.

"Azur! Now is not the time to—"

"As much as you'd like to show off for me again, darling," he said with a wink, "this is purely practical. We need to swim across the lake, and though your skin is immune to fire, your clothes certainly are not."

"Why can't we just fly over? Or teleport?" she asked, sounding more whiny than she'd intended.

He sighed dramatically. "Would that I could, but the ceiling is too low. I'd end up dropping you in the lava, and it's too far to teleport safely with the amount of magic I have."

He was right. The ceiling was only about five feet higher than the magma lake.

Ren was mentally unprepared for the moment that Azur pulled off his tunic. She tried to keep her expression neutral. His body was glistening with sweat from the heat, and she had to bite her tongue to keep her mouth from falling open. He then began to slip off his trousers, and Ren prayed that he couldn't feel her lust building.

"Do you need help?" he asked, noticing her hesitance. "I could oblige, but I'd hate to get you all bothered before we complete our mission."

He gave her a false sympathetic look.

"Only you could be so crass after fighting a dragon."

She huffed, pulling off her shirt and trousers.

Ren was not one for insecurity. Even her new scars didn't bother her. Yet, standing there facing Azur made her feel completely exposed. It was intimate in a way that even their sexual encounters hadn't been. They stood there for a beat, taking each other in. Her nipples hardened despite the warm air as she gave herself a moment to appreciate Azur's powerful legs. When her eyes finally trailed up his body and to his face, she realized he hadn't been scanning her body as she had been. His eyes were soft, and his face was pensive.

He lifted a hesitant hand and reached for Ren's abdomen, right where the scars had sewn her back together. She didn't recoil but rather breathed in deep—her breasts rising and falling. His hand lightly brushed the new red skin, a deep contrast to her usually pale complexion. The touch raised every hair on her body, and she closed her eyes briefly to savor the sensation.

"I hope you always remember, if you remember nothing else, that you are an exquisite creature," Azur said, suddenly serious. "You are a warrior and a musician. Capable of commanding armies and souls." He smiled to himself. "I hope these scars remind you that you are valiant—a survivor—and so much more than the things of your past. We carry scars, you and I, but for you, they don't define you. I am...envious."

She was stunned. His words were so tender and wholly incomprehensible. Before she could think of a response, he turned from her, folded their clothes, and tucked them and her piccolo under his arm before confidently stepping into the lake.

If it hadn't been for the shocking way the lava flowed around him, she would have probably stood there, motionless, for several hours contemplating the significance of his words. Before, the opinion of the god of evil wouldn't have meant anything to her. But his actions, as he had explained them, weren't altogether evil nor altogether good. That felt too simplistic. There was a line there, a line Ren wasn't sure she completely saw or understood. And who was she to decide where the line was, anyway?

She watched as the liquid fire coalesced and began to harden around his body before breaking away with his slow movements.

"This might be more difficult than I'd initially anticipated," he said with a grunt, "you might not be able to make it across without help."

Oh, fuck that.

True, it looked as if he was wading through thick mud, but she was too proud, and he was too smug for that.

"I'm sure I'll be fine," she responded as she slowly entered the thick pool.

While undeniably hot, the magma didn't burn away at her body. She couldn't say it was exactly comfortable—more like the hottest bath she could imagine. The worst part, however, was the difficulty she had lifting her legs. When she tried to move them through the pool, the magma began to solidify around her legs and mold to her body. She forced herself forward, only able to move a foot at a time.

She refused to look at Azur, who had stopped his own progress to watch her strain through.

"Just let me know when you're ready to give up, Elfy!" he said, finally turning to continue his trudge.

Her muscles strained as she kicked each leg out with all her might. The trek became more difficult as the magma reached her torso, for she could no longer use the momentum of her hips to push her forward and had to rely on pumping her arms.

By this time, Azur had made his way across the lake and was casually picking off dried bits of lava from his skin. She tried to focus on her goal rather than his toned back.

Droplets of perspiration were flowing free down Ren's body, but she spurred herself on, now over halfway across.

Azur dressed lazily, not even glancing back to see her clumsy movements.

Ren's body was tired, muscles screaming, but she refused to give up—spite being the powerful motivator that it was.

When she finally stepped onto the bank, she shamelessly fell forward onto the cool ground. She lay there, completely naked, gulping down full breaths.

Azur leaned over, his body shadowing hers.

"Ah yes, this position seems familiar. You looked very similar last night, if I do recall."

She shot him a menacing look before picking herself up and dressing.

"How much further?" she asked, trying to keep her breathing steady lest he know how exhausted she was.

"Just a few hours walk from here."

She groaned. "Walking is worse than the dragon."

He let out a low snigger.

"Don't be slothful, my darling," he said, winking.

Despite her protests, the hike was easy going, if a little sweltering, and Ren wondered if her fingers would start to prune from the constant perspiration.

As they walked, it occurred to Ren that this might be the last few hours she would have with Azur. Soon she would return to her family, her plane. A place where Azur could never follow. And she imagined inner-planar travel wasn't as easy as booking a six-week trip across the oceans. Besides, she wasn't sure what coming back even meant. She and Azur weren't exactly friends, and she couldn't see herself calling upon him for what—tea time?

Yet, Ren felt her heart split apart. One side of it felt an immediate panic at the idea of leaving The Hells. Leaving meant attempting to accept the life Renata had created—going back to her parents, her tavern, and trying to reconcile with Nephele. It meant abandoning any life that she could have created here for herself.

How Absurd! What kind of life could you truly have in The Hells?

Ren couldn't help but glance at Azur, who looked as if he was lost in thought.

So this might be it. This was her last chance to talk to the Devil who had taken possession of her soul. There was only one question she could think to ask him. A question that she felt like, if she had the answer to, she could move on with more peace.

"Azur? What's it like to," she licked her lips, suddenly nervous, "to be in love?"

She realized, blushing, how deeply personal the question was, but she had to know. Had to understand if going back to Nephele would be worth the risk.

The Devil stopped mid-stride and turned to her. Azur opened his mouth to say something and contemplated a moment before his words came out.

"I am the god of hate, Ren. Not love."

"But I know that you loved him—Ahdan. You—told me, yourself!" she sputtered.

Azur resumed walking. He was silent for so many heartbeats that Ren feared she'd upset him.

"I think perhaps you know just as much about love as I do," he said finally, with a small laugh. "But if I had to answer, I'd say that being in love is different depending on who you are and who you are in love with," he said thoughtfully. "Ahdan liked to say that love was invented in my realm." He smiled, suddenly wistful. "Ridiculous, I know.

He said love was envious. Desiring your partner and wanting them to desire you back. Gluttonous and greedy since you can never spend enough time with that person once you've truly fallen for them. Slothful because there is nothing more tantalizing than a lazy, lust-filled day never leaving the bedroom. It can be proud because that person can make you feel so worthy that someone that amazing has decided, above all others, to love you. And sometimes, in your worst moments, no one can make you feel more angry, more wrathful, than the person you have surrendered yourself to completely.

"I'm not sure if any of that is the best, most ideal love. Perhaps love should be pure—innocent and uncomplicated. But you've asked The King of the Damned, and I can't imagine anything other than love in this way. I can't run from what I am, even in love."

Ren thought for a moment.

"Maybe it can take parts of both. I could do without thinking I'll have a love with wrath, to be honest."

Azur laughed softly.

"Fair enough."

The final chamber was the first they had entered, and it was free of lava pits. The only light was shining from a complex carving on the stone floor. Upon closer inspection, the red light made a five-pointed pentagram.

"Before we can enter the final chamber, Someone has to temporarily surrender their powers. It's the only way The Ultimate Truth will appear upon the dais," he said, walking to the center. "No one who enters should have the power of the gods. It's a brilliant precaution to make sure no one can destroy it," he said smugly.

"Oh yes, very clever, Mighty God of The Hells," she said, rolling her eyes.

"You are clever for noticing!"

Ren watched as Azur crouched down and touched the ancient carvings. A gust of wind began to fiercely blow from the pentagram, Azur's dark curls lashing around his face. He closed his eyes and bared his teeth.

He looks like he is in pain.

A white light emerged from the pentagram and wrapped itself around Azur's body. The light curled and danced elegantly, but Azur continued to look anguished. His wings began to tremble, and Ren watched as they wilted, like two black petals, before falling off his back. Tears were now running down Azur's face, and he let out a dissonant yell as his horns splintered, crumbling to the ground. Azur's body convulsed—his godly form dying. The light was sucking every unholy cell from his body, and each little death reflected on his face.

Ren suddenly felt a burning on her neck. She reached up with a start. Pulling her hand back, she saw a smear of red. Her brand. While she hadn't thought about it since the night of the party, she suddenly felt exposed and insecure without it.

As soon as it came, the light blinked out.

Ren had to squint against the unexpected change in light, but ran in his direction despite her temporary blindness. Once her vision cleared, she could see that he was still crouched, yet his body hung completely limp.

She dropped to her knees and lifted his head. "Azur! Are you okay?"

She gasped. This was not the god she had come to know.

Still beautiful, but his eyes, usually iridescent like fire, were a dark shade of brown. His ears looked Human, and she could see through his agonized expression that his teeth had dulled.

"No. I'm...really not," he winced, struggling to stand, all pretense cast aside.

Ren could only imagine how much he hurt—not just physically. He was The King of Pride and Envy. He now stood in front of her, appearing completely Mortal. She wasn't sure if he was Human, as that wasn't one of his creations, but he wasn't totally Devil either. She felt the intense desire to comfort him for his loss. A loss of self and identity. She understood this, at least. But she didn't know what to say—her lack of interpersonal skills haunted her once more.

What do you say to a god who just became Mortal?

He strode off, advancing to the far wall.

"Let's get you home, Elfy," he said without meeting her eyes.

They heard a deafening scrape against stone as the two massive doors swung wide.

They entered, approaching a long stone bridge over a massive magma pool, which ended in a platform with a tall dais. The room was silent except for the clicking of their boots and the slight simmering of the flames below. Shadows shifted across the room as the fire burst and bubbled, making it difficult to distinguish different shapes. It was for this reason that it took the two a moment to realize that a figure was kneeling at the end of the bridge.

Leo.

Ren bolted to his form and grabbed the scruff of his neck.

"Where the fuck are my parents, you sack of shit!" she yelled, shaking him.

Every muscle in his body was trembling. Tears streaked his dusty face. He did not look at her—his face jerking back and forth, searching.

"Renata—I had to, he wouldn't—I couldn't—"

"Where are they?" she bellowed, pulling out the dagger and positioning it at his throat.

"Yes. Yes!" Leo exclaimed, excitement filling his face as he finally met her eyes. "Kill me, please," he squeaked. "It will be nothing compared to—now that I have—I failed him! failed him!"

Ren hesitated, trying to make sense of his words, but kept her dagger poised to carve him open.

"Ren, wait." Azur's eyes darted around the room. "He shouldn't be here. No one should be here."

From behind the dais, a figure emerged. His face was transformed, but it was indisputably the same being.

Nainaur.

CHAPTER 26

His hair was still gray, eyes still blue, but depravity was now present there. His smile was wicked, and his brows were perked up malevolently. The shadow of the flames underneath flickered about his face, giving him a ghostly halo.

Leo wrenched himself from Ren's grasp, indifferent to the dagger, which trailed a shallow slice across his throat.

Ren didn't move to pursue, too stunned by the scene in front of her.

Leo threw himself at the base of the dais, raising his hands in supplication.

"My lord, my king, I have been nothing but a loyal servant to you. I have brought you the girl—please have mercy!"

His voice shook, and Ren noticed the wet spots trailing down the back of his robes.

"You did *nothing* for me, Leonardo," Nainaur muttered, sneering. "You begged me for a task, and you, of everyone, should know the consequences of being such a *disappointment.*"

"But—you told me—you promised a place near you in The Heavens!"

"Leonardo, I owe you no thanks or credit," he seethed. "However, I have decided to show you the depth of my compassion. I will not kill you for your insolence."

Relief passed over Leo's face before Nainaur raised two hands in front of him.

"My savior, thank—"

But the words were cut off and replaced by a gagging sound. Leo's body twitched and writhed.

Ren didn't move. Her head swung back and forth between the god and the man. What should she do? What was right? Leo appeared to be a victim of the deity, but her heart clenched in rage when she thought of the deplorable choices Leo had made. She could kill him herself, it would be so easy, and she doubted she would feel even an ounce of remorse or regret at her decision. She might even enjoy the satisfaction of feeling her wrath manifest.

There it was again.

The question of whether these feelings or lack of feelings for this male teetered her across that line of malevolence.

A hard grip on her elbow stopped her wavering inaction as Azur stepped forward.

The two watched as Leo continued to writhe, golden light, like beads of sweat, began to trickle off his skin and float toward Nainaur. The god inhaled deeply, beckoning the essence, which swirled around his open palms and entered his nostrils. Nainaur's skin began to glow. He smiled and exhaled—making a contented sound while the light began to dissipate.

Leo collapsed.

"Sloppy, that one," Nainaur said, taking two steps off the dais.

Though prone, Ren could still see Leo's chest moving.

She pulled herself free from Azur and ran towards his body, turning him over.

His eyes were still full of tears, and they stared at Ren's face, looking past her.

Leo was a sleeper.

"Ren, run," Azur said, pulling Ren from the ground and standing in front of her.

"I wouldn't, my child. I will only kill you if you try," the other god laughed. "It would behoove you to listen to what I have to say."

He produced a large leather tome from behind his back.

Two more creatures emerged from the dais. They were unnaturally tall with gray skin and long fingers that curved into vicious points. They had no lips—only barbed teeth sticking out in every direction, and on their back were two large gray-feathered wings.

"Little brother, you remember Rafael and Michael, don't you? My Angels?" the god said, gesturing to the creatures.

"How did you do this?" Azur spat, gesturing with his head to Leo.

"You really are the most witless of our siblings," he said, opening the tome lazily and flipping through. "Almost as useless as those creations of yours. High Devils? That Xarek could barely string two words together. But the sleepers," he said, pointing to Leo, "these creatures are perfect. They are *my* children."

Azur blinked, confused.

"What are you saying? They are the product of my contracts."

The God of The Heavens waved a dismissive hand.

"Your contracts always were foolish, as were your creations. You and the others—harping on *free will.* Well, what did free will get you?" he queried, voice rising. "They all turned their backs on you and preferred to worship *me*—not that I can blame them."

Ren noticed that Azur's hands were clenched and shaking with rage.

"So I improved on them. Once you signed your contract with me, all of their agreements were under my ultimate control. I decided these *sleepers,* as you call them, were more useful in Hell than in Heaven. Now they work, they don't complain, they don't clog up my Heavenly Plane with their *souls*," he said, with an expression of disgust. "And most importantly, they bring me the vurmite. My power."

"Y-you did this?" Azur sounded breathless as he took one shocked step back. "You did this to them—to Ahdan. To all of them. You didn't let them move on."

Nainaur's smile twisted from ear to ear.

"I took particular pleasure in that one—*Ahdan.*" He said, savoring the name. "But I had to intervene. Love, as you have discovered since, is weakness, little brother. That bothersome Devil was a distraction. He stopped you from reaching your *true* devilish potential—"

Azur didn't let him finish.

He flung himself at Nainaur, arms outstretched, clawless hands twisted to rip whatever he grabbed. But Azur, without his powers, could not compete with a god.

Nainaur simply flicked his wrist, and Azur's body was shoved twenty feet into the air. His arms and legs snapped together as if by invisible restraints.

Azur roared in protest, gnashing his teeth, muscles straining. "Why?!" he demanded. "You just wanted control?"

"Tsk tsk, Azur. I can't reveal all of my secrets now, can I?"

Nainaur trailed a finger along the spine of The Ultimate Truth.

"After all, secrets—" his eyes flashed to his brother's, "are deeply personal."

Nainaur sighed. "It was all working perfectly—you made contracts, I made sleepers, and my power grew. For thousands of years! Until Faydir started to get ideas," he growled, ignoring Azur's bellows of protest.

"His children were *starving,* Nainaur. He discovered you—the loathsome thing you had become. The Ultimate Truth needed to be told—"

"*I am Truth,*" he bellowed, shaking the large cavernous room. "*I speak, and it is so!* You think you are justified in your betrayal of me? You all turned your back on me, and for *what?*" he snarled. "These pathetic creations? The parasites that drained your powers, making you barely capable of sustaining your Immortality?" He spat on the ground. "You disgust me, Azur."

"I will not let you destroy it," Azur said firmly, thrashing in mid-air.

Nainaur laughed maniacally.

"Oh dear. That isn't something you can stop."

"Let him go!" Ren hollered, glaring at the god.

Nainaur's soundlessly walked forward, closing the tome and tucking it under his arm.

"I would like to thank you, Renata. For leading me to Vutar'ka Zhartun. I knew that you wouldn't fail me."

"No-I-I didn't-Leo, he—"

Ren looked up at Azur. He was staring at her in horror.

One of the Angels stepped forward and pulled a black dagger out of his robe, the counterpart to the one Ren still held.

"They are twins, these daggers, they call to one another," Nainaur said softly, "I knew your innocence would be the perfect manipulation. I just had to give the dagger to that female near the tavern, and you would do the rest. Cursed objects are a wonderful way to make sure you always know where your quarry is. Almost like a brand," he said, eyes flickering to his brother. "You led me straight here."

Ren was horrified. She thrust the dagger from her, and it landed with an echoing *clank* on the stone floor. She hadn't once stopped to consider that the dagger hadn't been sent to her by Azur.

"You're quite prolific, Renata. So young for one with Elven blood, and already you've murdered *thousands* of innocents. And so *naive.* Like a child, you flounder. Trying to *speak* to the sleepers."

He scoffed.

"Is...that why you chose me? To find the tome? You could have manipulated anyone."

She barely was able to croak out her words, shame filling her chest.

"I knew *he* would have a soft spot for you." Nainaur shrugged in Azur's direction. "I knew of you long before I sent Leonardo to you. You were so *troubled* that day, stumbling into my temple. So fragile and desperate. I needed only to show you the way to my brother. I knew he couldn't resist your tragic little story and your desperate need for forgiveness and redemption—what he also needlessly craves."

"Stop!" Azur shouted from above, still struggling. "Don't," he said, with a look of warning to his brother.

"Or what? You are powerless here, *Pelegros.*"

"I will *end* you," Azur fumed, wrenching his head from side to side. "I will raise the planes against you and eradicate your presence from the known world. Then you will be *nothing.*"

"I am Immortal, Azur. No matter what you try to do to me, I am eternal!"

"And once I have ripped you from these worlds," Azur shouted over Nainaur's words. "I will obliterate all trace of you and your memory from the minds of Devils, Fae, and Mortals, and you will be what you've always feared—*forgotten.*"

A flash sparked in the elder gods' eyes. He lifted the tome once more.

"To think that Faydir gave up everything for this, and you did *nothing.* Bah! Sloth truly is one of *your* sins." He opened to a page in the tome. "And as Faydir says, ambition is *mine.*"

His hands, having once looked so soft to Ren, began to morph into golden talons and blazed with fiery light. His palms hissed as the brittle pages began to crackle and burn.

"No!" Ren shouted, throwing herself at the god.

But she froze. Restrained by the same invisible force that bound Azur in the air.

The two Angels sniggered.

"So excitable this one," he mused with a sinister grin. "Do not worry, my dear. You will be rewarded soon enough," he added, the edges of the pages curling as they ignited.

Ren could barely move her head, but she saw Azur floating only a few feet in front of her, eyes murderous. "Right, a reward like Leo's?" she gritted out.

The flaming tome continued to snap and pop as vapor began to emanate, sizzling sharply. The vapor swirled, taking on a purple hue, twisting and shaping into something oddly humanoid.

"Faydir! Glad you could join us," Nainaur said, feigning excitement.

Indeed, a translucent, distinctively Fae male was before them. His robes were in the fashion of centuries before and were the color of The Hells' violet sky. His hair was long and sleek, his eyes with the same ethereal shine as his brothers' and purple, like his robes.

"Faydir," Azur whispered. "You're alive?"

"Brothers," he said, his voice hoarse from disuse. "I placed my essence within the tome, the only way to protect its truth." He looked sorrowfully at Azur before turning his violet eyes to Nainaur. "Don't do this. Once upon a time, Naina, you were the sweetest of brothers. We lived together, loved together, and never wanted for anything.

"You helped Ziemia create the first gentle streams, taught me how to let the wind whistle through my glens. Why have you turned away from beauty? My soul suffers every minute I await The Ultimate Truth to be told. Suffers for what we have lost as a family. But, my sweet Naina, even you can change your past. Even you can make it right."

The heavenly god paused. His brow creased.

"My sweet Faydir," he said slowly. "Do you think I can be redeemed? That I deserve forgiveness after all I have done?

Faydir remained motionless, unblinking.

"I'm not sure I can answer that, for I do not know the true nature of redemption. Is this a power that the gods alone possess? The ability to look upon our creations and forgive them of the mistakes that they make? That is what they pray to us for. And yet, if this is so, who forgives us? Or is redemption always in the possession of the victim? If you asked the sleepers, could they forgive you? Are they even capable? In the end, I'm not sure it matters, Naina. You are my brother, and I will always love you, no matter the path you have chosen. We can fix this. We can find a solution together. That, I think, is the first step to absolution."

"No, Faydir!" Azur cut in. "Nothing on any plane of existence or in the power of any god could redeem what you have done, Nainaur," Azur snarled.

Nainaur's head snapped to him.

"At least you're honest, Azur. They say Devils are deceivers, but I've always thought that was too simplistic. I find that I'm much better at spinning a tale."

Ren was surprised that Azur didn't combust with all the wrath that was radiating off him.

"I believe you've both given me a lot to think about," Nainaur said, looking at each brother individually.

A pulse went through the air, and Azur landed on his feet beside Ren, who had also been released from her binds. Ren was sure Azur would have tried again to tear at his brother if a sudden crackling hadn't begun to emanate from Nainaur's fingers.

"Naina, no!" Faydir shouted, reaching for his brother. "Our creations—my people, deserve The Ultimate Truth! True Salvation!"

"You would have *destroyed* me!" Nainaur thundered, countenance all fury. "You lie to me, Faydir! You wrote this to kill me, to wipe my name from existence! And now, I will do the same to you and the pitiful remnants of your creations."

They watched in horror as the white flames spread from the tips of the pages and began to consume the tome. Faydir screamed in pain as his ethereal body began to erupt in white flame.

"Noooo, Naina *noooo,* it's not too late!" he shrieked, face melting from the burning radiant light.

Nainaur's expression was passive—stoic as he watched his little brother's god-essence be smothered in flames.

Azur pivoted to charge, but the two Angels lunged in front of him, blocking the path to his brothers.

Faydir continued to shriek, ripping at his face and robes, the inferno crawling up his hair, consuming his form completely.

Ren couldn't watch. The destruction of such a holy creature was too terrible. A violation of nature itself—incomprehensible.

The Angels released Azur as he stepped back, folding Ren's trembling body into his arms protectively. She could hear his heart beating erratically.

The sharp sounds of agony seemed to last forever as they echoed and ricocheted through every room in the volcano. When Ren finally looked up, there was no evidence that the tome, or Faydir, had existed. There were no robes piled delicately on the ground nor ashy remnants from The Ultimate Truth. Only the unmistakable smell of burned flesh lingered in the air.

There was the answer, Ren couldn't be evil. Not like this. If evil was a spectrum, she'd never come close to this—this absolute depravity. No matter what she encountered in life, she could never—would never, be this. To hurt someone for selfish reasons, to gain power, or to demonstrate authority. She couldn't know where Renata was on this spectrum, but it didn't matter. She—Ren—would not be this person.

Nainaur was standing with his hands laced in front of his stark-white robes. "I hate that it had to end this way, but it really was his time. As it is yours."

Ren swung her head towards the Devil.

"What is he talking about, Azur?"

"He wants to kill me," Azur said, brown eyes wet and full of hatred.

"Oh dear boy, you think so small!" he drawled. "I am going to kill everyone on this *plane.*"

His face twisted with sinister pleasure.

Ren was reeling.

"What?! You can't!"

"He *can*, Ren. He has the power of two gods now." His voice was quiet but strong.

"Learning, I see," he said, tapping his nose.

"I know you're ambitious, but why kill everyone?" Ren's face was reddening with panic. "Don't you want to...rule it or something??" she asked desperately.

"Too much work. I don't rule, I receive." He sighed. "And anyway, these Devils are too lost. Too dedicated to their *king* to give me the worship I deserve."

"Wait." Azur paused as though something had occurred to him. "You won't do it."

Ren looked between the two males, utterly confused.

"Tell her what you *really* want, Nainaur. Tell her what you want for saving me *and* my people."

Nainaur looked pleased.

"Ah yes, you see, deals are your specialty, and I simply couldn't help myself." He smiled a toothy grin. "It's very simple, really. I want Renata to go home, and in exchange, I will give her memories *and* allow the Devils to live."

"Home? To Vergessen?" she asked, voice heavy with skepticism.

She freed herself from Azur's embrace to look at the god full-on but kept a firm hold on his hand.

"Exactly, my dear! Back to Vergessen."

Ren felt Azur's grip tighten. The knot in her throat began to grow, sensing the trickery.

"I'm not falling for your lies, Nainaur. You would turn me into a sleeper!"

"Renata, Renata! There's that naivety again! I don't need to lie to you. If I wanted to turn you into a sleeper, I would." He tutted. "What I want is for you to leave—I want you to remember, and lives will be spared in exchange. It's that simple." His grin did not falter.

"To further demonstrate my benevolence, I'll even keep the more *unsavory* parts of your memories. Some of those you gave up. I wouldn't want to cause you any *undeserved* pain." His voice dripped with sarcasm. "All you have to do is go. Right now."

"And my family!" she blurted, "you will make sure they are safe?"

"It's always perplexing me," he said, tilting his head, "the way Ziemia created you Mortals to care so much about such trivial matters. But to answer your questions, yes, your family is already safe. They won't even remember their harrowing encounter."

Ren let out a shaky breath in relief. But she couldn't puzzle it out—it didn't make sense. What was he hiding? She couldn't see how this could possibly benefit him.

Then it dawned on her. Her family was safe. The reason she was determined to leave no longer mattered.

"Tell me why he wants this," she asked pleadingly, turning to look into Azur's brown eyes.

The expression they held was so much more excruciating than the acid burns. But those eyes, they knew something, and she wished she could read their language.

"I can't, Ren. Not yet," he whispered, voice cracking.

Ren's heart felt the insurmountable weight of this decision. She wanted to rage against Azur. To demand that he reveal what he knew. It was the end of the journey—she had to go back, back to being someone she didn't even know, and she *deserved* to understand the truth—to understand why she had to go through with this, to give up another part of her. A decision that, in an instant, no longer became hers. She was once again blown by the winds of the desires of others. Saving a Plane? Someone she cared about? It wasn't a decision at all. It was the only option.

And as much as she wanted to unleash her wrath upon Azur, to push him away in an act of self-comfort, push him away and deny that anything they had was real—she couldn't bring that anger to the surface.

As she gazed at The King of The Hells, she noticed then that he was, without his horns and wings, really just a man. The same pain, love, and regret existed within him. She thought in that instant that—perhaps in another life—on another plane, if he had been Mortal, she could have loved him. Perhaps they could take their sins and let them dance to the music of a life spent together. Accepting one another and maybe even someday growing strong enough to accept themselves.

"And," she rasped, "Azur will be okay?"

"I'll be fine, Ren," he said, lifting her hand to his lips to place a soft kiss there.

"Oh, he'll be fiiiiiine," Nainaur whined. "If I let him leave this chamber, he will get the powers he sacrificed back. I *do* appreciate that, by the way."

Ren wasn't looking or listening to the older god, only Azur, who gave a weak smile and inclined his head in encouragement.

"But I'll...never see you again!" she blurted, her hands beginning to tremble.

"You don't know that, darling," he said, voice soft as he reached up and stroked her cheek. "Your life is very long, and mine is...infinite. Our paths could certainly cross. Just try not to forget me? A third introduction sounds quite tedious."

The slight quirk of his mouth could not hide the grief on his face.

She threw her arms around his neck and kissed him. It was desperate and inelegant, but it might have been the most painfully beautiful thing she'd ever do. Tears were running down her face, and she couldn't tell if they were hers or Azurs.

When they finally broke apart, she did not look at him again. She thought that if she did, her entire chest would crack open.

She walked up to Nainaur.

"I'm ready."

The god didn't acknowledge her words. He simply flicked his wrist, and a portal appeared.

"You will arrive in your hometown with your memories intact."

The fiery portal burned brightly and gusted hot air, blowing her hair back.

"I will bless your path," the god said.

"Go fuck yourself," was the last thing Ren said before she turned, sparing one last, longing glance at the hard expression of King Azur Pelegros. That single second was unbearable before she threw herself into the portal. But in the fraction of a moment before her vision blurred, she could have sworn that the sad smile on his lips revealed two striking dimples.

EPILOGUE
Renata

1.

Renata woke up with a start, head pounding. She was in bed with the same familiar sheets she had bought at her favorite market.

"Finally! I've been waiting all morning for you to get up!" came a pleasant voice.

Across the room, sitting in a small wooden chair, was Nephele. His smile was so wide that his eyes crinkled at the corners.

"I woke up this morning to your letter!" he said excitedly.

Renata matched his grin and scrambled to the end of her bed.

"Why aren't you in bed?" she asked, flinging her hands around his neck and crawling into his lap.

He smelled of home and the nutty scent of fall.

Nephele wrapped two strong arms around her, and she heard him stifle a sniffle. She pulled back.

"What's the matter?" she asked, a crease appearing between her eyes.

Nephele's cheeks were pink, and his eyes were welling with emotion.

"You remember," his voice broke.

Renata squinted at her partner.

"What are you talking about?"

"Your letter said that you found a cure in Ataria. That you arrived last night. I'm so..." he sniffled, "thankful you're back."

She laughed.

"What are you saying? I've never even *been* to Ataria."

Nephele smoothed silver hair out of her face.

"Oh, songbird, your letter said you might still be missing some pieces—that the side effects of the healing would return your old memories, but you couldn't keep all of your new ones," Nephele explained to her how she had woken up almost a year before and how she had been summoned to Ataria to regain what she had lost.

"And it was...an illness? I've...never heard of such a thing."

Nephele shrugged.

"Me neither. We thought it was the trauma of the war, at first."

She shivered abruptly as a chill made its way down her spine.

The Great Fae War—scenes of her sitting around a camp covered in gore, visions of hard conversations with generals about compromises and collateral damage—the shine of a blade in her hand all flashed quickly in front of her vision. But they were just that—small flashes. Disjointed with little connection between.

"What's wrong, little songbird?"

"I...don't know," she said. "This is all very strange."

She reached up to touch her forehead—Nephele gasped.

"Renata! What happened to your hand!?"

He grabbed it and cupped it gently.

She saw with a shock that her hand was covered in unfamiliar red scars like splashes of discolored ink.

"Wha—?" she said, with a start, reeling back so quickly that she almost fell to the floor.

"Shh shhh," Nephele comforted. "Don't worry, my love. I know they're...uncomely, but we can fix them. You must have gotten them on your journey."

He bent his head to kiss her palm.

"I..." she said, unable to grasp the right response.

She felt unexpectedly defensive of her scars but said nothing.

Nephele didn't like them—and that was that. He had harped on her for months to get rid of the scar on her arm—but she couldn't. She had gotten it and kept it as a reminder of when she failed to...*failed to what?* She couldn't recall at the moment. No matter, surely all of her memories would return soon enough. No use in harping on the past, as he often reminded her.

When she came back to herself, she saw Nephele, the softest of looks on his face. The look of pure love and contentment. He drew a finger down her jaw and leaned in to kiss her, nuttiness filling her nostrils.

His lips, so familiar and usually so comforting, moved quickly and desperately. She could feel his wet tears on her cheeks and suddenly felt...embarrassed. She knew these lips, had kissed them hundreds of times, but it felt...awkward. Like she didn't know how to keep the correct pace.

She felt Nephele begin to coil his arms more tightly around her body, his kiss roughened as he started to squeeze her breasts.

Her body jerked back, and she stood up and took two hesitant steps back.

"What's wrong, songbird? We haven't...I haven't...gotten to touch you in so long. I was hoping—"

"Yes. I think I just need some time. I'm feeling a bit—"

"Out of sorts," he finished, standing and taking her good hand. "I am sure you need a—some time." He cleared his throat, trying to hide his displeasure. "Erm, perhaps we should go to Jamal's? I am positive he would love to see you. Perhaps you can play for him tonight?"

Renata's eyes lit up.

"Yes! That's exactly what I need."

Worry dissipating, she spun around to search for her piccolo. She bent to look over the bed and pushed aside some tattered travel leathers. Her room was small, barely big enough for her two pieces of furniture.

"Nephele...where is Calliope?

Nephele went rigid. "Your...piccolo?" he asked, voice raspy.

She giggled. "Who else would I be talking about?"

Nephele sucked in air sharply.

"Songbird, I was hoping you remembered."

From under the chair, he produced a small box, barely the size of Renata's hand, and passed it carefully to her. She hesitated—a ringing beginning in her ears. The last thing she remembered before opening the box was the soft texture of its lid, the last pleasant sensation she would have for the rest of the day.

Renata screamed.

Inside were what looked like jagged and misshapen splinters from a fallen tree. She tipped the pitiful remnants of her instrument into her shaking arms.

"What happened to her? When did this—"

Her voice caught in her throat, choking off her next words.

"I don't know," he said hurriedly. "I found it that way last night...."

She clutched the pieces to her face, feeling the wetness of her tears as her body shook with sobs.

"I'm so sorry, my love." Nephele moved to her side. "I know you enjoyed it."

"Her—not it."

Renata could barely get the words across her lips as she gasped for air.

Nephele grabbed her arms gruffly.

"Renata, no. Don't spiral—you are stronger than that," he said, shaking her slightly. "You will get through this. You should be over these little spells."

He let go of her arm and turned to walk into the small living area. When he returned, he held out a violin—newly shined and restrung.

"When I found the box with your letter, I decided to get you something to help you forget the pain. Do you like it?"

She swallowed, trying to look grateful and keep her breathing even. It wouldn't do to show her weakness in front of Nephele. After all, he was so kind to her today.

"I know it's not your piccolo. But you used to love the violin as a child. I remember you playing for the other children at school. Perhaps you could love it again?"

She recalled the images of the happy round faces of her classmates. Indeed, it seemed like everyone preferred it when she played the violin. She had only been playing the piccolo since Calliope came to her during the war. She was certainly better at the violin—more used to it. She looked at its shining exterior and flawless finish. She couldn't deny that it was such an attractive instrument. Perhaps she was just being dramatic, as Nephele said—she was being weak, and there was so much to love about the violin, wasn't there?

She loved it once. She could grow to love it again.

Azur

Azur Pelegros was standing among the splintered remains of his office. His power pulsed through him, face glowing like cinders, as he reached down and slung another desk across the room, the impact shattering it into hundreds of pieces.

"She's gone, Zem. Again."

His voice was hard.

Ziemia was sitting on the floor where her favorite armchair used to be.

"I know, brother—"

"No! You don't know!" he said, his fists shaking.

His talons dug into his palm, and blood was dripping onto the already ruined carpet.

She wrung her hands together nervously.

"Brother," she whispered, "maybe it's time we surrender. Just—let Nainaur have his way. He will only make it harder on us and our people if we resist. You have enough to worry about with the sleepers and now the broken contracts."

His red eyes flashed with warning, and he bared down on his sister.

"I will *never*."

His voice was deep and seemed to take on two different layers. One high and menacing, the other low and thunderous.

"I would rather raze the planes myself than let him win. Or before—"

Before I let him hurt her again.

Ziemia signed deeply and got to her feet.

"Then you know I will offer as much support as I can." She approached her brother and placed a delicate hand on his shoulder. "But you cannot let your wrath control you. You have responsibilities to *your* people. Ren is my creation, not yours."

Azur locked his jaw and snarled at his sister, her words unable to reach him through his fury. He knew that it was misdirected, she was only trying to help, but he wanted to banish her from his presence so he could revel in his sins. Let them feed his power.

"I want to help, Azur. I can't say I've always agreed with your decisions. But despite what you think." She lowered her hand to his chest. "You still have goodness inside. Light cannot exist without darkness. It is the way of our planes."

Azur scoffed in response.

"I no longer want goodness." He backed away from his sister. "I will destroy him, Zem, and those *fucking* Angels. I want to see the light fade from his eyes as he begs me to end it. And I know that when it happens, I will finally be happy. I will cherish his screams, and at last, my heart will be full. I will take everything away from him as he has taken everything from me. And she will be by my side."

Azur steadied himself, closed his eyes, and let the image flood his mind.

The goddess nodded slowly, acquiescing.

"Does she know? Now that her memories have been restored?"

Azur opened his eyes with a start.

"I don't know, Zem. I don't know what Nainaur chose to reveal."

"This will change everything—this was never something I had even considered possible." She paused. "But I shouldn't be surprised."

Azur smiled small to himself.

"So, you'll help me? You'll help me find my wife?"

RENATA'S ADVENTURE WILL CONTINUE IN HELL-SCAPE

ACKNOWLEDGMENTS:

In all honesty, writing Hell-Bound has been one of the most exhilarating experiences of my life. Watching my characters come to life, embarking on their own adventures, has been nothing short of thrilling. But like any worthwhile project, I couldn't have done it without the incredible support of a group of amazing people.

First, I want to thank every single person who has read my book (yes, that means you!) and every person who believed in me—even those who may not believe YET! I love you all, and your encouragement, excited faces, and "I'm so proud of yous" kept me going, even when imposter syndrome reared its ugly head.

Special thanks to Amanda A. who never stopped bugging me for the NEXT chapter, and the NEXT chapter after that. Honestly, I don't think I would've finished if it weren't for her infectious excitement. She's been there every step of the way, from the very first drafts to the promotional events, offering her gleeful support at every turn.

To Mary Beth H.! (As she is known exclusively to me), you were the first person I ever told about this book. I'll never forget sitting in Chili's, margarita in hand, when I described Renata's journey to you. You said, "Wow. I have chills right now," and in that moment, I finally felt like I could actually sit down and write this thing.

Huge thanks to my TTRPG teams for always getting me excited about storytelling, but especially to Atlas, who first helped Renata take her first steps into The Hells. Our Renata may have had a very different journey, but your campaign helped me realize just how much more I had to give her. I wasn't ready to let go once the campaign ended, and your support helped me keep going. Thanks for always going with the flow and putting up with my shenanigans.

To my amazing editor, Victoria: you've given me the best feedback and ensured this book could truly be epic. Thank you for your patience and dedication.

And finally, to my biggest supporter in life—my husband, Mau. You are, without a doubt, the best person I know. You've sat through countless dinners, patiently listening to me ramble on about my ideas, offering an encouraging nod or an infuriating joke in return. Whether it was about the book or life's chaos, you've kept me steady. Your love, laughter, and unwavering belief in me are the treasures I hold most dear. Thank you for inspiring me to always follow my dreams, no matter how big or small.

ABOUT THE AUTHOR

Bethany is a writer based in Santiago, Chile, and is the author of her debut New Adult fantasy novel, *Hell-Bound*. She holds a BA in English and an MLA and has spent several years casually developing stories. Her passion for storytelling grew when she delved into tabletop roleplaying games, where she created immersive worlds and narratives for friends to explore. Encouraged by those around her, she expanded one of her TTRPG campaigns into a full-length novel. Bethany's writing blends character-driven drama with fantastical elements, drawing inspiration from both her academic background and the collaborative spirit of TTRPGs.